Labor of Love

Port Provident: Home to Love

Kristen Ethridge

I0667193

Chapter One

IN LESS THAN TWENTY-four hours, Hurricane Hope would be too close for comfort to Gloria Garcia Rodriguez's island home. If it weren't for this sudden change in the storm's path, she never would have ventured to one of Port Provident's worst neighborhoods—somewhere she didn't choose to go even in broad daylight. And now with the gray clouds rolling in, casting the pallor of dusk around corners and throwing shadows on the ground, she welcomed her task even less.

On Monday, the Texas Gulf Coast looked in the clear.

On Tuesday, forecasters said the mass of clouds churning in the Gulf of Mexico had wobbled to the west.

And now, on Wednesday, the red line of the hurricane tracker drew a bull's-eye for Port Provident, Texas. If everything stayed on track, it would be here soon. The swirl of violent weather was too close and moving too fast.

Gloria walked up the narrow steps that led to the landing in front of apartment L5 and noticed the rust on the handrail and the peeling green paint along the wall. The worn-out building depressed Gloria as much as the thought of the impending hurricane. How would a building that appeared to be on its last leg on a sunny day fare when a major storm pounded it? Gloria didn't hold out much hope for the future of the small, dilapidated apartment complex or the residents and possessions inside.

She'd tried her phone to reach Tanna DeLong, a midwifery client due to give birth any day now, but there'd been no answer.

With the hurricane bearing down on Provident Island, Gloria knew she wouldn't be able to rest easy or evacuate herself until she'd ensured all her expectant moms were off the island and had a contingency plan in case they went into labor while evacuated.

Gloria easily reached the other two moms who were close to their due dates. Both planned to shelter with relatives in Houston, which was close enough for safety while traveling, but still far enough away to escape the brunt of the storm. There were plenty of hospitals nearby where either of those mothers-to-be could reasonably expect to be taken care of, should the need arise.

On the other hand, Tanna was younger—only nineteen—and didn't have family to take care of her. She'd come to Port Provident six months ago after fleeing an abusive boyfriend in Georgia. Apartment L5 was technically leased to a friend who'd offered Tanna a couch to crash on. At yesterday's checkup, though, Tanna shared with Gloria that her friend was picked up by the Port Provident Police Department on a drug charge and hadn't been home in two weeks.

Tanna was all alone, except for the baby in her belly. As a midwife for the past decade, Gloria always felt responsible for the safety of the mothers in her care, but somehow she felt unusually protective of young Tanna.

Gloria knocked at the door and waited for it to open, but it never did.

She knew Tanna had to be nearby—her red compact Chevy sat in the parking space closest to the stairs. She knocked again, and the thin wood quivered a bit under the force of Gloria's hand. The door opened slightly, the safety chain still connected at the top of the door. Tanna's left eye was barely visible, but not much more.

"Gloria? What are you doing here?" The voice from behind the door sounded unsure.

"The hurricane is coming and I need to make sure you're safe. All my other patients have evacuated. You're the last pregnant mama on the island and we've got to get you out of here. Can you open the door?"

A warm breeze whipped up and slapped Gloria in the face, a small sign of what was to come in the next few days.

"Get out of here? Where am I supposed to go? I don't have anywhere to go." She started to shut the door. Gloria quickly stuck her hand in and gripped the frame.

She reached up for the safety chain and poked it with a finger. "Undo this and let me in so we can talk, Tanna. We'll figure out something, I promise."

The crack in the door narrowed a bit. Gloria tried to figure out how she could wedge herself in the small space. She couldn't let Tanna cut herself off like this, not with her first labor and a hurricane coming together on a collision course.

"Tanna, please. Don't..." Gloria stuck her hand in the space and prayed Tanna wouldn't slam the door shut on the now-vulnerable fingers.

A scraping noise came from just above Gloria's head, and then the chain dropped free. The door opened just enough to allow Gloria a tight passage around her very pregnant patient.

"Oof. I'd really like to just go lay back down, Gloria. My back is killin' me."

"Your back? Upper or lower?" The door closed swiftly behind Gloria.

"Lower. Like right here." Tanna pressed the top of her pelvis with her fingers. "I can't get comfortable."

Gloria had seen the start of labor more times than she could count. Normally, it didn't faze her at all—it was just part of the whole process. But the average first-time mother in her care spent around fourteen hours in labor.

And according to the news reports, fourteen hours from now, Port Provident would be engulfed by Hurricane Hope.

Gloria took Tanna by the hand and led her to the couch. "Come on over here, Tanna. Let's talk. Tell me more about how you're feeling."

The young mother-to-be moved a small cushion behind her back and sat down cautiously. Still holding her hand, Gloria sat next to her and asked a few questions about what Tanna was feeling and for how long.

Tanna's water hadn't broken yet, but after observing her and timing things, then doing a quick check of dilation, Gloria made a very certain diagnosis.

"Honey, those aren't cramps. Those are contractions. You're in labor. It's still early and we have some time, but that's a definite rhythmic and measurable pattern you've got going there. I'm getting you out of here." Gloria reached in her purse for her cell phone.

"So we're going to the clinic?" Tanna's eyes darted, quick and catlike.

Gloria felt empathy for her. It was a lot to process.

Gloria did some processing of her own and furrowed her brow. "Well, no. The clinic is closed. It sits close to Gulfview Boulevard and Dr. Shipley was very concerned about flooding later."

She thought about calling the paramedics, but this wasn't an emergency. And it was far too early to take Tanna to the hospital. Women in this early of a stage of labor were sent home to wait and progress. Thanks to the imminent hurricane, she didn't know what to do. But she knew she had to do something. Thankfully, she knew people who would know the best options. Maybe instead of going to Provident Medical, which would surely be understaffed tonight, someone could get them an escort off the island and she could get a hospital in Houston to admit Tanna a little earlier than usual, in light of the circumstances.

Gloria pulled out her cell phone and dialed a number she knew could bring help. It rang four times before going to voice mail.

"Tanna, go pack a small suitcase with whatever you need. We're both going. Now. I know people."

She scrolled a little further through her contacts list.

Straight to voice mail.

Three more numbers, three more recorded messages.

Gloria was running out of numbers in her phone to call.

Gloria scrolled through her list again. Maybe she'd overlooked someone.

Well, there was one number she could call. She just hadn't planned on ever calling it again. In fact, she couldn't believe she hadn't deleted it out of her phone two years ago.

Gloria's fingers felt shaky as she connected the call. The phone stopped ringing and Gloria's best hope for saving Tanna and her unborn child answered. "Vasquez."

Although she hadn't spoken to Rodrigo Vasquez in longer than she cared to remember, his short salutation made time stand still, and Gloria realized she knew his voice almost as well as she knew her own.

"Rigo, it's Gloria. I need your help." There was no time to catch up, which thankfully meant they wouldn't have to discuss the night her husband died or why Rigo shut himself out of her life shortly thereafter.

"Gloria." Rigo paused. "Wow, it's been a while. What do you need?"

He didn't hang up on her, so that was a start. Even though merely rediscovering his number in her contacts list made her shake with fear and memories, Gloria knew calling Rigo was the right move. She had to do whatever it took for the health and safety of her patient—even if it affected the safety of her heart. Quickly, in her mind, she prayed he wouldn't leave her all alone again, not at this moment when she needed official help so badly.

"I need an escort off the island. I have a client in labor and I need to get her some place safe before the hurricane gets here."

"I'm in the beach patrol division now, Gloria, not back on regular patrol with Port Provident PD."

"Your aunt told me that at church a few weeks ago. But no one else is answering their phones and I can't call 9-1-1 for this, not with a hurricane on the way. I figure a first-time mom very early in the first stage of labor isn't an emergency priority, not with water already rising in the streets."

"No, you're right, it's probably not. I was headed to check on a report of surfers on the west end—no one's allowed in the water today. But I'll radio Davis. He can go issue their citation and I can be to you in a few minutes. Where are you?"

"In the Gulf Air Apartments on Avenue R. Apartment L5."

"On my way, Gloria—I'm close. Those apartments aren't even safe. You shouldn't be there to begin with. And they're not going to make it through the hurricane unscathed. Those units are owned by a slumlord and have been falling apart for years."

Through the phone, she heard the siren on Rigo's truck begin to wail. "That's why I called you."

"Tanna?" Gloria called down the small hallway of the dingy apartment. "Are you ready? It's time to go."

In his years patrolling a beat around the streets of Port Provident, Rigo Vasquez had been through some of the island's seediest crack houses, had shot criminals and had wound up with a few holes of his own, and ultimately watched as his best friend and patrol partner died.

But he'd never felt the slick, icy fear running through his veins like he did now, knowing Lieutenant Felipe Rodriguez's widow waited on the other side of the door at the top of the stairs.

Rigo looked around. The parking lot seemed completely silent—no one walked around and no cars were pulling in or out. Even so, Rigo's hand slid across the handle of the gun in his holster that he still got to carry as the new head of Port Provident's Beach Patrol, a division of the police force that wasn't just responsible for lifeguards and water safety, but also for keeping the island's beaches safe and mischief-free. Whenever his hand made that subtle shift, no matter how ordinary things looked, Rigo knew to trust his instincts.

Something wasn't right here.

And he was actually thankful. At least that sense of impending danger kept his mind off what he was about to do.

Face Gloria for the first time since the night his carelessness took everything away from her. Rigo knew he could never give her back her husband or her unborn child, and his gut squeezed tightly at the bitter memories.

But if he kept his focus and did his job, maybe he could get her out of here safely.

He owed that much to Felipe.

He owed that much to himself.

At the top of the stairs, the heavy feeling of instinct intensified, and he flipped open the holster to his gun. Instead of just touching the metal, he wrapped his fingers around it and slid it out. He couldn't shake the sense of being watched. Rigo pulled the gun up and held it steady as he investigated, walking from one end of the porch to the other. Everything seemed clear.

Still, it was time to get Gloria and her patient and get out of here because Hurricane Hope was picking up speed faster than any forecaster had predicted.

As unsettled as he felt about facing Gloria, he felt even more unsettled about the hairs on the back of his neck continuing to prickle.

He needed to do his job and quit thinking about the past. Gloria might be his partner's widow, but he needed to treat her like any other citizen of Port Provident.

"Gloria! Open up." He knocked on the door with his free hand, still gripping his weapon in the other.

Rigo felt his mouth go dry as he saw Gloria for the first time in almost seven hundred and thirty days. Not that he'd been counting. She'd changed, yet still looked completely the same. Her hair used to come down to her shoulders, but now it fell in layers just past her chin. It seemed lighter, too, with more honey than mocha. But with the summer days just now fading away, he figured that was the work of hours spent with sun and sand, not a salon.

Or maybe it was just the glow of the yellow bug light overhead.

He looked past her into the small, dark apartment. Noticing her hair was okay, he figured, but Rigo didn't want to see her eyes, didn't want to remember all the tears that he'd put there time and again. He wanted to get her and her patient to safety, tell himself it made up for the years of pain he'd caused and go back to his carefully orchestrated plan of quietly making amends while living separate lives on the small island.

"You ready?" He turned his head slightly left, then slightly right, telling himself he wasn't avoiding Gloria, he was just being careful.

"Yes." She let out a soft breath, like a feather floating away on the breeze. He wondered if she'd been holding it as she listened to his footsteps come up the stairs.

"Tanna? Come on, honey, we've got to go." Gloria's eyes darted around and she surveyed the landscape with a wary look, then she put her arm around a slightly built, very pregnant teenager. A scuffed-up suitcase rested at the girl's feet. "Felipe will keep us safe."

She'd called him Felipe.

He didn't think anything could have hurt more than two years ago when the ER physician came out to tell him that his lifelong best friend, his partner on the force, was dead. But now he knew he'd been wrong.

It was hearing Gloria call him Felipe.

It was knowing that he couldn't protect Felipe then, he couldn't protect Gloria now and he couldn't protect his heart ever.

"Rigo. I meant Rigo," Gloria said as they stopped in front of his beach patrol truck. She looked up at him, then just as quickly looked away. "This hurricane has me distracted. Thank you for coming when I called."

"Gloria, you know I'd do anything for you."

She stared at him, unblinking.

"So where have you been the last two years?"

She never missed a beat, and she was clearly still as direct as ever.

Rigo took a breath and stared into his cupped hands. He just wanted to get her and the young mother in his truck and get out of there, but he knew he owed her an answer that had already been put off for two years.

"A couple of steps behind, Gloria."

"What? I had no idea what your answer would be, but I at least expected it to make sense."

He promised himself a long time ago in a poorly lit, practically bare room that he wouldn't run from his past anymore. He wanted to break that promise. Badly. But he'd already broken too many promises where Gloria Garcia Rodriguez was concerned.

"I've been around, Gloria. I've just tried to stay out of your way since I've been back in town."

"Are you saying you've been avoiding me?"

Rigo shrugged. "It hasn't been coincidence that you didn't see me, Glo. But it hasn't been some ulterior motive, either."

"Then what is it?"

Rigo opened the door to the backseat as he tried to choose his words carefully. He hated that his concentration was divided like this. If the situation was serious enough that Gloria felt she needed an escort from law enforcement, he needed to give it his full attention.

But he couldn't just go through the motions when it came to Gloria anymore. She had hard questions and they were equally deserving of his undivided attention.

Silently, he and Gloria worked together, helping the heavily pregnant girl get inside the backseat of the truck. The rain began to fall more steadily from the solid wall of gray overhead.

"It's complicated, Gloria." He could feel the left corner of his mouth twist bitterly. "Can we just leave it at that for now? The only thing you need to do is get out of here and off this island. You still have about half an hour before they close the causeway. This isn't the time to conduct an interrogation."

She started to say something, but Rigo raised a hand and cut her off. "Not that you're not the best I've ever known at it. The CIA should have posted a recruiter at your door before you went to nursing school. They lost out."

Gloria rolled her eyes. "I don't know about that."

"I do. I know a lot about you, remember?"

Rigo's mind did a quick rewind past recent history and stopped on a sunny day in the late spring almost fifteen years ago. *Had it really been that long?*

In his mind's eye, he could see a version of the woman standing in front of him now, with hair teased a few inches higher and lipstick a few shades brighter. She stood at the end of the baseball dugout at Provident High School, just before practice was about to start. His arms wrapped around her waist, and he could almost feel the softness of her curves again under his tight arms, muscular from hours in the weight room and swing after swing that sent baseballs flying over the outfield fence. He remembered her saying something completely serious about where they'd be in the future, and as usual, he'd laughed it off.

"Glo...I've told you a thousand times. You're not going to be happy taking over your parents' restaurant. You just need to be around babies. Lots of them." He leaned down and kissed her lightly on the mouth, teasing her out of her scowl and back into a smile. *"Preferably mine. After I make it to the big leagues, you can stay home, knee-deep in being a mom, and we'll pay someone to take over the restaurant. Just because being a* madre *is a traditional role, it doesn't mean what's in your heart is less valuable than being some big-shot career woman. Just be who God made you to be—and He didn't make you to be a restaurant owner. Don't let anyone tell you what's in your heart is wrong. Trust me. I know you. I know you better than you know yourself, Gloria Garcia."*

"Maybe you do, Rigo. Maybe that's why we'll be together forever."

Gloria got in the truck without any assistance from him and Rigo pushed the daydream away like the windshield wipers he'd been using all afternoon. He forced himself to gain control of his thoughts, to put them back into the here and now. Gloria had called Rigo today only for Tanna's protection.

Not her own.

He could only assume she'd been honest about dialing his number because she didn't have any other options right then. She didn't call because she needed him in her life.

Felipe's death was in the past. Felipe and Gloria's son's final breaths were in the past.

And Rigo Vasquez needed do his job, take Gloria and her client back to Gloria's house so Gloria could collect a few belongings and get off the island.

Once he knew they'd be safe, Rigo knew where he needed to go—back to Gloria's past.

Chapter Two

AFTER GETTING GLORIA and her patient settled, it was time to get back to work. And Rigo knew beyond a doubt that today would be unlike any other he'd ever had while at this job—as though the surprise call from Gloria hadn't been enough of a shock.

Provident Island Beach Patrol's headquarters took up the top floor of a three-story concrete behemoth of a building which sat directly on the sand, about fifty feet back from the shoreline. The ground floor was open, ringed with chain-link fence and marked off by the giant concrete pillars that kept the building high and dry. Beach Patrol used the area to store their equipment, as did some of the other vendors who worked out on the sand. The second floor housed bathrooms, showers, and a grill and gift shop for tourists who came to Surfside Beach, the most-visited beach on the island. Long known for its amenities, Surfside Beach was a popular destination for beachgoers from all over the country from Spring Break to Labor Day.

Today, though, the beach was empty. As Rigo walked from his truck to the area under the building, rain fell on his head with a stinging slap. The air around him had begun to turn angry. Most everything had been transferred to higher ground except one last ATV they used to patrol up and down the beach during the season. Hidden back in the corner, Rigo guessed it had been overlooked by the lifeguards who had helped move the rest of the equipment to the Park Board's storage lot in the middle of the island.

Chances were that if Hurricane Hope truly came in as a Category Four hurricane, all of the beach patrol ATVs, lifeguard stands and other equipment would be ruined, no matter where on the island they were housed for safekeeping. Category Four storms brought feet upon feet of storm surge, and very little on the island would not be touched by it in some way, Rigo feared.

He took the elevator up to his office on the third floor and grabbed the ATV keys. Rigo looked around. One of the lifeguards had packed everything up and moved it away from the windows, which a city crew had boarded up yesterday. The room was dark, which echoed the foreboding in his thoughts. This building had withstood numerous storms. It only made sense that it would stand up to Hurricane Hope, too. But this time, for some reason he couldn't explain, he wasn't so sure. Everyone in Port Provident would know sooner rather than later, though.

He picked up the small, framed picture of his mom that was still sitting on the corner of his desk. He'd always loved this picture of the two of them at a baseball tournament in his youth. Cancer took her when he was just eighteen, but it hadn't robbed him of the memory of her steady, sweet smile. He shoved the picture in his pocket, turned off the light and locked the door.

He didn't know if he'd ever unlock it again.

Taking the ride back down the elevator, Rigo realized it would probably be one of the last rides he'd get to take for a while. He held out absolutely no hope for the squeaky old elevator, which had to basically be overhauled at the end of every season because the saltwater in the air rusted out just about every part and sand wedged in every nook and cranny. No way it would survive a hurricane.

"Goodbye, old girl," Rigo said as he got out of the elevator and gave the buttons a small tap. He quickly tossed the picture of his mother on the front seat of his beach patrol truck and headed back to the storage area underneath the Surfside Beach Pavilion to move the ATV.

The wet sand made the ATV's tires a bit sluggish, but Rigo was able to get some traction and speed as he headed toward the main road leading to Gulfview Boulevard. He needed to cross Gulfview, stay on Palm Avenue, and go about fifteen blocks until he reached downtown Port Provident. Normally, the trip wouldn't take more than 15 minutes. But today, with pelting rain and the occasional wind gust, he figured it would take more.

At the stoplight, Rigo tightened the hood of his rain jacket around the baseball cap he was wearing to keep the water out of his eyes as much as possible. This particular ATV had a sun cover on it, and while there wasn't a drop of sunshine in the sky anymore, it did keep some of the rain out. Just not much.

Rigo noticed that the water was quickly rising in the streets. It looked to be about six inches deep and climbing. He knew he needed to get the ATV to the lot soon and then figure out how to get back to the beach to pick up his truck before the tide got too high. He jammed the ATV in gear as hard as he could, pushing the little green four-wheeler to move. Water sprayed from around the tires, splashing Rigo constantly. The streetlights still worked, but there was virtually no traffic. At each intersection, Rigo looked both ways but never slowed down as he plowed through red and green lights alike.

As he pulled into downtown near his destination, Rigo noticed a small waterspout twisting out of the water in the harbor and hopping easily onto the waterlogged street, then spinning dizzily along. Hurricane Hope wasn't playing games. A gust of wind knocked into the waterspout, shearing the little twister and stopping its momentum.

Thump. Thump.

What on earth?

He couldn't tell what it was, but he didn't dare stop to find out. He knew he was just one step ahead of being swept away or blown away. Or both. Rigo pulled through the entrance to the Park Board's lot on Twelfth Street and when he'd parked the ATV, he stood up and checked the cover above him.

Two sand trout lay on top of the soaked brown canvas. They'd been sucked up by the waterspout and dropped on top of the ATV when the spout died out.

Wow. It was raining fish.

A fishnado. He didn't even know what to think about that.

Rigo pulled his radio out of the plastic bag he usually carried it in to protect it from water while out on patrol. He hoped that the cloud cover hadn't totally shut down the radio frequencies yet. Service had been spotty all afternoon and was getting worse.

"This is Vasquez. Dispatch, are you there?"

Static crackled, then faintly, Rigo heard a voice. "10-4, Chief. Can you give me a 10-8?"

"I'm at the Park Board lot. I just had to bring over the last beach patrol ATV. Is there someone in the area who can take me back to get my truck?"

"There are some officers in the area assisting citizens to the shelter at Provident High. I can divert one of them to come get you, Chief."

Rigo could barely pick out enough syllables to understand what she was saying. He hoped the dispatcher could hear him better. Otherwise, he'd probably be standing here for a long time.

"Thanks. I'll be at the back of the building under the cover. Tell them to pull up in the lot if they can."

"10-4 Chief. Someone will be there shortly."

Rigo stood under the cover, back flat against the wall. He didn't know why he was trying so hard. He was already soaked. A few more sheets of rain couldn't possibly make him any wetter.

As he waited for the Provident County Sheriff's Department car, Rigo tuned to the maintenance department's frequency and punched the talk button.

"Williams? Are you still there? This is Vasquez." He hoped the answer would be affirmative. He didn't have the right keys to lock up this lot. Not that a lock would matter much in the face of the biggest storm the island had seen in his lifetime.

"I'm over at the warehouse, Chief. Almost through."

"Great. I'm just leaving the Park Board lot. Everything's here. Can you come lock up?"

The voice crackled in the speaker. "No, sir. Dalton says I need to get out of here—they're closing the causeway."

Rigo stopped in his tracks. Rain pelted him. "They're what?"

"Closing the causeway in just a few minutes. The winds are too strong for cars to be at the top of the bridge now. Did you know the storm's only twenty miles an hour away from sustaining Category Four winds?"

He got back on the ATV and turned back toward the beach pavilion to get his truck, consigning the four-wheeler to wash away with the eventual tide. He hoped the little utility vehicle could get him back. He bowed his head, not just against the force of the blowing rain, but in a silent prayer that he still had enough time to rescue Gloria and get her off the island.

Gloria knew she should pack, and quickly. But she couldn't stop herself from looking out the window and watching the storm clouds roll in. Tanna had the TV on in the living room, and as Gloria walked past, she recognized Rick O'Connell from National Weather News reporting live from the barrier wall on Gulfview Boulevard. Rick O'Connell's presence was like the sign that the storm was going to be big. He never went anywhere that wasn't going to be a really big deal.

A heavy mist was falling on Rick and his bright yellow raincoat. He wasn't wearing the hood, though, and his trendy longer haircut was blowing back and forth with the gusts.

It was weird to think this was all happening right outside her window—literally—and yet, she was watching the ever-heavier lines of rain and buffeting winds on TV, as though it could have been anywhere in the world.

She'd been through a number of hurricanes since her family moved to Port Provident from Mexico when she was a child. They'd lived on the Yucatan Peninsula, so she'd seen a few there, too. Gloria considered herself a hurricane pro at this point. Go to the local big box store. Buy plenty of batteries, bottled water, a new flashlight or two, and load up on the nonperishable food. She had a great mini propane stove that she'd boiled many a pot of water on to make post-hurricane ramen noodles. She knew when to fill up the bathtub and had studied the required elevation survey of her lot when she'd moved into the house. She had moving things to higher ground down to a science.

But this time, it wasn't just about her. She had a pregnant teenager in her care—and that girl could go into the next stage of labor and become a mama at any minute.

"Gloria. You're still here."

She jumped at the sound of a deep voice as her front door opened.

"Rigo." Ice caught in her throat at the reappearance of the man who'd kept popping into every thought she'd had for the past half hour.

"They closed the causeway early. I headed over here as soon as I heard they were going to, but the official word came down just as I was turning into your neighborhood." He shut the door behind him with a soft click, then walked to the window and stood near Gloria. Tanna got off the couch to take a look, as well. They watched in comfortable silence for a few moments as the sheets of rain beat against the small window and loose palm fronds swirled in the streets below, blowing and tumbling in the wind. "You need to get out of here."

Suddenly, Gloria became aware that something was very wrong.

"Rigo! You're dripping on the floor!" A puddle had begun to collect over the sturdy work boots he was wearing.

He shrugged, a sheepish grin catching the corners of his narrow lips. "I'm soaked to the bone, but that puddle isn't me."

"Gloria?" Tanna's usually soft voice jumped an octave. "I think that's me. I think my water broke."

Gloria's heart sank. A crack of adrenaline to match the lightning bolts outside shot through her body. "We've got to get her to the hospital. The clinic is closed, obviously."

Rigo shook his head. "Can't. I heard it on the radio on my way over here. Their power is already down and their main generator failed. They have only the absolute bare minimum amount of backup power. It's a good thing they evacuated all the critical patients this morning and discharged everyone who could be sent home. They're not accepting any patients right now. I'm afraid it's going to get more dire before this night is over."

Gloria settled Tanna on the sofa, then carefully watched the mother-to-be, checking her rate of breathing and the time between the pulse of her contractions. Everything was kicking into gear.

So was Hurricane Hope. A gust of wind shook the front windows to the house.

Gloria looked around her little home. She'd never stayed in it through a storm as big as what the National Weather News reporters were saying Hope would evolve to. She thought back to that elevation certificate they'd had to obtain as part of the home's purchase. The home was behind the barrier wall that ran behind the beach and protected the majority of the residential areas of the city, but a generous storm surge would put several feet of water into her home.

She'd made a career from out-of-hospital deliveries at the birth center. She was confident in her skills, but she always operated from the vantage point of caution.

And right now, caution had been thrown to the wind and blown miles away. The little home on Travis Place was no place for Tanna to labor and give birth.

Gloria paced, three steps forward, followed by three steps back. "But if the causeway is closed, we're trapped on the island and we can't stay in a one-story house. I don't want to take her to the shelter of last resort at the high school, either, if I don't have to. Too many people. She doesn't need an audience. Stress can slow down labor and complicate it, putting us in an emergency situation. This is stressful enough. I don't want to add to it."

Rigo looked out the window. "I've got the beach patrol truck. It's a four-by-four, so we should be able to get back to Tía Inez's house just fine. But not if we wait too much longer."

Gloria's head snapped around. "Your aunt's house? What do you mean?"

"You said it yourself. You can't stay here and the shelter isn't ideal. But I don't know what kind of night I'm going to have. I figure I'm going to be rescuing some pretty stubborn people who should have already left from their homes. But there's no one more stubborn than my aunt." Rigo smiled. "Inez has lived in Port Provident for every one of her seventy-three years. And as she told me just yesterday, she hasn't left for a hurricane yet, and she doesn't intend to start now. Her house survived the Great Storm of 1910 and every other storm since, and she doesn't believe it will fail her now. You can stay with her and take care of each other. I don't expect the water to get up to the second story. It never has before—the house is at a pretty high point."

Gloria stood still, although her mind raced like never before. She always had a plan. She didn't know if the fact that she didn't have one now scared her or infuriated her.

But maybe it wasn't a failing on her part.

Maybe it was that there were no plans that made sense for delivering a baby in a hurricane.

The only thing that made any sense was Rigo—and she didn't know if that scared her or infuriated her, either.

Rigo raked a hand through his wet hair, sending a small stream of water down his shirt and to the floor to join the widening puddle. "You're not going to have lights or running water anywhere you go, not even at the shelter. I think Inez's house is your best option right now. Relatively private, and as safe as you're probably going to find without being at the shelter or leaving the island—which you obviously can't do now."

Rigo had on a Beach Patrol T-shirt and black pants. But the shirt was white, and the water had rendered it practically see-through and as close as a second skin.

Just for a second, Gloria stopped running birthing scenarios in her head and caught herself staring. *He clearly still works out as much as he did at eighteen on the baseball team.*

Gloria shook her head to clear her derailed train of thought.

"What, you won't go? You don't really have a choice, Glo." Rigo looked at her, then Tanna, then the door. "The water is rising. Your house is in one of the most flood-prone areas of town. Your street floods when someone leaves their sprinkler on too long. It's not safe."

"Gloria, please? Can we go there? Please." There was no escaping the mix of pleading and rising panic in Tanna's voice. She'd never been through a birth or a hurricane before. She had to be terrified.

Gloria knew her first responsibility was to the safety of her patient and the unborn child. Now was a time to be decisive.

"I need ten minutes to gather my things," Gloria said to Rigo. Tanna's shoulders relaxed slightly.

"Five. I don't think the truck will be able to handle us staying here for ten. The water's already risen two inches up the tires while we've been standing here talking. I'm close to being worried about the truck starting again." He narrowed his eyes and stared at her straight-on. "Felipe would want you to take care of yourself first and get out of here as fast as you can. Stuff can be replaced. People can't. You know that."

Ferocity rose in Gloria, like an angry cat who'd been out on the streets too long. "Felipe? You lost all right to speak to me of Felipe when you led him into an ambush, then didn't even have the decency to show up at his funeral. Believe me, Rigo, I know you can't replace people."

Her breath came out in short bursts through flared nostrils. Her jaw muscles clenched together. She knew she was right on this, and she would not back down. Felipe and his memory belonged to her. Not to the so-called best friend who bailed.

She would not back down. Not even when she saw what looked like hurt in his eyes.

Rigo turned away and looked back out the window. "It wasn't an ambush. Gloria, it was a traffic stop gone very, very wrong. You know that. The official investigation told you that."

She knew every word of that report by heart. "Semantics don't matter. He should have been there at the hospital. With me. With Mateo. You knew he was on his way to us in the hospital. You should have called someone else for backup."

"There was no one else I trusted like Felipe. Something didn't seem right about that stop. He was the best cop I knew. I trusted his instinct. I knew they had drugs in the car. I knew something was going on. What I didn't know was that they had a guy with a gun who was going to pop out of the trunk and start shooting." He paused, then looked at her, but his brown eyes were blank. "Felipe was my partner. My best friend."

Gloria felt her heart drain, as if she'd been shot point-blank in the chest. "No. He was *my* partner. *My* best friend. My husband. And now he's gone."

She couldn't control herself. She buried her head in her hands. She would not cry in front of Rigo. "The memories in this house are all I have."

She heard his shoes move, heard the lap of the water puddle as the work boot raised out of it and took one step closer to her. She heard the damp shirt pull as Rigo's arm reached out for her. Then he stopped.

"Five minutes. I'm going out to start the truck while you pack and gather what you'll need for the birth. Then we've got to go. I'm not about to leave you here so you can drown and go join him."

Rigo walked back out in the rain, and Gloria took in one more panoramic view of the main area of the 1930s-era house she and Felipe had loved so much and bought not long before that terrible night when all her dreams shattered like a dropped mirror. They'd spent countless hours painting and fixing it up, participating in the shared dreams of new homeowners and expectant parents who were finally going to meet a baby after so many roadblocks along their path to parenthood.

Even years after that terrible night when everything changed, Gloria had never had enough heart to change Mateo's room. The walls had stayed light blue. Just the way Felipe painted them, in those last three weeks before he and Mateo never came home again.

And in the remainder of the time she'd lived there, surrounded by painted walls and painful memories, there hadn't been a hurricane anywhere near Port Provident. So, everything had remained neat as a pin, and more or less just how it had been the last time Felipe walked out the door to go on patrol and Gloria had gone out to get a quick check from her OB because her kick counts were off.

She turned her head and saw that her street was now best described as a river. Rigo wasn't exaggerating about the situation getting more dire by the minute. The water covered the front yard and would most likely continue to rise, then be creeping under the front door sooner rather than later. And when that happened, her orderly little house and orderly little life—the one she managed so tightly and fiercely because the alternative was too much to bear—would change tonight. And just thinking about it made an indescribable heaviness fill her chest like thick cement reaching slowly to all corners of a mold.

"Gloria? Is everything okay?" Tanna gestured from the striped sofa in the corner. "I knew I'd be nervous when labor finally got here. I just never imagined I'd be this nervous."

"Well, Tanna, there's a lot going on. It's understandable that you're scared. But I'm here and I'm not leaving your side and we'll get through this together." With a shaky exhalation, Gloria followed behind Tanna, feeling as though she was leaving all the hopes and dreams of her past in the boggy front yard. But she couldn't show that burden to Tanna, who had enough worries of her own today.

"Lie down while I gather my things. I'll check your dilation and other vitals as soon as we get to Inez's house. We don't have the time to do it right now. You're going to do great, mama. Babies have been born in all kinds of conditions, and the vast majority of them throughout history haven't had electricity, either. Your body knows exactly what to do, and it's telling us that it's almost there."

Gloria opened the door to the storage closet in the hall where she kept the suitcases and pulled one out along with the plastic storage bin of birth supplies she kept packed at all times. Everything she needed—even shots of Pitocin in case of bleeding and a small tank of oxygen for mom or baby—was inside.

She laid the suitcase open on the queen-size bed in her bedroom.

She made herself keep going, pulling a few shirts and shorts and pairs of sturdy shoes out of the closet. She grabbed a pair of pajamas and carefully folded them on top of the stack. Then she went into the bathroom and filled her toiletries bag with a few overnight essentials.

Gloria decided to walk through the house to see if there was anything else she needed to take. As she passed by her desk, she reached in the drawer and grabbed the folder that Felipe had always kept their important papers in. She knew some of what was in there, but truthfully, not all of it. Her sister, Gracie, had been her rock in those days when the world spun off its axis. She'd handled the finances and the insurance and the details. But Gloria figured since Felipe had said it was important, she didn't need to take the chance that the contents of the folder would be waterlogged.

From the bookshelf, she grabbed her own Bible and the family Bible, given to her by her abuela in Mexico. She picked up a few other things here and there and tucked them into the suitcase, but she didn't have a plan. Mostly, an item made it in the suitcase if she happened to lay eyes on it and it registered through her daze as important or memorable.

Gloria walked robot-like through each room of the house, not seeing much, until she stepped into the small blue room and stopped. She hardly ever came in this room. Most weeks, she just ran the vacuum across the carpet as quickly as possible.

Some weeks, she still had to stop the vacuum in the hall.

Although Gracie had come and taken down the crib and some of the other baby furniture during those nightmare weeks after Mateo died, the rocking chair had never moved from the corner. Without realizing what she was doing, Gloria crossed the room, sat in the chair and started rocking.

She picked up the oversize light brown teddy bear from the floor and cradled it in her arms, the same way she'd been able to hold Mateo—just the one time, with his eyes closed and no butterfly whispers of baby breaths in his lungs.

Fire pushed into her throat and collected like lava. Hot, slick, overpowering. The memories burned her mind and her soul.

This room was the last connection she had to her son who died before he'd ever had a chance to live. Her darling baby. The only baby she would ever have.

Aside from that occasional vacuum, she mostly avoided Mateo's little room. But it was always there, virtually untouched. She'd never had the heart to completely dismantle the last remaining link she had to her son.

What if she woke up tomorrow and it was gone?

What if she woke up tomorrow and the last place she could feel Mateo's presence and see Felipe's labor of love in every stroke of paint on these walls...what if it was all gone?

Gloria hugged the teddy bear fiercely, then leaned over and bit the stuffed ear tightly to muffle the sobs that she couldn't muster the fight to keep inside.

Tanna waddled into the doorway. "Whose room is this?"

A cottony feeling choked Gloria's throat and she tried to wipe off the tears with the bear's ear. She hadn't talked about her son to anyone in so long. She didn't know if she could utter his name now. "It belonged to my son, Mateo."

Gloria's low, gravely tones muffled in the stuffing of the bear.

"Did he evacuate already?"

Gloria lifted her eyes heavenward. "I guess you could say that. He's in Heaven. He left a while ago."

She struggled to hold her emotions inside. Tanna had her own journey to motherhood today. She didn't need to know the details of how Gloria's son was stillborn.

Gloria turned and climbed on a nearby box, stretching her arms as far as she could to tuck the bear on the top shelf of the narrow closet.

"I'm so sorry. I didn't know. I didn't mean to interrupt." Tanna frowned and looked around the perfectly arranged room, so clearly at odds with a baby being gone for years. "I just came to tell you that Rigo's at the door. We have to go."

Chapter Three

RIGO CONSIDERED GLORIA and Tanna one more rescue in a long line of them he'd be doing for another couple of hours. The 9-1-1 switchboard was overrun tonight with people who thought they'd throw bravado in the face of Hurricane Hope, then found her might thrown right back at them with wind-whipped fury. He got the two ladies dropped off safely at Tía Inez's house and then got right back in his truck and out on the streets to do what he could.

He didn't like that there were still people on the island, but there was nothing he could do about it. When they had to shut down the causeway early due to the increasingly dangerous winds, everyone left on the island was staying, it was just a matter of where. Anyone who called for a rescue was being taken to Provident High School. The water in the streets was now over Rigo's knees and, at six foot two, he estimated that it was getting close to three feet deep where he was. He knew it was deeper in many areas and most of the rescues were being done by boat.

He didn't know how much longer they'd be able to rescue stranded citizens. At some point, those in charge would call off the rescues because they would start to endanger those conducting them. But until that call was made, his beach patrol team was on the front line. As seasoned water rescue professionals, they were deferred to by even the high-ranking members of the police and sheriff's departments at times like these.

Still, eight people couldn't save the world.

But they'd keep trying until they were told to stop.

Conditions around the island were deteriorating rapidly. As he tried to decide where to head next, he looked in the distance to the lights on inside the Grand Provident Hotel, where city officials had set up their command center. As he watched, the lights flickered, blinked twice, then all went out, taking the streetlights and the rest of the electricity with them.

His radio popped once more with static. The command center would be running on generator power now, and like the radio's reception, it was spotty. Rigo could barely make out the words. "Attention all units. The power grid is now down." The whole island was now in darkness, just awaiting the wrath of Hope. "You are mandated to take shelter."

He'd been working the *La Missión* neighborhood, checking every home in the community where he'd grown up for people staying behind and urging them to move to the shelter. Gloria and Inez were alone in a sea of water with a very pregnant woman in a house four blocks behind him.

The command center, where he was expected to be as the storm blew in, was about twelve blocks ahead.

In his younger days, Rigo knew his reputation had been something of a hothead. And those hasty decisions had impacted Gloria's life not once, but twice. Once when they were eighteen and he left her behind with a broken heart. And again, two years ago, when her life was shattered and he didn't have the courage to face her. He'd come back to help take care of his aunt and to do the right thing, now that he'd cleaned up and gotten his life on the right track.

Gloria didn't know he'd changed, and no words he could say would convince her. Only actions and time could make up for the hurt he'd caused. He wasn't going to leave Gloria to face one more uncertain night by herself.

Rigo knew he'd come back to follow the rules, not to hide anymore.

"This is Vasquez. I can't make it back to the hotel."

"10-4, Vasquez. Can you get to the shelter at the high school?" The voice on the radio went in and out as the weather conditions cut the ties of electronic contact.

"No. I'll take shelter at my aunt's house in La Misión neighborhood. I'm not far from there."

"10-4. God keep you safe, Vasquez. Get here if you can."

"Amen." Rigo agreed out loud into the night and hoped that God could hear him over the howl and thrash all around.

The radio's crackle went silent and Rigo knew this was it. The fury of nature had been building to an extreme all day, but it was now about to be unleashed in a way that Port Provident hadn't seen since 1910.

Without streetlights, it was impossible to judge the depth or speed of the water. Rigo hadn't been lying when he said he couldn't make it to the Grand Provident. Conditions had been precarious for hours, but now it was definitely not safe to drive. He pulled his truck into what was left of the closest driveway, climbed into the truck bed, and untied the small boat he carried. A flat-bottomed jon boat, it was convenient for search and rescue because the design meant he could maneuver easily in shallow water. He generally carried it everywhere in the bed of his work truck. He'd hauled it out a few times already tonight when he couldn't reach someone begging for help. Water and waves slapped at him from the sky and the land and he struggled with the plastic boat in the whipping wind.

With a growl, he righted the boat on the surface of the water which now stood more than bottom-of-tailgate deep. He got himself inside, powered up the small trolling motor and set off in the direction of Tía Inez's house.

Alone on the waterlogged streets, he had everything to lose.

And everything to prove.

"Gloria?" Tanna's voice sounded shrill with panic. "The contractions. They're stronger." Ever since Tanna's water had broken, all of the telltale physical signs had followed quickly one after another. This baby was coming and wasn't waiting for a sunny day.

And then there were the other signs.

The full moon. The drop in barometric pressure. Many people wrote off babies being born at a full moon and other weather-related times as nonsense. But Gloria had seen it too often for the old wives' tale to be nothing but coincidence. If a mere lunar phase could push the right buttons to send a mama into labor, what would the conditions that brought on a hurricane do?

Tonight, Gloria and Tanna were going to face the greatest storm Port Provident had seen in almost a century and they were going to face the greatest force Tanna had ever known as she brought her baby into this crazy, rain-soaked world.

And they would do it with no power, no modern conveniences and no medical backup.

It would take every ounce of skill and training Gloria had. She knew this test would actually take more than that. It would take every word of prayer Gloria knew to utter. Except she didn't know how to utter many anymore. Since the night she'd lost both Felipe and Mateo, she'd become convinced God had better things to do than to work in her life the way He used to. He'd taken everything and she hadn't known what to say back to Him in reply.

They were pretty far apart these days, Gloria and God.

And now there stood the wrath and fury of the storm in the gap. There was no bridge that could cross that. She was alone with one pregnant woman and one elderly aunt who went to bed an hour ago saying she "always liked sleeping to the sound of the rain."

Crazy lady.

Of course, Gloria wondered what was more crazy: Inez's idea of ideal sleeping weather or Gloria's idea that she could deliver this baby under these circumstances.

She felt pretty sure the answer was not Inez.

There must have been a lot of cries being lifted from the citizens of Port Provident tonight. Gloria didn't think it mattered much, but the icy chill in the pit of her stomach and the howl of the wind outside came together and nudged her to add one more request from Port Provident to Heaven.

"*Querido Dios, dear God, give us the strength we need to get through tonight*." She closed her eyes and let out a sigh. "*Please*."

She didn't have anything more to add. Talking to God for basically the first time in two years was much like placing that call to Rigo earlier. Awkward. And just a reminder of the bad times, when she was all but abandoned by someone she thought would never leave her.

"I'm coming, Tanna. I'll check you again. You may be getting closer to transition." Gloria tried to master the fear inside. First-time labor brought enough uncertainty to a mama. Tanna at least deserved a midwife who sounded confident, even if the midwife was scared to death on the inside of the conditions all around.

Gloria looked over the railing and down the stairs. On the level below, the water had risen to more than a foot deep. Gloria could no longer see the baseboards, and the electrical outlets would be next to go incognito. Since the turn-of-the-century home stood on pilings that were about six feet high, plus the slope of the lawn down to the street, Gloria estimated the water was easily more than ten feet outside.

She rummaged through the boxes that had been stowed earlier at the open area at the top of the stairs, both for easy access and the hope they'd remain high and dry. Inez had earlier packed a box with food and some supplies like batteries and candles, and there was a smaller box that Inez said Rigo had packed with things like a hammer and a small plastic sheet that could be used like a tarp. Shortly after arriving at the house, Gloria pulled together another box with sheets, blankets, a coil of twine, scissors and some bottled water, just in case she needed to use it. And she'd also placed her box of midwifery supplies alongside these critical supplies.

As she grabbed a sheet and a new pair of disposable gloves, something crashed into the front door with a thud.

Her breath came short. Surely someone wasn't trying to break in on a night like this. Was it debris? The thud hit again and rattled the doorknob, then the front door swung partway open. The sky behind it glowed strangely red and a familiar figure stood silhouetted in the frame, water lapping almost to his knees.

"Rigo. You got my message?" She'd never been more thankful to see him. Not when she was madly in love with him as a teenager. Not even when he showed up at the seedy apartment complex to help get Tanna to safety. The world seemed to be collapsing all around her, but at least she wouldn't be alone as Tanna's labor progressed. His presence was better than nothing.

Maybe a lot better than nothing. But she didn't want to admit that quite yet, not even to herself.

"The power's out completely now. I couldn't make it up to the command center at the Grand Provident. The streets are like rivers. I barely made it back here. Is Tanna okay?"

At that moment, Tanna let out a low moan. The guttural noise told Gloria's trained ears that Tanna was moving toward the next phase of labor, the one where instinct and the body took over and left the thinking, controlling mind behind.

"Yes, she's been having steady contractions since we got settled and things seem to be picking up. I was just gathering what I needed to check her again."

Gloria needed to get to Tanna but stood rooted, drinking in the sight of Rigo's silhouette, dark with untold layers of rain, framed by crimson in the sky behind.

"Rigo?"

"Yes?"

"Why is the sky red? Is that normal?"

"It is if a marina is on fire." He kicked the door shut with his foot and began to cross the room toward the kitchen as he answered. "Although I've been told the sky color in hurricanes can range from midnight blue to teal and even shades like pink."

"The marina is on fire?"

"Yes. The whole thing. The fire department can't get to it, so they're just letting it burn. It will be a complete loss."

She rolled her eyes in disbelief. More destruction, in ways she never imagined. "Gracie's sister-in-law has a really nice boat down there. Jake used to take us out on it sometimes."

"I'm sorry, Gloria. I'm afraid that boat is gone. They're not expecting anything to be left. One of my guys talked to an assistant fire chief about an hour and a half ago and told me. I'm coming up. Is there anything you need?"

She needed to stop thinking about the way looking at his silhouette in the fire glow a few minutes ago made something else inside of her spark. She'd taken notice of him then, and she had to remind herself that at age eighteen, she'd promised herself she was never going to take notice of him again.

She shook her head, not trusting herself to answer with words.

As Rigo waded across the entry and placed his shoe on the first soaked stair, a crackle sounded behind her. She turned around to see a blue glow spit out of the holes in four of the wall outlets. A loud pop accompanied the flash, then water shot from the outlets like the jet on a Jacuzzi tub.

"Rigo! The house!" Gloria screamed, terrified she was about to find herself in the same situation as the doomed marina.

"Gloria. I need your help down here. Now." In that instant, Rigo had transformed from civilian to peace officer. There was no questioning or disobeying the tone in his voice. "It's the pressure. It's building up in the walls. Those holes are the best way for the water to relieve the pressure."

"Gloria? Gloria? What's going on?" Tanna shouted from the bedroom.

"It's just the water, Tanna." Gloria couldn't believe that she had the ability to sound calm. Her throat was full of fear and her veins coursed with adrenaline. "Rigo's here. We're coming. Just move into whatever position makes you the most comfortable."

Gloria skittishly made her way down the stairs, afraid of the blue of the outlet sparks and the red of the marina fire and the ice in her heart and her stomach and the tips of her fingers.

Rigo grabbed Gloria's hand as she made it to the bottom of the stairs. Even though he was leading her into who knows what kind of chaos, she felt better just having his hand wrapped around hers. She could feel a callus at the base of his ring finger and vaguely wondered what had caused it. It hadn't been there before.

Time had changed them all. In big ways. And small ones.

"Where are we going?"

"My boat. I tied it up on the porch. But I need to get it inside."

She cocked her head in disbelief. "You want a boat inside the house? You're crazy."

He turned and looked straight at her. "Maybe. But that boat may be all we have in a few hours—I don't know what's going to happen next. I have a pretty good idea, though, and

I can't afford to lose the boat. It's small enough that it fits in the bed of my truck and light enough that I can maneuver it myself. If we can get it on its side, it will go through the door. The trolling motor just clamps on. I can unscrew it. I just need you to hold the door and help me guide it through."

Water pushed in waves, as the Gulf of Mexico had literally come to their door. It was rising more quickly now. Hurricane Hope was being anything but ladylike. She was making her force known.

Rigo untied the rope mooring the small craft to the banister near what had been the front steps. He guided the boat to the door and braced it against the frame, then turned himself, grabbed the edge and heaved the boat onto its side, using the frame of the door for counter leverage.

Gloria had never seen so much strength used at one time. He was probably right that he could easily move the boat to where he needed on an average day. But in these conditions with the water rising and the wind whipping, the strength he needed to pull off the feat she just witnessed had to be nothing short of superhuman.

Was that God answering her earlier prayer for strength for them all tonight?

Had He really heard her over the howls of the wind and the cries all across the town? Was He really there?

Gloria ran up the stairs as fast as she could as Rigo stayed behind to tie the boat to the banister and move everything back from the small entryway so the vessel wouldn't flop into it and cause damage. Gloria wasn't sure it mattered. Everything on the first floor of Tía Inez's house was going to be a total loss anyway. At the rate Hurricane Hope was growing, Gloria wondered if even the ceiling down there would be safe.

She wondered if any of them would be safe. Or would this be the time the house that made it through the Great Storm of 1910 met its match?

Entering the bedroom, Gloria found Tanna lying on the bed, propped up with some pillows. Several candles had been lit and set on various surfaces. The room had a warm glow that brought Gloria's blood pressure down several notches. It wasn't the birthing center, by a long stretch, but as long as there were no complications, everything should work out. She didn't need to let the panic and what-ifs take over. That wasn't doing anyone any good.

Inez had apparently woken up. She sat next to the laboring mother, holding her hand.

"Just breathe, *niña*, breathe." The calm in the older woman's voice contrasted sharply with the chaos Gloria had just witnessed below and could still hear from outside.

Inez looked up at Gloria and smiled. "It's okay. I've done this six times before."

Rigo's voice came from the doorway. "Six times? I thought you only had five kids, Tía."

She smiled. "Five kids. Six hurricanes, nephew." Stroking Tanna's hand rhythmically, she continued. "Birth and hurricanes are a lot alike. They're intense and sometimes unpredictable. But they only last for a few hours, and after it's over, the sun comes out again."

Tanna moaned and rolled a bit from side to side.

"But you're so calm, Inez. You even took a nap! I couldn't sleep if my life depended upon it." Gloria wished she could have looked out a window, but everything was boarded up.

"Go ahead. Hold my hand. It's okay." Inez rubbed Tanna's back while the young woman grunted through a contraction, a sheen of perspiration bubbling up just below the line of thick, dark hair at the top of her forehead. "Well, it's what Jesus did. It's never a bad thing to follow his example."

"'Put your hand in the hand of the man who stilled the waters,' hmm, Tía?" Rigo sang the line of the children's song but stayed put in the doorway, clearly wanting to be near the light and the company, without coming too close to the action.

"Rodrigo Vasquez." Inez's calm voice was replaced with a snap of reprimand for her nephew's mocking tone. "One of these days, you'll learn. Every Sunday morning I go to church, and there's a reason why. I didn't make it to this age all on my own. And neither will you."

Gloria would never admit to Rigo's aunt—or her own family, for that matter—but lately, she found herself more aligned with Rigo's doubt than the confident faith she saw mirrored around her. She'd known Inez for years. The older woman, as far as Gloria could tell, lived a fairly uneventful life. She always saw her at church and on the occasional trip to the grocery store, and she knew that Inez spent a lot of time with the ladies of the women's Bible study group Gloria's own mother attended. A lot of tamale making, knitting and chatting over slices of flan.

If she lived Inez's life, it would probably bore her to sleep. Even in the midst of a hurricane.

But thankfully, a midwife's life was far from dull. Babies were never predictable about when they were going to be born. Sometimes they decided to stay and bake for days after their due dates. Sometimes they decided to come in the middle of the night. Sometimes they clearly all decided to deprive their midwife of rest and come one right after the other.

And sometimes, they decided to come in the middle of a natural disaster.

"Rigo, would you mind stepping out for a minute? I need to check Tanna. I think we're getting close."

She turned to her patient. "Unless there's an emergency, Tanna, I'm going to follow your lead. You do what's most comfortable for you and I'll let nature take its course." As she bent over and did a quick check of Tanna's progress, Gloria laughed a little.

"Hmm?" Tanna shifted her weight as Gloria stepped back from the bed.

"I was just thinking," Gloria said. "I'm perfectly comfortable letting Mother Nature take her course with your birth, but to the core of my being, I wish she'd quit taking her course with this storm outside. I just want it to be over. The good news is you've progressed more quickly than I expected you to, so Mother Nature will be through with you shortly, in all likelihood. You can push whenever you feel ready, Tanna. I won't hold you back."

"Mmm-hmm." Tanna breathed low and slow through a contraction, then looked up when it passed. "I guess I don't get my water birth after all?"

Tanna had wanted to use the deep water birth tub at the birthing center since her first appointment. "I'm afraid not in that way. There's plenty of water outside and downstairs, but Inez filled the bathtub with water earlier today for drinking and emergencies."

"Peace." Inez wiped Tanna's head with a wet washcloth. "Breathe deeply and think of peace."

The next contraction started. Tanna bore down, gripping Inez's bony hand, but Rigo's aunt never flinched. Gloria was amazed at her strength and her demeanor. She wondered if she could bring Inez to attend all her births.

Tanna made instinctive reaching motions with her hand. The birthing waves were taking over, bringing her closer to motherhood.

Rigo stood just outside the doorway, and Gloria called to him. "Rigo. Grab her hand. She needs something to push against."

The man, who'd stared down criminals in the line of fire and who'd already saved grown adults and children alike from the clutches of near-drowning tonight, hesitated. In addition to being a certified peace officer, she knew he had to be a certified EMT for his job. Surely he'd had some training for this. Gloria looked up from where she'd been focusing, monitoring the baby's progress. "Go on. She needs you. Just stand back by her head. You're not going to see anything from there."

Gloria hastily threw a towel over Tanna's knees and belly to preserve her modesty. Rigo stood by the headboard and looked toward the doorway, but reached out his hand and provided more than enough support to give Tanna the leverage she needed.

She'd prayed for strength for everyone earlier tonight, and this was the second time she was seeing it in action. Tanna's focus amazed Gloria, even as the world ran out of control and the wind battered the house, causing it to sway gently on the pilings. She'd attended more than a thousand births in her career, and thought she'd worked in every kind of condition possible—highly advanced labor-and-delivery suites, standing by in Caesarian sections, working the past two years at an out-of-hospital birthing center at the edge of Provident Medical Center's footprint, and she'd even been present for a few planned home births.

But until today, she'd never supervised a birth in a candlelit room with not even the most basic of equipment or running water. Tanna, the young nineteen-year-old who, nine months ago, Gloria initially judged as a good candidate to ask mid-delivery for a transfer to a hospital to get an epidural, was showing strength through adversity tonight.

With one last forceful push and a punctuating explosion of breath, another refugee from the hurricane's fury shot into the world. Gloria picked up another towel from her box of supplies with one hand as she held the little squealing baby with the other.

It was a triumphant moment, made all the more incredible not just because of the amazing nature of birth, but because of how amazing it was to have this birth in the middle of this particular storm.

The hurricane may have been named Hope, but as Gloria lifted the mewling baby and handed it to the euphoric, exhausted mother on the bed, she knew she was holding hope in her arms.

"Congratulations, Tanna. It's a boy! And a strong one, too. Do you want to cut the cord?"

Tanna shook her head, unable to tear her gaze from the tiny stranger that she already knew so well. "No. I couldn't have done this without you and Rigo. I'd be alone in that awful apartment if you hadn't come to check on me, and who knows what would have happened if Rigo wasn't there to protect us."

Gloria met Rigo's eyes and felt something chip at the heavy cement that had poured in her heart hours before when he walked back into her life. Tanna saw Rigo as a hero. And maybe she was right.

She handed Rigo the scissors she'd found in a downstairs drawer upon their arrival. She'd sanitized them in some boiling water before they'd lost all the utilities. They were just common household scissors, but they'd have to do. She had one plastic cord clamp in her box of tools but couldn't find another at the bottom of the box with the dim half-light. Instead, she tied a length of twine tightly, using it as a makeshift clamp. "Do you want to do the honors?"

It felt so strange to be standing over a baby, sharing in a cord-cutting ceremony with Rigo. All those foolish teenage dreams and plans she'd once had for the future popped in her mind like kernels of corn.

"Sure. Wow." Rigo took the scissors, and with one steady press, snipped the baby's last physical tie with Tanna. Rigo stared at the little infant as though he was seeing one for the first time. "I've never done that before."

"Not even with your paramedic training?" Gloria took the baby and towel-dried him. His hair stuck up in ten different directions. She laid him on the bed and began folding an oversize washcloth around the baby's legs and safety-pinning it shut, in an old-school fashion. Without diapers, it was all she found on hand earlier. It would have to do for now.

"No. I don't think I've really done much past treating things like puncture wounds and doing CPR and chest compressions. That's most of what you see on the street and on the beach. Not a lot of babies being born in the sand dunes."

He intently watched every move Gloria made. "What are you doing with that? That's my sock."

His curiosity was so intense it made Gloria chuckle, a welcome feeling. This day needed some comic relief. It was now almost one in the morning. Today had been too long and too life-changing.

"I don't have a hat. An old tube sock seemed like the next best thing to keep his head warm. Is this one of your favorites?"

Rigo shook his head. "Not anymore."

Inez slid off the bed and walked out to the hallway. "I'll find something for her to eat in that box I packed. There's some peanut butter and a bottle of coconut water. We need to keep her strength up and the coconut water is full of electrolytes."

Gloria finished bundling the baby tightly in a blanket. It seemed to have once had Winnie the Pooh scenes all over it, and had probably belonged to one of Inez's children or grandchildren. Now it was soft and faded from wear and love. The baby settled and made a smacking sound.

"Here, Rigo, hold him while I check Tanna quickly." Rigo held his arms out. "Not like that. He won't bite. He doesn't have teeth. Haven't you ever held a baby before?"

"Well, no. Not really." Rigo's eyebrows raised slightly in a position that seemed to say, *What did you expect?* without uttering a single word.

"Bend your arms. Here, like mine. You need to cradle him. He's completely floppy. You have to support his head."

Gingerly, she laid the baby in Rigo's arms. It felt strangely powerful.

She leaned over and pressed her fingers across Tanna's tummy, checking her progress as she prepared for the afterbirth. Everything felt fine. Within minutes, all stages of labor were completely finished.

Gloria shifted an old shower curtain from under Tanna. It had kept the bed protected throughout labor. Too bad, she thought as she looked at Rigo gazing at the little baby in the hazy puddles of candlelight, there wasn't something equally convenient to shield those walls she'd built up to protect herself from memories of Rigo for the last several years.

"Rigo, you can hand the little man back to his mama. Tanna, why don't you start to try and feed him? I'm sure he'll appreciate the comfort and it's important to start a good nursing relationship early."

Inez came back in, peanut butter jar in one hand, a sleeve of crackers in the other and a bottle of coconut water tucked under an arm. This had undoubtedly been the most unconventional birth Gloria had ever attended, but she wasn't sure she could have asked for a better crew to share it with.

"I'll help her with that, Gloria, while you clean up. I've got some experience with this." Inez placed the food on the bedside table and got Tanna set up with pillows tucked securely behind her. "You can hand the baby to me, Rigo."

Slowly, Rigo moved toward his aunt.

"Something wrong?" Gloria looked up and caught Inez studying her nephew's face. It was as blank as the wall behind the bed.

He continued to stare at the baby, almost tracing the little smacking lips with his gaze.

"No," he said quietly. "Not at all." He laid the baby in Tanna's open arms. She cuddled the little bundle tightly against her chest.

Rigo backed up and headed toward the door, then turned back to the bed. "Tanna, do you have a name for him?"

The baby squirmed, drinking in his mother's scent.

"No, not really." She tore her gaze away from the tiny face in her arms for just a second. "Gloria, earlier when we were at your house, what did you say your baby's name was?"

Sadness pierced Gloria's heart. She'd never spoken of her son in front of Rigo.

She needed that strength she'd prayed for. And she needed it now.

"Mateo," she said, her tongue stumbling over every syllable. "His name was Mateo."

A smile crossed Tanna's face. "I like it. Mateo Rodrigo, for you both."

White-hot shock pierced her heart. Tanna didn't know their history. She just thought she was doing them a great honor.

Gloria prayed for the second time today. For the second time in the past two years.

Oh, please, God, don't let me fall.

Gloria picked up the crumpled linens and brushed past Rigo and into the bedroom across the hall, where she could silently crumple herself, away from the eyes that had seen some of the most hurtful moments of her past.

Chapter Four

AS THE IMMEDIACY OF the birth wore off, Rigo had time to notice the demeanor of everyone around him. There wasn't really much else to do besides sit and wait. The baby was peaceful. Tanna was euphoric, brushing the baby's downy hair with the tips of her fingers, over and over again. Tía Inez was in her element, delivering advice and suggestions.

Gloria seemed reflective, quietly tidying things up as best she could, keeping the makeshift birthing center comfortable by relighting the candles when they burned low and writing down details of the birth.

As he watched Gloria at work earlier, he found himself unable to take his eyes off her. He'd pursued his career in law enforcement and rescue because he liked the thrill, the chase. The constant of never knowing what would come next—and the adrenaline buzz that came along with it.

Gloria was different, though. She directed Tanna's birth without lights, without equipment, without conveniences, in a manner that connected strongly to birthing women throughout the ages before hospitals and delivery rooms. In spite of the uncertainty, he never saw fear when Gloria was in that room. She had to have been scared by the hurricane—he knew he was—but even so, he only saw the actions of a woman who was uniquely called to do that very career. Not because she chose it. Because it chose her.

The stubbornness he used to chide her for. The single-minded focus he used to try and break through his teasing. The drive to accomplish exactly the path set in front of her. It was all still there, more than a decade later.

So, too, were the things he'd been attracted to as a teenager. The soft glow that caused her topaz eyes to glitter when she got truly excited about something. The fierce protectiveness that took complete care of and responsibility for anyone in her inner circle. And the petite frame that made her look like a tiny, sweet package, like a *dulce de leche* candy you could tuck in your pocket and carry with you. Looking at Gloria, people might first disregard her—until they later learned they did so at their own peril.

He'd figured she'd changed over the years, like everyone did, although he hadn't been close enough in a long time to know for sure. He'd left to pursue a crazy youthful dream. Then, she'd kept her distance from him when he returned and was on the force with Felipe. Afterward, Rigo had his own strength to find, and had removed himself from Port Provident and Gloria's circle entirely.

But now back, face-to-face with the woman who appeared in all of his best memories—and at the center of his worst—Rigo saw nothing had changed.

She was a truly unique mixture of dewdrop soft and hurricane fierce.

Just like what was going on around them.

Even the wind seemed to be slowing outside. Rigo left the room and sat at the top of Inez's staircase, watching the water level bob and shake around the steps below. Swarms of bugs floated on top in little clumps. He checked his watch. It was 2 a.m.

Rigo's ears noticed a change outside. He clicked the switch on the old weather radio he'd brought out of the room with him, hoping it would spring to life and confirm what he thought was about to happen.

"The National Weather Service is reporting that the eye of Hurricane Hope will make landfall within the next twenty minutes. Citizens of Port Provident are still encouraged to exercise extreme caution during this time."

Rigo shut off the radio. He'd heard exactly what he needed to hear.

"Gloria," he shouted. "Gather up what you need. Everyone needs to put on their sturdiest shoes, quickly. The eye of the storm is almost here. We're taking Tanna and the baby to the command center at the Grand Provident Hotel. It's the safest place on the island for them. For all of us."

From the bedroom, he heard his aunt's steady voice. "I told you He'd calm the storm."

Rigo didn't want to point out that every hurricane had an eye. It would have been disrespectful to suggest such a thing out loud. Besides, he didn't have any time to waste.

Wading through the chest-deep water in the front of the house, Rigo tried not to think about the possibility of rats or snakes taking refuge in the living room. He'd already seen the bugs, small armies that had hitched themselves together to float in baseball-sized groups. That was enough. He reached blindly below the surface of the water, trying to grab the doorknobs to the double doors and force them open. The water level was the same outside as inside. Dormer windows and the angles and points of roofs were all that he could see on the smaller, one-story craftsman-style homes and cottages. Everything looked like children's toys in a very dirty bathtub.

"Is everyone ready? We've got to go."

At the top of the stairs, Rigo could make out three dim shadows. Inez stood in front, with Gloria providing a steadying hand behind the older woman's elbow. "Tanna, stay here. I'll come back to help you and the baby," Gloria said.

Rigo stood on the bottom stair and tried to hold the small jon boat steady where it floated, tethered still to the banister.

"Gloria, reach out and hold the boat. I'll come up and lift Tía in."

He switched places with Gloria. Even though she stood two steps up from where Rigo had been, the water came almost to her chin. But she kept a steady grip on the lip of the boat, pushing it up against a wall for more security. Rigo lifted Inez and slowly turned on the step, careful not to slip and fall. He sat her gently on the small platform in the front.

"Ok, Tía, can you make it to that second little bench? Just hold on tight. Crawl if you need to."

Inez nodded her head and began to inch, crab-like, toward the back of the little craft. "I can do it."

"Stay there, Gloria. I'll get Tanna." Rigo walked to the top of the stairs, water rolling down his back. He'd spent most of his life in the water, surfing and lifeguarding, but he wasn't sure he'd ever been as thoroughly soaked as he was right now.

Carefully, he picked up the dozing bundle from Tanna's arms. Her eyes widened with fear—not only for herself, but now for her new child. "I'm going to hand him to Tía," he said.

Step by step, he made it down the slick wooden stairs. "*Holá*, Mateo," he whispered. "It's okay. You're going to be safe. I won't let anything happen to you."

Rigo was scared to think about the five of them floating in the small boat through what had been the streets of Port Provident, especially if the eye was narrow and closed soon. But he was even more scared to keep a newborn and its mother in a flooded, bug-infested house with half a hurricane still left to go.

He leaned as far across the boat as he could get, and Tía reached out her arms. Little Mateo was on board. Time to get Tanna.

Her feet were unsteady. Placing an arm under her knees and one under her arms, Rigo scooped her up and made his way down the stairs again. Resting her on the front platform, he tried to scoot her as far in as possible. He held her hand as she wobbled toward the seat next to Tía, then took her baby back in her arms.

Only one more passenger to get aboard and then they could leave.

"Let me help you, Gloria." She'd climbed a few steps higher, and the boat started to bob once she lifted her hand off the hull.

Rigo put his hands around Gloria's waist tightly. He remembered picking her up and swinging her around during summers at the beach. There wasn't anything else similar to those days right now, except confirmation of his earlier train of thought.

In more ways than one, Gloria hadn't changed a bit.

On the other hand, he sure hoped he had.

He'd been to places he wasn't proud of and done plenty of things he'd regretted, and one day, he knew he'd need to come clean to Gloria if there was any hope of putting things right between them. But for now, he'd do the next best thing and keep her and those who depended upon her safe.

Gloria got settled on the small bench seat next to Tanna. Rigo untied the boat from the railing, turned it around and swam behind, pushing it through the oversize frame of the turn-of-the-century door. The edges of the boat brushed the edges of the door. It barely fit, with only a feather's width to spare.

"Everyone duck." The women in the boat bent their heads low. Their bodies cleared the top of the door frame by just about a foot.

Well, that was a first. He'd spent his whole life on the coast, but never before had he floated a boat out the front door of a home. Tying the boat hastily to the railing of the porch, Rigo climbed up on the rail, then worked his way into the boat, untying it once he was safely inside. He sat in the back next to the trolling motor and fired it up. He was soaked to the bone with sticky, salty brackish water.

"Everyone ready?"

No one replied. The only affirmation was the nodding of heads. Everyone indicated they were ready, but like Rigo, he imagined none of them knew exactly what for.

The sky on the horizon line glowed teal, almost as crisp and shining as the water off the Baja Peninsula on Mexico's Pacific Coast, where he'd once loved to surf. He'd never seen colors like that in the air before. Above him, he could see stars. A few seagulls squawked and circled overhead, likely as disoriented as he was.

"The eye of the storm. Not many people on earth can say they've seen this," he said to the passengers.

Gloria looked up at the sky, her face showing amazement in the soft moonlight and turquoise glow. Tanna kept her head down, looking at baby Mateo.

They headed south toward the Grand Provident Hotel, where Rigo hoped there would be power from backup generators, some drinking water and a plan.

Inez's hands were folded serenely in her lap. She didn't intently stare like Gloria, nor was she avoiding the view like Tanna. She seemed calm, almost like this was an everyday occurrence for her. A gust of wind touched the back of Rigo's soaked shirt giving him a chill, and he could see Gloria's short hair ruffling with the breeze.

This respite from the chaos wouldn't last much longer. They needed something stronger than just himself to get them all to the Grand Provident, but even after Inez's words to them all earlier, he knew he couldn't do what his heart was telling him to do. Not in front of Gloria. He didn't know exactly why. He'd started attending the earliest services at *La Iglesia de la Luz del Mundo*—that service chosen specifically because he knew Gloria attended the later service, and he hadn't wanted to cause a scene or be in her way.

But still, he just couldn't be close to God while he was close to Gloria.

"Hey, Tía, I think you'd better pray."

"I have been all night." She smiled a knowing smile. "Haven't you noticed He's been here?"

Rigo's hand slipped a bit off the motor's handle. He hadn't quite thought of it that way. Mateo broke the night's temporary stillness with a little wail, a further reminder that he came into the world with a healthy set of lungs.

Even though he had to navigate through the help of street signs just barely poking their green metal rectangles above the waterline, the trip was relatively uneventful and took less time than Rigo had planned.

They motored up to the parking lot behind the hotel. Rigo hopped overboard and waded to a palm tree, where he tied the boat. He saw others with flashlights standing on the wall surrounding the pool area of the hotel, presumably also watching the once-in-a-lifetime experience of standing inside a hurricane's eye wall. He waved his own flashlight in signal to the group above. Two men threw their legs over the wall and started down the side of the waterlogged hill to come help.

Maybe Tía Inez was right. Maybe—just maybe—Rigo noticed, God really had been with them all night.

A few emergency doctors from Provident Medical had assembled a small clinic inside of one of the meeting rooms in the hotel. They quickly escorted Tanna and the baby up. One doctor insisted on checking Tía Inez out, as well. Gloria handed over her notes from the birth, relieved to have other medical professionals confirm that both baby and mother—and aunt—had checked out fine. Assured that the two women and youngest refugee would be taken care of and transported to a hospital on the mainland for observation as soon as the storm cleared, Gloria let out a breath she hadn't realized she'd even been holding.

The past several hours had all run together. All of her training had kicked in and she'd just done what she needed to do. But now the immediate danger was no longer resting squarely on her shoulders and they were safe, surrounded by local officials, police and doctors in the safest building in town and she could release that burden. Gloria tried, but she couldn't even feel relief. All she felt was tired.

Inez reached toward Gloria from the couch she had been instructed to lie on. "Gloria, come here."

Gloria slipped her hand into the older woman's thin grasp. Her hand felt cold. So much time spent in wind and rain. Gloria wondered if any of them would ever be dry or warm again. Or safe. Would the memories of tonight mark them all forever?

"How are you feeling, Inez?"

"Like a drowned rat." The older woman shuddered, making her gray hair shake. "I think I saw a few on the boat ride over here, too. Yuck. But they're bringing me some dry clothes. That should help. I think they're bringing some for you, too."

Gloria wondered what kind of dry clothes they had in a hurricane command center. Probably not anything that would show up on a catwalk—in Paris, France, or Paris, Texas. "I'm glad you're okay, Inez."

Inez smiled. The deep lines around her face stretched out, and Gloria could see the neighborhood beauty she used to be. "You don't have to be afraid to be around Rigo, you know."

"I'm not afraid of him." Gloria tried not to snap. Just because she didn't want to spend any more time than necessary around him didn't mean she was afraid of him.

"You're afraid of something. You know, God doesn't give you a spirit of fear. He gives strength to His people."

The corner of her mouth twisted downward. Gloria didn't want to talk about God and she didn't want to speak badly about the woman's favorite nephew, but Inez had to know the history. Everyone in the *La Missión* neighborhood knew the story behind Gloria and Rigo, from high school until after Felipe's death.

She was the star of a real-life soap opera in her own backyard.

"No, really, I'm not afraid of anything." Gloria tried to sound reassuring. She tried to end this line of conversation. Couldn't they talk about something more palatable? Say, the hurricane winds, which were again howling outside, wrecking even more of their hometown?

"Gloria, I know a lot has happened between you and Rigo."

Could Inez read her mind? Maybe not, Gloria decided. "A lot" was mild compared to how she would have described it.

Gloria waved her hand, noncommittally. "It's in the past, Inez. Really. We don't have to talk about it."

Inez shook her head again. "No. We do."

The strength in her voice hit Gloria like a punch to the stomach. Clearly, Rigo's aunt was going to have her say.

"You think he's responsible for Felipe's death. And your son's. You think he left you high and dry after high school and again after the funeral." Her gaze was unwavering. "Don't deny it. I know *su madre*. Your mother's submitted many a prayer request to our Bible study group on your behalf over the years."

Gloria had no choice but to silently nod. Every word was true.

"And, Gloria, maybe he could have done things better over the years. Maybe you could have, too. He's had to learn a few lessons—some the hard way. But the simple fact is that God can work all things to good for those who love Him. The Bible says so. The question is, do you love Him?"

She wasn't expecting the conversation to take this turn. She felt her heart miss a beat.

"Who? Rigo?" She had, once.

"No, silly girl. God. Do you love Him?"

She had, once, too. Now she didn't know Him anymore. She sat in church, week after week, month after month, year after year, too afraid to not go. And too afraid to let her guard down and ask for the help she needed.

"I did. But then He took everything away from me." Her voice sounded quiet, even to her own ears. The syllables sounded flat. Just like her spirit the past two years.

Inez gave her hand a light squeeze, just like Gloria had seen her do earlier today to comfort Tanna through the pain of childbirth. It felt unexpectedly reassuring. "Just like you, I've lost a husband. And I've lost a son. I know how much it hurts. Remember what Job said?"

Gloria shook her head.

"God gives, and God takes away. And that He does, *mija*. It's part of life. And we won't always know the reason on this side of Heaven. But I do know that it is so. Just like this hurricane will sweep out the old and in time, bring in repairs and new buildings and a fresh look to Port Provident—I know it will because it's happened after every single hurricane. Something so terrible as that wind and water outside can spark something new. The same is true in our own lives."

Gloria stayed unusually silent. She didn't even know how to take in what Inez was saying. Part of her wanted to bristle at her words and her assumptions about Gloria's heart and life. But that prickly feeling was smoothed over a bit by knowing she was just an old woman who wanted to do some good.

If only words could wash away things as easily as the rain. But even though she wanted to believe what Inez was saying, it just wasn't that simple.

"If a hurricane tears off a roof or washes away a building, you can fix it up or build it back. It just takes some time and the right materials." Gloria looked down at her feet. She couldn't meet Inez's gaze. "But Felipe and my Mateo, they're not coming back. There's no work I can do to change that."

Inez put a finger under Gloria's chin and pressed upward, forcing her to look up.

"You're right. There's nothing you can do. But that's not what I said. I said *He* works all things to good. Why don't you try letting *Him* work for a change? You don't have to do everything. Think about what I'm saying." She pulled her hand away. "Now, then. It's been a long night for all of us. I'd like to get some rest. Can you go see if they've found my dry clothes?"

Gloria left Inez's makeshift bed in search of the young doctor who had been attending them earlier. As she stepped into the main hallway of the hotel, she spotted Rigo talking with some officers near a table covered in piles of papers. He'd changed into a new pair of swim trunks and a T-shirt with a blue Port Provident Beach Patrol logo on the back. A pair of cheap black flip-flops had replaced the soggy work boots on his feet.

She was drawn to the cuts on the back of his tanned calves. Some were superficial scrapes, but a few were deeper and covered with new scabs. Clearly, they'd all happened sometime between shuttling her and Tanna to safety and protecting all of Port Provident from Mother Nature. She knew all the salt water he'd walked in had to have stung each and every one of those scrapes and exposed them to infection. And yet, he never said a word.

What had Inez meant when she'd said he'd had to learn some lessons the hard way? Not for the first time in the past day or so, Gloria wondered just where Rigo had been for two years before he returned to take the chief's role at Beach Patrol. Was that what Inez spoke of? Or something else?

Dr. Stephenson, the young ER doctor who had been checking on Inez, turned the corner. In her hands was a pile of shorts and T-shirts with some socks on top. Gloria chuckled inside at the thought of proper Inez Vasquez in a pair of board shorts and an old T-shirt instead of the floral embroidered dresses she wore every day of her life. But at least they'd be dry.

"Gloria. I finally found what I was looking for. I have clothes for you and for Mrs. Vasquez and Tanna. For now, we're just going to have to use what spare towels and T-shirts we can find as swaddling and diapers for the baby. We should have everyone taken care of in no time." Dr. Stephenson reached out a pair of blue shorts and a T-shirt and handed them to Gloria. "I think the shorts are going to be a little big for you, but they have a drawstring, so you should be able to get them to fit, more or less. Most of the spare clothes they had in the work room were in men's sizes. Here's a blanket, too, in case you're still cold."

Gloria smiled. It would be good to peel off some of the layers—almost like shedding a very sodden layer of skin. "Thanks, doctor. I'm just going to step into the bathroom across the hall and change. Do you need me for anything?"

She shook her head, making her brown ponytail bounce. "No, we're good. I'm going to make sure that Mrs. Vasquez and Tanna get a nap, since we still have a few more hours before we can even think about getting them out of here. The best thing for them will just be to rest. For you, too. Why don't you come lie down on one of the couches in the clinic, too?"

It sounded appealing, Gloria had to admit, since she felt as if she hadn't truly rested in days. But she knew her body's signals pretty well and she knew she was still too keyed up to sleep just yet. "Maybe in a little bit. I'll let you know."

"Okay." Dr. Stephenson turned and headed back toward her patients in the clinic. Gloria walked to the bathroom and into the handicapped stall to give herself more room to change. Everything was wet and brown from the muck of the past day. The whole outfit reminded her of nothing but chaos, and she discarded it all in a heap on the tile floor. She slid a pair of too-big socks on her feet and wiggled her toes in the warm softness.

When she was done changing, Gloria threw the blanket over her shoulders. She kicked the wet pile of clothes out of the stall with her foot and took her tennis shoes to the hand dryer. She tried to convince herself that a couple of cycles of hot air had made her shoes a little less wet. But she decided against putting them back on just yet. She held them, pinched between two fingers, then awkwardly picked up the stack of wet clothes and shoved them in the trash can.

"Good riddance," she said as the door shut behind her. "I don't ever want to see—or smell—you again."

As she approached the makeshift clinic, she saw Rigo just outside the door. "Looks like everyone is doing well. All three of them are resting, and the doctor said they should be fine. She's eager to get Tanna and the baby off the island for observation once the coast is clear, though. She's insisting Tía go, too, because of her age. I don't want to be the one to tell Tía that when she wakes up." He laughed and shook his head.

Gloria nodded in agreement, remembering their earlier conversation. Rigo's *tía* had a will of iron. She would almost assuredly put up a fight and insist that she was perfectly fine. But considering the conditions that would be revealed on the island once the storm passed, it would be better for her health to leave.

"Hey. Nice shirt." Rigo pointed at the small logo on the front of Gloria's new clothes.

She'd been so grateful just to have dry clothes that she hadn't really even paid attention. She was wearing the same design as Rigo, a Port Provident Beach Patrol logo shirt. They looked like twins. Gloria couldn't stop the loud laugh that popped out of her throat.

"What's so funny?" Rigo looked at her, slightly sideways.

"Remember junior year when I asked you to the Sadie Hawkins dance and we wore those ridiculous matching, rainbow-striped, rugby jersey shirts?"

Rigo leaned his head back and rolled his eyes. He laughed right along with Gloria. "And the khaki pants with the woven belts and loafers. I hated Sadie Hawkins—no offense. It was bad enough having to wear a penguin suit at prom, but having to dress alike for Sadie Hawkins was just too much."

But then he broke into a grin and bared his front teeth. The white of the enamel stood out brightly, surrounded by his deep black far-more-than-five-o'clock shadow. She felt warmer, all the way down to her chilly toes in the new, dry socks.

"But the company more than made up for it. Thanks again for asking me. We did have some good times, didn't we, Glo?"

A lot has happened between you and Rigo...

Inez's recent words rang in Gloria's ears.

A lot *had* happened. But if she was honest, it wasn't all bad. Well, maybe those rugby shirts were.

But they had years of history. And maybe it wasn't fair for her to erase all the good from her memory and cling only to the bad, like a drowning person clutching a life vest. Maybe it wasn't fair to have turned her worst moments into her defining moments in her relationship with Rigo—or with anyone, for that matter.

"Yeah, we did. A lot of them, actually." It surprised Gloria that the words didn't turn her throat raw. The yawn that followed, however, didn't surprise her at all.

"You're tired, Gloria. You need to get some rest." Rigo reached up and readjusted the blanket she was carrying, gently dropping it across both shoulders. It felt like a gentle hug, comforting and warm at the same time.

"I am. But I can't sleep. I'd say there's just something in the air, but that's an understatement. There's a lot in the air. About a hundred and ten miles per hour of something."

Rigo put his hand on her shoulder and guided her to a couch against the wall of the main hallway. "Why don't you lay down here? I've just checked in with the folks I needed to talk to and I don't need to check back in for a while. We're going to meet with the dive team in about an hour to put together a plan for rescuing people who stayed in their homes and got trapped by the storm surge. I've got some time. How about I just sit here with you until you fall asleep?"

The other end of the hallway bustled with action, but down here by the clinic, it was quiet. And although the couch was tufted and upholstered with a thick brocaded fabric, it looked like the most comfortable bed she'd ever seen.

"But you don't have to..." She started to protest, reflexively.

He put one finger to his lips and gave a quick "Shush."

"I don't have to. I want to. Now lie down."

Gloria did as she was told, tucking her knees up for warmth and adjusting herself to get as comfortable as possible. Rigo pulled the blanket down around her and tucked it securely under her knees and feet. She felt like a child, when Mamí would tuck her in at bedtime.

Rigo sat on the floor and leaned his head slightly on the edge of the lower cushion. He reached up and took her hand as it lay on top of the blanket. "You're completely safe now, Gloria. Just rest and get your strength back."

She wanted to pull back, but it seemed rude. He wasn't doing anything but trying to help her get to sleep. As the mild haze of sleep began to take over, Gloria noticed that it felt completely comforting to have her hand resting in his, almost as though hands had some kind of muscle memory for movements and feelings of decades ago.

They were surrounded by the finest team of emergency personnel Port Provident could offer. City government, police, fire, EMS, doctors. All of Port Provident's leaders were here, staying busy with what needed to be done.

The firefighters moved along the hallways, checking for stress fractures in the walls of the hotel as it was battered by the storm. Others, like Rigo's colleagues, were meeting in huddled groups, mapping out a game plan for how they would assess damage and rescue citizens once the sun rose and the winds and the waters receded.

All of them were at the top of their game tonight.

But could any of them rescue a broken heart?

Gloria fell asleep before she could determine the answer.

Chapter Five

BY EIGHT O'CLOCK IN the morning, the Grand Provident Hotel seemed close to bursting at the seams with activity. Everyone was just waiting to get the all clear that winds had dropped below the seventy miles-per-hour mark that signaled the shift from hurricane-force winds to a tropical storm. At that point, another type of flooding would begin as rescue workers would head out to see what was left of Port Provident and how her brave citizens fared.

Rigo was nowhere to be found. Gloria hadn't seen him since she woke on the couch several hours ago. Inexplicably, she felt better than she had in days. She must have slept more deeply on that short, bumpy sofa than she ever thought possible.

"Gloria!" Tanna stepped into the hallway, carrying her newborn son, who had already seen more in a few hours than many people saw in a lifetime. "Dr. Stephenson says they've arranged for us to be transported to Mainland Regional Hospital. As soon as the causeway is cleared, they're going to send someone for us. I can't thank you enough for what you did. When I first met you, I knew you were going to be special—but you've been far more than that. You kept me safe from the storm, and you made sure Mateo arrived safely. I don't know anyone braver than you."

She leaned in and hugged Gloria with one arm, careful not to squish the baby.

"When Mateo is older, I'm gonna tell him about you and tonight. And the first Mateo. I won't let him forget."

The words wrapped Gloria's heart like a healing bandage. They touched her. To know that somehow, her own little Mateo would live on in spirit beyond just her memories felt like a blessing.

She couldn't think of anything to say other than simply and softly, "Thank you."

Gloria had attended numerous mothers and patients throughout her career as a nurse and midwife. She hated to say she'd forgotten many of them, but it was the truth. Tanna, though, and this little Mateo...never. They would stay with her the rest of her life. Just like her own Mateo would.

Tanna headed back to the command center's clinic and Gloria went in search of a familiar face. Maybe she'd see a friend from the police force and they would be able to give her a lift home as they dispersed from the hotel.

She had to find out the answer to the question that had burned in her heart all night: Was Mateo's room saved? And she didn't have time to waste, or the not-knowing would drive her crazy.

"Gloria! Hey...wait up." Rigo jogged down the hallway when he saw her. "I came by a while ago to check on you, but you were still asleep. They just gave us the all clear. I need to get out there. We know there are people trapped in their homes. I've got to round up my beach patrol lifeguards. Several of them said they were staying behind at a house. They can help with rescues today."

She grabbed at Rigo's arm. "Can you take me with you?"

"I don't think it will be safe for you. You're not trained in rescue." She could see hesitancy in Rigo's dark eyes. "The best thing for you is to go with Tía and Tanna and make sure everything is okay."

Gloria shook her head, the flattened layers of hair flopping out of control across her face. She pushed her bangs back with a forceful hand. "No, that is not the best thing for me to do. I need to get out of here."

"Why, Gloria? What's gotten into you? There's no need to bite my head off. I'm just trying to help you."

A little ashamed of the tone that had overtaken her voice, Gloria tried to moderate her reply. "I need to go home."

She could see compassion in Rigo's face. The lines of tension between his eyebrows faded. "Glo. You own a one-story house in one of the most flood-prone areas of town. There's probably not much left. Why don't you let me check it while I'm out today and I'll report back to you?"

It was a generous offer, to be sure, one that thousands of Port Provident homeowners who'd evacuated would likely wish they could take advantage of. But for Gloria, it wouldn't do. She thought of wiping her tears with her Mateo's stuffed bear yesterday, and she couldn't stomach thinking about what had happened to what she'd left behind.

Exhausted by the past two days, and heartsore from the past two years, a cry tore from Gloria's chest. "Noooo. I have to know. Myself. Now."

Rigo took one step forward and gathered her in his arms. She leaned against him and her tears began to turn his dry shirt wet. "Shh, Gloria. It's ok. What do you need to know? Whatever it is, I'll help you find it."

"Mateo's room." Her voice was muffled against Rigo's broad chest. She wanted to collapse on the floor in a puddle, but his arms wouldn't let go. "I have to know if it's still there."

Rigo swayed back and forth, rocking Gloria gently as her heart cracked with a mother's renewed grief. "Shh. It's okay. I'm going to tell Tía and Tanna goodbye. Get your shoes on, then meet me in the clinic. We'll go together."

The water was only about mid-thigh-deep at the palm tree where Rigo had left his little boat tied up, instead of the chest-deep it had been only hours before. He couldn't believe it, but the small craft was still there. He boosted Gloria in and ungracefully wiggled himself in, as well. The boat swayed with the movement but thankfully didn't dump them back out.

Gloria remained silent, and now that Rigo had seen through that window she'd opened to her heart, he understood why. He didn't understand from personal experience, as he'd never been a parent. He didn't really even see it in the cards for him. He'd had girlfriends over the years, but the only girl he'd ever truly loved was sitting across from him in a beat-up plastic boat, cruising debris-laden waters with him.

And he was not the only man she'd ever loved. He knew that, and when she'd called him Felipe in the apartment parking lot, he was reminded of that reality.

He wished he could tell her where he'd been, where he'd gone after Felipe's funeral...but no, this wasn't the time or place. The truth would not set anyone free in this case. Not now, maybe not ever. And maybe struggling with that and never having the right chance to tell her would just be his cross to bear.

"Where did the lifeguards stay?" Gloria finally spoke up as they navigated the waters near Pirate's Point.

Rigo shook off the apprehension in his thoughts and pointed to a two-story white house in the distance. "Here in Pirate's Point. That's Caleb Simpson's parents' house. It's pretty new, so it's built to the latest construction standards. I think it's on pilings that are about twenty-one feet tall, so they should have been safe from most of the flooding."

As they approached what had once been Blackbeard Boulevard, Rigo caught a whiff of something in the air. Something that wasn't raw sewage or dead fish—the two most common odors of the morning.

"Do you smell that?"

Gloria's nose wrinkled. "I do. What on earth…?"

"Vasquez!" A shout came from the tall white house. "Hey, man, up here!"

Rigo looked up. On the deck were eight of his most seasoned lifeguards. And a rounded, black kettle-style grill.

"We've got steak! Are you hungry?" Caleb brandished a pair of tongs over his head. "Woo-hooo-woo! We made it, Chief!"

Well, I'll be, Rigo thought. They did make it. And they were throwing a party to celebrate survival. Suddenly, the small box of neon-colored children's cereal he'd picked up at the hotel wore off and he was starving.

"Glo? You hungry? Can we stop for a few minutes?"

She looked up at the teenagers on the porch, then back at Rigo. A smile full of sunshine slowly crossed her face, lighting up her features, from her wind-tossed dark honey-colored hair to her tawny eyes. "We're all survivors." She took in a deep breath and then let it out. "I don't think we should miss this moment."

They moored to the tall staircase and then angled themselves over the handrail and climbed up. The teenagers greeted them with sports drinks and bags of potato chips and pulled two more steaks out of a high-end cooler packed with ice. Rigo cracked the seal on the orange sports drink and polished off half of it in one gulp. He ate a handful of chips, then finished off the drink and looked around for a trash can.

"Down there," Caleb said.

"Where?" Rigo looked below the house, but all he could see was murky water.

"Out there, in the street. There goes a Dumpster."

A giant green metal trash container bobbed along in front of the house, dislodged from its proper place behind some building around the island. Who knew where it had come from, or where it would ultimately come to a stop when the water receded. Rigo cocked his arm back and threw. The plastic bottle sailed through the air and landed right inside the Dumpster's open door on top.

"He shoots, he scores!" Gloria clapped behind him. "Nice work, Chief Vasquez." She hadn't relaxed much since he'd walked back into her life. He remembered how she'd cheer for him at high school baseball games. What he hadn't remembered was how good her cheers sounded.

He knew it was all his fault and he had to live with that. But he also knew he'd missed her support over the years.

"Thanks. It's crazy to see something that large just floating around."

As they cut into the T-bones and crunched on chips, Rigo relayed the updates from the command center to his team. He informed them that Texas Parks and Wildlife would be bringing air-powered boats across the bay and onto the island in about an hour. They would be pulling up to the Pirate's Point marina a few blocks away. The lifeguards agreed that they would be ready and waiting to assist the boats with patrol and rescue of anyone who still needed it.

As they wrapped up the meal, Rigo turned to Gloria. "Okay, we've been here long enough. Let's get you home."

It promised to be a long day ahead, but at least they were better fed than most on the island this morning, and he'd gotten to see Gloria's smile when she was briefly distracted from what was waiting next.

Rigo's boat made it back out of Pirate's Point and lasted until about halfway to Gloria's before the water became too shallow for the motor. Painfully reminded of the thoroughly soaked clothes from yesterday, Gloria was thankful when Rigo said he'd use the boat's stowed paddles to get as far as he could. She offered to help, but Rigo told her to relax for a few more minutes. There would be plenty to do once she got home, he reminded her.

As though she could forget what was ahead.

"I think this is as far as we can go, Gloria. We'll have to walk it the rest of the way." Rigo reached out and grabbed the pole holding up a stop sign about four streets away from Gloria's house. He looped some rope around the pole and tied up the boat. "Not like anyone's going to notice another boat in their front yard, anyway."

Gloria looked around her. She knew most of the residents of these homes. They'd had block parties together, watched homes for each other when people went on vacation, hunted for lost dogs through the lawns and the tight alleyways. It was a small neighborhood, with streets named in tribute to the heroes of the Texas Revolution. There was a spirit of community here that Gloria had always felt.

Today, though, she felt nothing but wind and the remaining light rain. The soul of the neighborhood seemed gone, washed out the open doors and windows on most of the homes, flung helter-skelter with the mess of thousands of pieces that had once made up people's lives and now littered yards, streets and alleyways.

But in spite of the overwhelming evidence that confronted her at every glance, Gloria couldn't focus on what she was seeing. Not right now, at least. She kept putting one foot in front of the other and hoping that Rigo would think the wetness on her face was from the weather.

Gloria knew better, though.

The one thing she didn't know was what would be left when she turned the corner and saw 909 Travis Place.

"Almost there, right, Glo?" Rigo splashed alongside her. Unlike Pirate's Point, the water had receded quickly in this area after the storm pushed through. There was only a foot or so left covering the streets. It was enough to soak her socks and shoes again, but at this point she was too focused to even really notice.

Gloria nodded, then pointed. "As soon as we turn the corner, we should see it."

It didn't take long to walk the remaining half a street until the intersection with Travis Place. Gloria closed her eyes and took a deep breath. Rigo came up behind her and squeezed her right shoulder tightly. "It's going to be okay, Gloria. Whatever happens, you're not alone."

She never thought she'd have felt this way again, but she was grateful for Rigo's presence. Since she'd dialed his number in an act of last-resort desperation, he'd been nothing but a rock for her. He'd been the Rigo she'd once thought he was, until he left and changed everything she thought about him. The years had taught her who the true Rigo actually was, but just for a moment, it was nice to have the untarnished Rigo back.

Gloria opened her eyes and looked up. Her front door stood open, pushed by the pressure of the storm surge. In her yard was a tangled mess of fencing, couch cushions that didn't match anything in her own home, paper dropped in wet clumps and even someone else's cherry-red forty-gallon ice chest. Just as on all the other streets they'd recently passed, pieces of board and roof shingles were everywhere. Neither of them could look up and take in the full landscape around them because they had to watch their feet. Rigo had his work boots back on, but Gloria only had her athletic shoes. Nails and debris were everywhere and they'd poke through an unsuspecting tennis shoe easily. And with no likely way to get a tetanus shot on the island right now, the outcome wouldn't be good.

"I've seen this before." She felt as flat as the crushed palm fronds submerged beneath her feet.

"What do you mean?" Rigo stepped into the intersection. There was no chance a car was going to come by, so he was completely safe.

She gestured broadly with her arms. "All of this. It looks like something out of the history books. I feel like I'm looking at pictures of the Great Storm of 1910."

"I can't fault you there. I don't think I've seen anything like it in my life. Unreal. If you live here long enough, you've seen a hurricane or two. But never like this." Rigo turned around and faced Gloria. "Well, are you ready?"

She answered without hesitation and plowed across the spongy grass that had once been her perfectly manicured front lawn. Her shoes were sucked down by the mud beneath with every defiant step. "No. But we're here. Let's just go."

Since the front door stood wide-open, Gloria walked right through without pause.

Just dive in and you'll figure it out, Gracie was fond of saying when she didn't quite know how to do something. Gloria wished her sister was here right now, instead of taking refuge more than two hundred miles away in San Antonio.

But Gloria wasn't alone. Rigo stood right behind her. If she'd leaned just slightly back, she'd find her shoulder blades resting on his chest. He was so close that at any other time, she'd accuse him of invading her personal space.

Instead, once again, she was grateful for the old Rigo. The Rigo who'd seen her through plenty of teenage turmoil was now here for the greatest challenge of her adult life since that day when he'd just disappeared. Maybe she could turn his solid physical strength into emotional strength.

There it was again. Ever since she'd uttered that short, plodding plea of a prayer at Tía Inez's house, she kept being reminded of displays of strength.

Maybe God had been there since Felipe and Mateo died. Maybe she just hadn't been listening.

No, that wasn't it—she'd been in church every week. God knew where to find her. She'd done what she was supposed to do. So, clearly that wasn't really it. She just didn't know what made today different from any other day, with all these mental coincidences.

The water had receded out of the front room. The couch was at an angle in the center, lying on its back. It looked like a sponge. There was no discernible waterline on it, just cushions of sodden foam and fabric. Tables had toppled, and she saw her washing machine on its side in the dining room, leaning against the overturned table. There used to be four chairs, but she could only count two right now. She figured she'd find the others later. Or not.

"Look up here, Glo." Rigo stood against the wall near the front door. A brownish line wiggled across the wall about a foot above him, not far from the ceiling. It looked like a child's bad watercolor painting. "This is your waterline. I'm six-two. It had to have been almost seven and a half feet in here."

Gloria's jaw fell open, stunned. If she'd stayed here like she'd tried to insist on doing...she couldn't even think about it.

"Wow." Rigo let out a low whistle from where he'd tiptoed over to the doorway to the kitchen.

"What?" Gloria crawled over a set of golf clubs that hadn't ever belonged to anyone who'd lived in this house.

She got to the doorway and saw what Rigo meant. There were just no words.

"Your kitchen."

Or rather, what was left of her kitchen.

The water had floated the refrigerator, then apparently, as it receded, it dumped the fridge on its side, tearing off the door. Glass jars were broken and their contents spilled everywhere. Food that had neatly been stacked on shelves only hours before was now a virtually unrecognizable, disorderly mess. It smelled of backed-up sewage with a strong overlay of mustard and pickle brine.

Leaning over, Gloria pulled open the knob on one of her lower kitchen cabinets. Brown water felt gritty as the small wave poured out onto her feet. Pots and pans were upturned and the shelf that held her lids had fallen down, the wood glue holding the cheap particle board eaten away by the time submerged in the pungent water and the exposure to whatever had been floating in it.

"I don't know what I was expecting, Glo. It wasn't this. I watched the force of the water all night long. I saw it move cars on the streets. I sat at the top of the stairs, watching Tía's furniture swirl in the haze below. But this..." Rigo's words trailed off. His eyes took in the whole scene, wide with disbelief. "I don't know why, but I just didn't expect this."

Gloria laughed, a small noise that sounded distant to her own ears. "You know, Rigo. I think I did, in a way. I expected to walk out the door when we left here yesterday and never see my life normal again."

She stepped carefully toward the hallway. The floor of her house lay buried under a thick gray silt. It spread across tile, hardwood and carpet, making everything not only incomprehensibly dirty, but slick and dangerous. The soles of her shoes had no more traction on these mud-smeared floors than if she were walking on the bottom of a pond covered with sludge and seaweed.

"Come on, we're not through." She waved him back toward the bedrooms.

Her bedroom appeared just as decimated as the rest of the house. The bed was no longer on its frame and her dresser had dumped over, spilling out nightgowns and shorts and socks all over the floor. A brackish brown stained deep into every piece of fabric.

"There's not enough bleach in the world to make this right. Guess I'd better get used to this Beach Patrol shirt. Seems like it's all I have left, except the few things I took to Inez's house."

"Let me check the closet, Glo." Rigo stepped on top of the mattress. It squished and spit water up as his shoes smashed across. "Wow. The waterline was above all the hangers in here. I don't think anything is salvageable."

She bit her lip so hard it stung and choked on the cotton rising in her throat.

"It is what it is," she bit out. The matter-of-factness in her voice surprised her. Gloria knew she didn't feel as confident as her tone implied. "The worst part is I hate shopping. How many women would do anything to be able to go on a shopping spree and replace their whole closet? I'm probably the one woman in America who is just ill thinking about it."

"Most of my clothes were in the little storage unit in Tía's backyard. When I moved back, she said I could have a place to stay with no questions asked until I found something of my own. The only catch is the room that's temporarily mine has a pretty small closet. There wasn't enough room there for all of my things so I had to store them outside. So, we'll probably be shopping together." Rigo gave her a smile, and she knew he was doing his best to let her know she wasn't alone.

One more room to check.

She'd strode purposefully through the front door earlier, but now all of her confidence was eroding quickly. Gloria forced her feet down the hall, and Rigo dogged each step. She could feel the light touch of his fingers grazing the rougher skin of her elbow. The soft tickle mixed with the adrenaline already swirling through her and made her pause for a millisecond. She couldn't tell if the touch from Rigo set something off or if all of her senses were on heightened alert.

The plain white door had been parted from the bottom hinge. It hung limply askew like a flag on a windless day. She walked across the sludge on the floor and stopped in the doorway.

The stripes were still there. But like everything else in her life, they'd changed for the worse.

"This isn't Mateo's room." A sob caught in her throat. It scraped as it rose from the depths of her soul. "This is just as dead as he is. Gone. All gone."

As limp as her body had become, Rigo turned her easily and held her as the minutes and the sobs passed by. Time seemed to stop. She didn't know if she was eighteen again or if she'd instantly aged to eighty. The crushing despair she felt sharp as a hot poker in the marrow of her bones seemed to indicate the latter.

She'd lost her husband and her baby two years ago, but today was the day when her heart was mortally wounded. Her memories, the only things that had held her heart together for the past two years, were wiped out and torn away.

Gloria walked inside the room, her path marked indelibly by footprints in the muck atop the carpet. She opened the door and reached for a box on the top shelf. "I put this up here yesterday. It was as high as I could reach. I thought it would be safe there."

The cardboard box ripped as Gloria tried to tug it off the shelf.

"Let me." Rigo reached and pulled the small cube upward. The box and the paint had soaked together and didn't want to part easily. "Here you go."

Gloria took it between her hands and the once-rigid cardboard lost shape at her touch. Without thinking, she sat on the floor. The silt and the sludge seeped into the fabric. She knew it was turning the bottom seam of the Beach Patrol shirt the same withered brown as the rest of her clothes, and she didn't care. Everything was a sea of brown and she didn't think the world would ever hold color again.

She reached inside the box and pulled out a small stack of photos. Rigo squatted down in front of her to look.

The photos were no longer individual, but stuck together in a messy clump as hardened as glue. She tried to peel the top one off the pile, but the colored ink of the image on the photo below stuck to the back of the print above and peeled, ruining them both.

"Why? Why?" The words ripped her throat with the harsh pull of barbed wire and tears flowed anew. They seemed stronger than even yesterday's downpours from Mother Nature. "These were the pictures I had the hospital photographer take of Mateo right after he was born. My son is gone, Rigo. He's gone and he's never coming back. Why did God have to take my memories, too? Couldn't I have at least kept those?"

Rigo gently lifted her fingers from the photos and placed them back in the box, then returned the box to the shelf.

Gloria stood up and tried to reach for the bear she'd cuddled yesterday before escaping to Tía Inez's house. Her hands brushed the uppermost curve of the bear's ear, touching wet fur.

"Oh, Teddy," she said, not even caring that Rigo heard her directing a conversation to a stuffed bear. "Oh, Teddy. You're ruined, too. Everything's gone." Her voice dropped to a whisper.

Rigo gently placed a kiss on the top of Gloria's head. It felt so simple, so unexpected. And instead of being angry, she felt a small grain of comfort where he'd touched her. She could feel a warmth right there, where they'd connected. It contrasted with the chill running just under her skin, causing goose bumps to ripple up and down her arms.

He took a step back. "Glo, I'm sorry. I just...I don't want to upset you even more."

She wiped her forearm across her nose. "You didn't."

"I wish I could do something. Even saying that sounds inadequate."

Gloria brought her gaze up and looked at him straight-on. The color in his eyes almost matched the pupil. She knew this look. A long time had passed since she'd last seen it, but she'd never forgotten how his eyes deepened in color when he was truly moved or serious about something.

"You have. You made me get out. If I'd stayed here, Rigo, like I'd planned, I'd be dead. That waterline—look at it. I'd have drowned, along with Tanna and the baby. You saved my life."

"I finally got my head on straight, Gloria. When I came back to town to take the beach patrol job, I told myself that I was going to stay out of your way. But if I ever had the chance to see you again, I wasn't going to let you down one more time. And then you called out of the blue and gave me the chance to make good on that promise to myself. We'll get everything sorted out here, and then I won't bother you anymore. But at least I got to do right by you once."

It probably wasn't the time. And standing in the middle of her ruined house amidst her shattered dreams definitely wasn't the place, but maybe...if those reminders the past few days had come from God, maybe He would give her just a little more strength to ask that question that burned in her mind and her heart.

"Where were you instead of at Felipe's funeral? What could have possibly been more important than paying your last respects to the man you called your best friend, the man who felt the same way about you?" She stared hard, looking for a change of color in his eyes, but one didn't come. They stayed steadily dark and soulful. "I deserve to know. Where have you been the last two years?"

There. She said it. And she was able to master the weakness in her knees as she asked the question. Her pounding heart didn't fail her. She had found the strength to say what needed to be said.

Or maybe, more accurately, she'd been *given* the strength to say what needed to be said. She wasn't sure. But either way, it was out there.

He didn't turn away or hesitate. It was as though he knew it was coming.

"I've thought about telling you a few times since you called me yesterday, but obviously a hurricane makes things even more complicated than they already are." He paused and her eyes followed the twitch of his throat as he swallowed while he gathered his thoughts. Gloria didn't know if she was more nervous anticipating what he would say next, or if Rigo was, summoning up the courage to say whatever he'd been hiding. "But I can't put this off anymore. You deserve to know. The morning of Felipe's funeral, my father drove me to Houston and checked me into a substance abuse rehabilitation treatment center, where I lived for four months."

Asking hadn't made her weak in the knees, but hearing the answer sure had.

"You went *where*?" Her mind drew a blank, as though she were unable to take it in.

She'd known this man for years. She'd been in love with him for a time, even. She thought she knew him pretty well. But apparently he'd been keeping a big secret from her for a long time.

"Rehab." Rigo's voice sounded crisp, matter-of-fact. "It's not something I'm proud of. In fact, it's been something I don't talk about. A few people high up at Port Provident PD knew when I went on leave, and later resigned, and then I had to answer questions when I came back for the beach patrol job. Other than that, no one knows. But you're right. You deserve to know."

"Rehab?" The taste of the word was bitter in her mouth. Gloria's voice sputtered like a stalled car until she found the right words. "For what?"

"Alcohol. Lots of it." He sat down on an overturned bookshelf. It wobbled a bit unsteadily under his weight. "I'd been drinking for years. Since I left town the first time and went to Baja, actually. You remember the North American Lifeguard Championships, right?"

More than a decade had passed since that time in her life, but she wasn't surprised to realize it still seemed like yesterday.

It still *hurt* like yesterday.

"You mean when you told me you were going to be gone for a week and just never came back? Your first disappearing trick? Yeah, I remember the North American Lifeguard Championships."

"Well, it was in Mexico, right? Kids from all over the US, Canada, and folks from Mexico. We were all there surfing and swimming and showing off. The drinking age there is eighteen, and the locals wanted to show the rest of us a good time. I'd never had a drink before in my life."

Gloria nodded. "You'd been totally dedicated to working out and living clean so you could be in the best possible shape to play baseball."

"Right. But Lady Tequila...well, she made it easy to be friends." He shrugged. "And before I knew it, I'd signed up with

Mario Portillo to teach at surf school down there and I wasn't coming back. You know the rest of that story."

She closed her eyes and the pages of the calendar flew back in time.

"'Hey, Glo... It's Rigo. Look...um...hey...I'm gonna be staying down here for a while with my new friends. You take good care of yourself and go live your dreams. Um...love you. Be good, okay?'" Gloria chirped the awkward message back to him, pitch-perfect. Rigo flinched a little as her words hit his ears. Clearly, he remembered them, too. "You left a message on my parents' answering machine full of cheap bravado. I stole the tape out of that old machine and played it a hundred times. I kept thinking it would say something different. *You left a message*, Rigo."

He raised his eyebrows. "I was a coward, Gloria. If the bravado sounded cheap, that's because it was. It wasn't me talking. It was a bottle. I was already hooked. I'd closed the door on God, on you, on baseball, on everything I'd been here in Port Provident. All for what I'd been told was going to be an endless good time. Life was supposed to be a party. But leaving you that message was the hardest thing I've ever done."

Gloria wanted to shake him. "Then why'd you do it? Why'd you stay down there and leave me here?"

"I don't know, Gloria. I really don't know." His voice sounded worn out, as if he'd asked himself the same question before and came up with the same unsatisfactory answer.

She wanted to stop, but there was more she still needed to know. "But eventually you came back."

"Sure." Rigo laughed without mirth. "My dad stopped paying the bills and the pesos I was making at surf camp didn't go that far. And once a cop, always a cop. My dad thought the discipline would do me good, so he pulled a few strings and got me in the police academy. Just like Felipe always said he was going to do. I wasn't too far behind him."

He closed his eyes, looking as though he was caught in the trance of memory. "And away from the crowd in Mexico, I was able to stay away from all the drinking. I did pretty well for a few years. But then Felipe came to work one day and announced that you all were finally having a baby. He was overjoyed. And that was the night I fell off the wagon. Hard."

Gloria looked around the little dirty nursery. The one event she'd longed and planned for, the single thing that had brought her the most joy, brought Rigo the exact opposite. She broke into his story with memories of her own.

"I moved from being a regular L & D nurse to getting my nurse-midwife certification after my third miscarriage. My doctor told me I couldn't have children. It was my way of coping and getting closer to something I could never have myself. And then one day, it just happened. We were overjoyed. But you, well, I just thought you were being a jerk."

"That sounds about right." Rigo stood up. "But it wasn't without good reason. I'd messed up. I'd let you go because I wanted to 'find myself' on some beach in Mexico. But all I found was I was nothing without you. By the time I'd realized that, you'd moved on. With my best friend. The stand-up guy who never did anything wrong. Until the night he took a quick detour on his way to the hospital to help me take in a carful of kids who were transporting drugs off the island. When the doctor told me what had happened that day, the weight of my role in it dragged me all the way down to the bottom. Riggins was working off duty, watching the door at Molly McLeod's bar downtown. He called my dad when I fell off a stool at the bar that night and passed out on the floor. Before coming to pick me up, my dad called a rehab center. And that was that. I agreed to go without putting up a fight, except that I made him promise not to tell you or anyone where I was. I'd skipped town before. No one would suspect anything out of the ordinary if I did it again."

After he finished speaking, Rigo stood still as a statue. His arms were crossed in a posture that would commonly be called defensive. But after hearing everything he'd just laid bare, Gloria knew the only thing he was trying to defend was his heart.

She knew because she tried to put up her own defenses every single day.

"I didn't know," she said quietly.

"I didn't want you to."

"And yet, when I called you, you still came."

"I owed you that much. And I needed to see for myself if I could be okay around you. If I was going to be back in Port Provident for good, I needed to be okay with the fact that I might run into you one day. I needed to make my peace with the past. And I needed to make any amends I could to you, no matter how small." He ran his fingers through his hair, once on the left side, and once on the right. "I decided I was never going to find out if I was strong enough to see you and be okay if I didn't just take the chance."

Gloria reached out shyly and took his hand. She pressed his fingers with her own. They felt solid. "I've heard that we can't have strength if we have a spirit of fear." She remembered Inez's words from early this morning.

"I've feared being honest with you for a long time, Glo. I'm glad I don't have to do that anymore." He didn't move his hand. She could feel the connection between the two of them. The goose bumps on her arm receded.

Maybe last night washed away the need for that fear and that space. Maybe, just as Port Provident was going to have to do, maybe they could start over, as well. They'd never be who they used to be—but Rigo was right. They shouldn't have to fear running into each other on the street.

A ray of light hit the miniblinds and filtered into the small room. It was only a small flicker of sun after a huge storm, but it made its presence known. Just like the strength she'd felt earlier after praying, this tiny streak of yellow-white came into her life at just the right time. She didn't feel quite as lonely as she had in months. Years, actually.

"I'm glad, too, Rigo."

Chapter Six

RIGO DROPPED GLORIA off at Inez's house and then went outside and peeled off the boards from as many windows as he could before he went out to meet his lifeguards to work search and rescue. Alone with her thoughts, Gloria noticed Inez's downstairs wasn't in any better shape than her own house, but the upstairs had at least been untouched and would give her a safe place to stay while she worked out a plan.

Kicking pots and pans released from Inez's kitchen cabinets out of her way, Gloria walked around, opening windows in all four directions in order to catch whatever cross breezes might come that way. Victorian homes had to be retrofitted to have any kind of modern conveniences, but the one thing they all came equipped with was large windows designed to maximize airflow. Some of the windows stuck, the wooden frames warped softly from their recent hours under water, but with a little elbow grease, Gloria was able to get them all opened fully.

"Oh, good. I tried that earlier and couldn't get any of them to budge." A voice behind Gloria made her jump. She pressed her hand to her heart.

"Inez! What are you doing here? You scared me to death."

Inez looked at Gloria as if she was crazy. "This is my home. Where did you think I was going?"

"I thought the doctors from the clinic were taking you off the island for observation and treatment." Gloria's gaze wandered upstairs. "Tanna isn't here, is she?"

Inez waved her hand in front of her face, shooing away Gloria's crazy idea. "Of course not. About an hour ago, the winds died down enough that a helicopter could land on the pad behind the Grand Provident. They took her out on one of those medi-copters. They wanted me to go, too, but, *ay yi yi*...there's nothing wrong with me. So I flagged down an officer friend of Rigo's to drop me off."

The older woman had even changed into different clothing and somehow managed to fix her hair. She must have superpowers. Gloria knew that she herself looked as if she'd been narrowly pulled out of a floating Dumpster.

"Did you get a shower?" If so, Gloria was pretty sure she'd never been more jealous in her life.

"I got a bucket of water out of the tub and tried to clean up a little. Now I just have to figure out what to do down here."

Gloria had known Inez casually for most of her life but had never spent much one-on-one time with her. Clearly, though, Gloria was finding out why much of the neighborhood depended on her. She was a force of nature.

"Have you seen your house?"

Gloria tucked a wayward strand of her still-hurricane-styled hair behind her ear. She nodded soberly. "Yes. There's not much left."

Inez nodded. "*Lo siento*, Gloria. I'm very sorry. But you're welcome to stay here as long as you need to. It'll probably be a mess all over the city for a few days. Usually is with these things."

Inez leaned over and picked up a spindly wooden chair from the ground and turned it upright, then sat down.

"How many hurricanes have you been here for, Inez?" Gloria leaned up against a wall. It still felt faintly damp.

"Oh, well, let's see…I'm eighty-three now. My parents were young when the Great Storm of 1910 came through, so I've heard lots of stories about that. Last night reminded me of some of those." Inez started naming off names. "There was Carrie, Elise, Linnie, Elaine, Carlene and Jovie. And then several tropical storms, too. So I've probably seen ten or so good storms in my day. They come through every few years, even though it's been quiet here for a good long while now. It's just part of living on the coast. I love it here, though. You just have to take the bad with the good."

Gloria laughed without mirth. "Boy, isn't that the truth?"

"It is." Inez's tone left no room for disagreement. "And I know you've had a run of bad the last few years, Gloria. I know Rigo has had a lot to do with that. But rarely is anything all bad or all good. This hurricane is the same way. It seems bad now, but watch and see. Port Provident will come out and be better than before. And so will you. And Rigo."

"I just wish I knew what to do next." Hot air blew through the windows in a huff, bringing the smell of stagnation into the room from outside. In a way, it reminded Gloria of her own life. Stagnant. Without a whole lot of direction. "No husband, no child, no home, presumably no job for the near future, since I'm sure the birth center will have to be rebuilt. What do I have to call my own?"

"Maybe you're asking the wrong questions, *mi querida*. Maybe it's not about you."

Gloria had no response, despite the loving endearment Inez had used to address her. What a terribly odd thing for the older woman to say. It felt like being in school all over again, being chastised for not following directions. All she needed was a chalkboard to write her name on.

"You don't like that I said that, do you?" Rigo's aunt balanced her elbow on the chair's narrow armrest and tapped her chin with her fingers.

The silence fell with weight around the room as Gloria started and stopped ten different responses in her head. The challenge made her prickle with a bit of anger. She'd just lost everything. Why *couldn't* it be about her, just for a minute?

"Do I really need to answer that?"

Inez tapped her chin again. "Well, no. But you ought to at least think about it. Rigo's made mistakes, Gloria. But he's also had to pay a price for them. He lost his best friend, and he does blame himself. But since he's come back, he's been a different man. He's been commended by the city for his work on the beach patrol. He hasn't even missed a week of church. He has to go to the eight o'clock service because of his other obligations, but he goes every week. And he comes home and earns his keep around here with me."

Gloria didn't really want to hear about all the changes in Rigo. It was easier for her to believe he was the same impulsive, self-centered man she had believed him to be since the day she listened to that message on her answering machine. It made it easier to be around him now if she knew she was getting ready to close the door on him again. She'd only called him because she was panicked and out of numbers in her phone to call. And like he said, he'd only answered because it gave him a chance to make amends.

He'd come clean about the past, and he'd helped her during the recent craziness, but now that the hurricane had passed and they'd cleared some of the heated air between them, Gloria didn't really want anything to do with him in the future. She'd gotten the answers she needed and she'd survived the storm.

And she knew Rigo didn't want much of anything to do with her, either. He said it himself. His goal was for them to be okay with coexisting in the same relatively small city.

But Inez wasn't finished. She caught Gloria's gaze and locked on to it with her own dark eyes. "And something else—he lost the woman that he loved. Truth be told, I saw how he looked at that woman last night. I think he still loves her. And I think she's the last piece in the puzzle of putting back together his life. You know, Gloria, forgiveness is a gift you give to yourself along with the other person. It means you can both move on without living in the past."

Gloria shook her head. She could feel pinpricks of anger under her skin. "I understand that Rigo's your nephew and you want to help him. But my son is in the past. My heart is in the past."

Inez stood with purpose and without acknowledging Gloria's words. "I'm going down to *La Iglesia*. Do you want to come with me?"

No. Gloria didn't want to have any opportunity to continue this pointless conversation. "To the church? How are you going to get there?"

Inez raised one foot and then the other, clad in white leather tennis shoes that clearly hadn't seen the light of day more than once or twice. Low-heeled leather pumps were more in line with Inez's fastidious style. "Well, I'm going to walk, of course. It's less than six blocks."

Six blocks of boards, nails, shingles, palm fronds, household goods and who knew what else. She couldn't let an eighty-six-year-old woman make that walk alone. She'd just have to do her best to change the conversation.

But to what? As much as she didn't want to talk about Rigo or forgiveness or the past, Gloria definitely didn't want to talk about the weather, either.

"Okay, I'll come with you." Gloria felt almost as reluctant about this as she had about entering her waterlogged house earlier.

"*Bien!*" A smile lit Inez's face, making her cheeks stand out like small apples. "You're probably too young to remember Hurricane Jovie too much. That was the last big storm to make landfall here. But those of us who stay always go check in at the church and start seeing what we can do to help."

"Yeah, I was about ten when Jovie came through. I just remember cleaning up a big mess at Mamí and Papí's restaurant. They opened back up the next day, cooking fajitas on a charcoal grill." She'd almost forgotten those days after Hurricane Jovie. Thinking about it reminded her of how proud she was to be Mamí and Papí's daughter. They'd put a bunch of food in coolers and iced it down with dry ice before the storm. Then the next day, as crews worked to restore the power, they'd showed love for their community in the best way they knew how—a hot meal. They'd only settled in Port Provident a few years earlier and wanted to support the rebuilding of the place that had allowed them to rebuild their own lives after coming from Mexico.

"I remember when they did that. Your mother has a heart as big as the sky. And your *papí* has never met a stranger." Inez opened the door. "Now, come on. Let's go see what we need to get started on. It's going to take the strength of everyone working together to bring back Port Provident."

Strength. There was that word again.

Gloria was beginning to think maybe it wasn't just a verbal coincidence anymore.

But why? Why now?

A small crowd of about twenty people stood on the lawn of La Iglesia de la Luz del Mundo. In English, the name meant The Light of the World Church, and it had been a staple in Gloria's community for several generations. Gloria could make out Pastor Marco Ruiz at the center of the small group. He was waving his hands animatedly, just as he did every Sunday in the pulpit.

What would he do now? It looked like the church had been hit pretty hard. The landscape had been ripped up and a patchwork of holes showed where shingles on the roof used to be. Based on her observations at Inez's house and inside her own home, if it was this beat up on the outside, Gloria knew the church had to have taken a knockout punch on the inside.

"Inez, Gloria! Praise God. You're safe." Pastor Ruiz navigated around a few of his parishioners and came to give both women a tight hug.

"Pastor. It's so good to see you. I knew the church members who'd stayed would be gathering here, so Gloria and I came to join you." Inez patted him on the shoulder, then walked over to the group. Gloria recognized several faces from the Bible study group Inez shared with her mother.

Thinking of her mother made Gloria's heart ache a little bit. Although she was thankful they were all safe in San Antonio, the Garcias were rarely apart. Not knowing when her parents and Gracie and Jake and their new baby, Gabriela, would be able to return to Port Provident only increased the sense of loneliness Gloria had felt since she'd stepped in her home earlier today.

Her memories were gone, and for the time being, her family was, too.

"Gloria, come on over. We have drinks and crackers." Monica Hernandez reached into a cooler and pulled out a plastic bottle filled with purple liquid. Normally, Gloria tried to drink only water and the occasional iced tea, but this second sports drink of the day seemed as good to her as a ritzy sparkling water poured over ice with a fancy lemon twist. It looked divine, and she took it gratefully, gulping it down in just a few swallows after she ate a handful of trail mix and saltine crackers.

It wasn't quite the steak she'd shared with the lifeguards earlier, but it settled her mildly rumbling tummy, and it was nice to be surrounded by familiar faces.

"Have you heard from your sister?" Monica asked.

Gloria picked up another small bag of trail mix from the table nearby. "She and the baby and Jake were headed to San Antonio with Mamí and Papí when I last talked to them."

Pastor Ruiz turned and joined the conversation. "That Gabriela is *muy bella*! Such a beautiful girl. I'm glad they're all safe. Jake's family will be busy once the rebuilding starts.

There are a lot of houses and buildings that will need to be brought back to life. I'm sure the foundation will be active with grants and other programs, too. Maybe I can talk to him about helping us here. From what I saw around the neighborhood, the residents of the *La Misión* area are going to need a lot of help. And *La Iglesia*..."

The pastor waved his hand in the direction of the mud-splattered building as his words trailed off. He didn't need to say anything. If a picture was worth a thousand words, seeing this kind of destruction for herself had to be worth a million.

"Is there anything left, Pastor?" Gloria asked, almost certain of the answer.

He shook his head. "No. Not much. All of our seats were completely soaked. All of the electronics were standing in water, so they have to be ruined. The cross is still standing on the back wall, though. I guess that's all we really need, right? As long as we have Jesus, we can rebuild the buildings and the lives of the people in them."

Gloria nodded in casual agreement.

There were going to be long days ahead for Port Provident. Who knew when the electricity would come back on or when they could do something as simple as take a shower again? Rebuilding seemed like a distant idea. Kind of like kids always waiting for Christmas. They knew it was coming eventually, but it was so far out on the horizon.

"I'm hoping that everyone can return to the island soon," Pastor Ruiz continued. "We're stronger when we're all together."

Gloria's head snapped up toward the sky. "Really? Again?" She spit the words out under her breath.

"Did you say something, Gloria?" Monica asked.

"Not really. The strangest things keep happening to me the last few days. Everywhere I go, it seems like someone is talking about strength." She hesitated even saying it. They probably all thought she was crazy. But she figured she couldn't look much crazier, since she'd just been caught red-handed talking to the clouds above.

"Maybe it's just your subconscious talking to you, Gloria." Monica screwed the orange lid back on her drink bottle. "You know, like when I got my new car last year. I thought I was getting something unique. Next thing I know, I see a green Volkswagen convertible at every stoplight. I still don't know if there was some kind of Beetle convention on the island, or if I just became more aware of them."

Gloria picked through the trail mix bag, looking for raisins. "I've had that happen to me before, too. But this is just getting weird. It's like you know how they say 'be careful what you ask for'—well, I guess I got it."

A chuckle came from Pastor Ruiz. "Oh, I think we all prayed for strength when those winds were howling."

Gloria knew he was probably right. Everyone probably telegraphed a prayer to God to help them make it through the night. Even nonbelievers did that in times of extreme stress, so it wouldn't be too unusual. But she'd become a cynic, a lapsed believer, and it had been a long time since she'd really talked to God about anything.

"It's just that..."

"It's been a long time since you've prayed for anything?" The middle-aged man's eyes conveyed a tenderness and understanding that made Gloria feel anything but strong. Her knees softened a bit and she adjusted her stance.

"How did you know?"

He clapped a hand on her shoulder and patted it twice. "I'm your pastor. I've known you a long time. In the good times and the bad. And I know you've just been going through the motions since Felipe and the baby died. Your body is here every week, but your heart isn't. God knows it, too."

Of course He knew. Gloria might feel disconnected, but she still remembered all those childhood Sunday school lessons. God knew everything. It made her stomach turn with shame and dry saltines.

She'd tried to hide in plain sight when really, she should have known better.

Instead of moving away, Pastor Ruiz took one step closer.

"But, Gloria, it's okay. Even the Prodigal Son ran away. What was important was that the son came back." The pastor patted Gloria gently again. "It's important that the daughter comes back, too."

Gloria's throat scraped with dryness. She was at an unusual loss for words.

The silent pause didn't seem to bother the pastor. Instead, he used it to make a graceful exit and leave Gloria alone with some heavy thoughts.

"I see my aunt over there. I'm hoping she has an update from city hall. When you need a shoulder to cry on or someone to talk to, I'll be here. I think we've got a pretty long road ahead. But I meant what I said. We're stronger together. A cord of three strands is not easily broken, remember?"

She nodded as the pastor walked back across the lawn. He'd said those same words at her wedding.

But Felipe was gone. And Gloria had been so sure God was, too.

If these feelings and words *were* nudges from Him, what exactly was He trying to tell her? Gloria felt as confused as she had the first time she'd stepped back into her home alone two years ago.

If a cord of three strands was stronger than a cord of two strands, Gloria wondered what that meant a strand of one was.

Leave it to La Iglesia de la Luz del Mundo. The members could turn anything—even a community post-hurricane check in—into a social event. Rigo had been helping with relocating some supplies from a staging point downtown when he saw Councilwoman Angela Ruiz, the pastor's aunt, and gave her a ride over there from city hall. She'd been hunkered down with city leadership on an emergency strategy planning session and had immediately been swarmed by the cluster of her constituents on La Iglesia's lawn, all of them desperate for any information.

With cell phone towers destroyed and the power grid still offline, the citizens left on Port Provident were totally cut off from the rest of the world.

Rigo saw Gloria, standing alone, holding an empty drink bottle. She looked distant, as if she was there, but not really *there*. It worried him a little bit. He was used to the Gloria who would always step in and take charge—like she'd done for Tanna and the baby.

"Glo?" Rigo walked toward the corner of the building she stood near. "You need anything?"

She rolled the bottle back and forth between her fingertips. He recognized it as nervousness. She'd always played with her hands when she was lost in thought or agitated about something.

"Um, no. Not really."

Rigo gently plucked the bottle out of her hands. "Something's on your mind."

"Maybe." She smiled a half smile. "What do you think about strength, Rigo?"

He didn't know where she was going with this. "I think Island Workout Club is pretty destroyed. I drove past it earlier."

The half smile grew into a Cheshire grin. "I wasn't talking about going to the gym. Not that kind of strength. Besides, if I need to exercise, I have a feeling there are plenty of two-by-fours for me to lift around here."

Gloria ran her hands through her hair and twisted one of the locks around her finger. Rigo recognized that gesture, too. He knew she'd changed over the years—they both had—but under it all, the same Gloria was still there. She'd put up defenses, to be sure, but at this moment, it was as though he was looking through a crack in her mortar and saw the teenager she'd once been, innocently fingering her hair as she gathered her thoughts.

"So what do you mean?"

"It just feels like I'm hearing it everywhere these days. Trouble is, I don't feel like I measure up."

Rigo cocked his head. "How could you not measure up?"

She looked down at her feet and dug the toe of her tennis shoe in the squishy mud. "There's so much to do now. I tried to rebuild my life once before and I don't think I was very successful at it. Look at them." Gloria pointed at a group of church members, standing in a circle with bowed heads, holding hands. "They know exactly what to do. And they believe God will get them through all this mess. I...I don't think I do anymore. I'm scared of having to rebuild again."

Rigo placed two fingers under her chin and raised it. He wanted to see her face. He knew he had been behind the blows that had broken her spirit. "I'm sorry, Gloria. It's my fault."

"You're responsible for a lot of things, Rodrigo Vasquez, but this is between me and God."

He'd been in a number of scrapes over the years. Stupid bar fights in Mexico. Tangles with young punks as a cop. And more than one beat-down by an aggressive jellyfish while lifeguarding and surfing over the years. But nothing stung like Gloria's words.

"If I'd never left for Mexico, I'd never have broken your heart the first time. And if I hadn't called Felipe for backup that night, well, I don't know if it would have saved Mateo, but at least Felipe would have been there for you. He died because I called him for help. If I hadn't called Felipe, your heart wouldn't have broken again."

He dropped the plastic bottle on the soggy ground and took Gloria's hand. It trembled like a baby bird, and Rigo knew he'd caused that, too. He'd probably said too much. But he might never get the chance again. "I don't have any right to ask this, because I know I'll probably never be able to forgive myself for that. But I hope that one day you can forgive me."

Gloria exhaled deeply. She closed her eyes slowly, as though a fighter's punch had just connected with her head. She exhaled again.

Time seemed to stand still as Rigo waited for whatever she was going to say next. If she cut him out of her life again, he would just have to be okay with it. He'd had the opportunity to do what he said—apologize to her—he couldn't ask for anything more.

But still, the silence didn't fall softly. It landed stark and unmoving around them.

Gloria took in one more breath, then flicked her eyes open. They were clear and unblinking.

"Forgiveness is a gift you give yourself. It lets you move on without living in the past. That's what your aunt says."

She laid her other hand gently on top of Rigo's.

"My home is nothing but a leaky roof and wet walls. My keepsakes are stained with mud and they smell of sewage. I don't have much left. So I'm going to have to rebuild, whether I like it or not. I don't want to live in the past anymore, Rigo."

Gloria squeezed his hand and looked him squarely in the eye. Rigo felt his shoulders tense and his teeth grind together.

"If I'm going to move forward, I don't think I have any other choice. I have to forgive you."

To replace the flooded truck he'd had to leave in the streets the night of the hurricane, Rigo had been given another one, which rode out the hurricane in one of the upper floors of Provident Medical's parking garage. As he patrolled the beaches, making sure everyone continued to stay out of the water, Rigo couldn't stop thinking about Gloria's declaration. He thought about the soft touch of her hand and how it still fit in his like it had during summer strolls on the beach. He liked the feel of her palm brushing against his. He liked the memory.

But he felt burdened.

Lord, make me worthy of her forgiveness.

He'd been there and seen for himself the anguish when she realized her carefully constructed memories had been sloshed with mud and tide. He knew she'd had the bandage ripped off her heart today and the pain was real. He knew what it had to have taken for her to offer forgiveness on today of all days.

But maybe, he thought, maybe this was the only day she could have done it. Maybe she needed to lose all the things that bound her to the past in order to walk freely into the future.

Lord, make me worthy of her forgiveness.

The words seared into his mind as he headed back for the rest of his twelve-hour shift, driving slowly around the debris still jumbled in the middle of almost every street.

He knew whatever future Gloria had wouldn't be with him—she may have uttered words of forgiveness, but that didn't just rub out the years like a big pink eraser from their school days. But seeing her today, holding her hand, watching her absently twist her slim fingers in her butterscotch strands of hair—it made him wish he hadn't been so stupid.

It made him wish he wasn't such a fool to want something he could never have.

He should have been content with her forgiveness.

But Rigo couldn't stop himself from wishing he could once again have Gloria's heart.

Chapter Seven

THE SUN ROSE EARLY on Sunday morning. The city's electric grid had experienced a catastrophic failure during Hurricane Hope, as the salt water flooded the mechanics that had sustained the Port Provident community for decades. No one thought the storm would do this kind of damage, and even three days after the storm, the residents who remained on the island were still without basic services like lights and water—because the pumping stations could not come back online without the power to run them.

Because of the lack of infrastructure, the city leadership kept a police officer posted at the base of the causeway bridge connecting Provident Island to the mainland. They were not ready to have a swarm of residents come back and strain the infrastructure reboot even further.

The La Iglesia congregation refused to be deterred, though, and assembled a small group of metal folding chairs on the front lawn.

"It feels good to be together with *familia,*" Inez said as she took a seat. "Save the one on the aisle, Gloria. I'm sure Rigo will be here soon."

After a twelve-hour shift, Gloria was sure Rigo would probably be resting. In fact, she hadn't heard a sound out of his room at the top of the stairs this morning. She assumed he'd come in at some point in the middle of the night and crashed. She knew she was exhausted, and she couldn't imagine the level of stress that was on him, being faced with hour after hour of patrolling the streets and trying to make sense out of the chaos left behind.

As the small gathering of people settled into their seats, Pastor Ruiz walked to the front, holding an acoustic guitar. He sat on a chair facing the group, and without any fanfare, began to strum his guitar and sing a familiar, old hymn. With no choir, no other instruments and no boosting speakers, each word of "His Eye Is on the Sparrow" struck straight to Gloria's heart with the force of a swinging pickax, chipping away at the shell she'd created and sustained for the past several years.

"When hope within me dies, I draw the closer to Him, from care He sets me free," Pastor Ruiz's deep, rich voice sang. Gloria felt her eyes closing, to block out everything but the sound of the words. "His eye is on the sparrow—and I know He watches me."

When she opened her eyes, she saw two nondescript brown birds perched in a nest near the pastor. They'd been exposed to the elements of Hurricane Hope, and yet, they made it through.

Her own hope had died on that hot August day in the past. But instead of taking refuge in God—who'd created the Heaven where her Felipe and Mateo now lived together—she'd shut Him out. She'd thought it would shut out the hurt. But she'd been wrong. She should have drawn closer.

It took an act of brutal nature to get her attention. Gloria could feel a weight being lifted. The feeling was real. Her shoulders pushed up straighter. It took coming face-to-face with Hope to make Gloria realize the simple truth of a song that had been sung for more than one hundred years, of a Bible verse that had been read for more than two thousand.

He'd provided refuge and a fresh start for those birds when the storm raged.

Why wouldn't she be any different?

His eye was on the sparrow, and for the first time in a long time, as the early morning sunshine washed down and warmed a battered and sodden congregation, Gloria knew without a doubt His eye was watching her.

She'd been gone for a long time. The sun's rays felt like a hug. She let the warmth wrap around her and indulged in the sensation for a moment.

Just as she'd forgiven Rigo, she knew she, too, had been forgiven for being away.

From deep inside, Gloria felt a smile rising. It danced along her lips and turned up the edges.

It had been a long time since joy had taken wing from her heart. It felt good.

Rigo slipped into the aisle seat next to Gloria. The pastor had started speaking, and he knew he should be listening, but Gloria attracted all his focus.

Her eyes were closed, and sooty lashes lay dusty on her cheeks. The corners of her lips curved upward and a glow spread across her smooth caramel complexion. Normally, he'd blame the Texas heat and humidity for any kind of glow this time of year, but Gloria hadn't broken a sweat. This seemed to come from inside.

The very sight of her made him forget the time that had passed, the mistakes he'd made and the small cornerstone of rebuilding they'd laid between them at that first informal gathering after the hurricane on this very lawn. He wanted to reach over and hold her hand, just like he used to do when they were teenagers. But he knew he couldn't do that.

Gloria said she'd forgiven him. Not that she'd forgotten.

She must have felt his gaze on her, because her eyes fluttered, then she turned her head and looked at him. Her smile wrinkled a bit, as if she were a little shy.

But she didn't look away. Her eyes looked like warm maple syrup, amber brown with a hint of crystalline light in the depths.

It made Rigo realize he hadn't heard a word the pastor had said. And if Gloria kept her eyes turned toward him, he wasn't sure he ever would.

He thought he'd never see that look again. It made him grateful, all the way down to his toes, to have had the opportunity to see it again.

Lord, make me worthy of her forgiveness.

Yesterday's refrain came back to him. And maybe, just maybe, looking over that unsure smile and those maple eyes, framed by that point of her hairline that came down and gracefully shaped her face into a heart...maybe he wanted it even more today than he had yesterday or when he'd come back to the island.

But what could he do to show her that her forgiveness was not misplaced? What could he do to nurture that seed of forgiveness into a sprout of trust?

Pastor Ruiz closed his brief sermon and asked the church members to join him in prayer. Rigo bowed his head without hesitation. He knew there were so many needs in the community that the pastor would cover—but he had one of his own that he needed to ask God first.

"*Sobrino*," Tía Inez's voice came through loud and clear, addressing Rigo with the Spanish word for nephew. "Are you able to stay for lunch with all of us? Or do you have to go back to work?"

Rigo did a double take. "I have a little break, but how is anyone serving lunch?"

He knew his tone held more than a healthy dose of skepticism. The ladies of the church could make something out of pretty much nothing, but he didn't know how on earth they could pull together a meal for thirty or so people when there hadn't been power or water for days.

Gloria must have picked up on his disbelief because she laughed. "The FEMA folks came by earlier and Pastor Ruiz talked them into leaving a couple of boxes of MREs for everyone."

The MREs had already become something of a legend around town. The Federal Emergency Management Agency had staged trucks of supplies in Houston when Hurricane Hope's path became clear, and they were able to quickly get water and boxed meals in to those who had stayed behind. Because the causeway had been torn up, everything came across from the mainland by boat. Once the causeway was repaired, other agencies would be bringing catering-style trucks with hot meals, but they weren't expected until tomorrow at the earliest.

For now, they all ate field rations and tried to wash the salty cardboard taste that lingered behind with a bottle of water and gratitude for the opportunity to eat a meal of any kind.

"Venga!" Inez's shout told everyone to come on. She waved her hands toward a table near the parking lot, which had now become a staging area for debris being brought out of the church. "Come grab what you want. It's time to eat."

Rigo and several of the others picked up folding chairs and moved them closer to the makeshift dining area.

"Here you go." He unfolded one next to Gloria. "Mind if I sit with you?"

She shook her head. "Not at all."

"Tía? What about you?" He set a second chair for himself next to the one he'd put down for Gloria.

She pointed toward three ladies her own age near a pile of shingles. "I'm going to sit with Maria and Juana. Can you bring a chair for me?"

"Sure." He picked up another chair, then turned to Gloria. "While I'm over that way, I'll go get our entrees."

Each box of MREs contained twelve different meals, so he'd have to see what looked most edible of the variety.

Apparently Gloria's thoughts ran along a similar wavelength. She called after him with a small chuckle. "Don't get any of the cheese and egg omelet ones, okay? I hear they taste like sawdust."

"Your wish is my command," Rigo said, bowing low. If only she knew how sincerely he meant that oft-used phrase.

Lord, make me worthy of her forgiveness. Could an indestructible meal pouch be part of that? God had used food memorably before. Loaves. Fishes. Why not MREs?

On the other hand, Rigo had already sampled a few of these. Undoubtedly, the disciples had much better eating with fresh bread and the daily catch. There wasn't anything redeeming about today's lunch, except that it would be filling.

Rigo presented the beige plastic packet to Gloria with a flourish. "Today, for your dining pleasure, The Hurricane Hope Café is pleased to present beef ravioli."

"Sounds tasty." Gloria tore her bag open. Rigo sat down and did the same.

"Actually, I'm told this one is the best. I had tuna last night. I'm probably not going to be picking that one again. Do you know how to work these?" Rigo pulled out the food pouch, the heating element, a cardboard sleeve and a slim white pouch with a few ounces of water.

Gloria dug around in her bag and followed Rigo's lead. "No, not yet. Inez and I have been sharing ramen noodles and soup we've been preparing over the propane camp stove."

"Well, these are pretty simple. Pour the water in this large green plastic pouch. It'll cause a chemical reaction that will heat your food. Slide the sealed food pouch inside and fold it over. Then stuff it inside this cardboard pouch. Like this." Rigo reached over to help Gloria put everything together and brushed her hand. The green plastic pouch didn't hold the only chemical reaction around here. Rigo was keenly aware of Gloria's nearness and his own desire to stay close for just a few seconds longer.

"There. It takes about five minutes for everything to get hot enough. But in the meantime, it looks like we have a lovely pretzel appetizer to go with our bottled water."

He laid the pouches of heating food on the ground, then cracked open the two bottles of water he'd also brought over and handed one to Gloria.

"It's not exactly a cold bottle of Topo Chico," he said, naming the popular Mexican mineral water he knew Gloria was partial to. "But it'll do."

Gloria took the offered bottle and then raised it. "A toast?"

The scene made Rigo chuckle. "Of course. To what? Hurricane Hope?"

She looked around. "How about just to hope? And a new start."

"I'll definitely drink to that," he said. They tapped water bottles. "To hope."

Rigo looked at his watch. "I think it's been five minutes." He reached down and picked up Gloria's MRE in the cardboard and plastic cooking pouches and handed it to her.

"Wooo! *Caliente*!" Gloria bobbled the hot pouch in between her fingers. "Ouch!"

The steam rose out and scalded Gloria's fingers.

Rigo set down his water bottle, took the MRE from her hands and balanced it on the ground against the plastic bottle. He took Gloria's hand in his own and held it up, fingers spread wide. "Here, let me."

He blew gently, then took Gloria's water bottle and splashed some water on them.

"Better," she said, nodding. "Thank you. That took me by surprise. I didn't expect such a strange-looking little thing to get that hot."

"I'm glad you didn't hurt yourself." He handed the pouch back to her. It felt good to just be interacting normally. There was no drama of labor or howling winds or looking at hurricane damaged dreams. Just two people sharing a meal and a conversation. "You know, when I take a girl out on a date, I like to serve up classy meals without injury."

Rigo stopped himself from saying anything further. He knew he shouldn't have made the joke as soon as the words left his mouth. Gloria mixed the contents of her MRE's food pouch with a spoon, and he couldn't see her expression due to the short layers of hair falling in front of her bowed head.

"Do you go on a lot of dates?" Her voice could best be described as monotone.

Even in Mexico, when he stumbled from bar to beach trying to find himself, there hadn't been other women. And certainly not after he returned to Port Provident, where the memories of Gloria littered every corner and danced between every grain of sand.

No one measured up to Gloria. So he'd stopped trying to fill that hole a long time ago.

"It's been a while." He hoped she didn't press him to define it any further.

"Me, too." The monotone quality still clung to her voice. "You know, we went out for Italian on our first date. This ravioli isn't as good, but all things considered, I won't hold it against you."

She looked up through her downcast lashes. He could see a faint twinkle in her eyes. Whether it was the shine of the sun or the light of a good memory that caused it, it made Rigo glad. He'd say he'd missed this Gloria, the girl whose name "glory" seemed to perfectly reflect her spirit. But in truth, he'd carried this Gloria in his heart since he was young.

And he wanted her back.

Lord, make me worthy of her.

Not just her forgiveness. He knew now he wanted all of her. He didn't deserve her after the self-centered mistakes he'd made, but he'd gotten out from behind a bottle and he'd gotten his life straight. And if he got a second chance with Gloria, Rigo didn't want to let it slip through his hands. He wanted to be ready. He wanted to be worthy.

He looked at her shy smile, lips full and slightly curved. He wanted to kiss her again like he did when they were eighteen and the whole world was at their feet, before he second-guessed himself and broke her heart. And then didn't do or think enough to keep it from breaking again.

"Thanks," he said. He owed her so many apologies, but he didn't know if he'd ever have the words. If he kissed her, maybe he could make her understand.

A makeshift church picnic wasn't the place and this wasn't the time. But if he ever did have that chance again, he didn't want to take her in his arms for granted. *Lord, make me worthy of her.* It seemed like the only thing he could ask.

"What's your schedule look like today?" She set the bag, now empty of highly processed pasta, down at her feet and took a sip of bottled water.

Rigo finished a bite before answering. "I just got off. I'm not back on shift until tonight. What are your plans?"

Gloria leaned her head back and rolled it from side to side. He could see the tension in her shoulders. "I don't really know. I was at the restaurant some yesterday, pulling out what I could, so Mamí and Papí can get back open sooner. Wow, the smell of the food rotting without refrigeration was terrible. I just piled it out on the curb—I didn't know what else to do with it. I hope I never have to do anything like that ever again. I probably will be at Mamí and Papí's house today, seeing what all needs to be done there. Who knows when they'll get back from San Antonio..."

The sigh at the end of her sentence told him Gloria had more to say. "But what?"

She raised her eyebrows. "That obvious I was hiding something?"

The MRE had come with a pack of gum. Rigo unwrapped one piece and popped it in his mouth. The crisp minty flavor cut through the lingering ravioli taste. He offered another piece from the pack to Gloria and she took it.

"A lot has changed," he said, looking around what had once been a neat, organized neighborhood less than a week before. "But you haven't."

"I'm not so sure about that. But I am sure I'm avoiding my house. I've seen it. I know what I'm up against there, and I just can't. Not right now." She scraped her hands through her hair and tucked the flyaway layers behind her ears. "I know avoiding it isn't going to make it any easier or smell any less. But I just don't know when I'll be ready to go back."

"Glo, it's okay." His fingers wrapped around the edges of the chair and he locked his wrists tight. It took all the strength he had not to reach out and try to wipe the apprehension off her face. "The recovery hasn't even really started yet. There's going to be plenty of time to do what needs to be done. In typical Gloria fashion, you've taken on the restaurant and your parents' house. You've been to Gracie's, too, haven't you?"

She nodded. "They have a baby. They're going to need help."

"So do you, Glo. One thing at a time. You don't have to bear everyone's burdens."

"I don't really think of it that way." She bit down hard on the gum in her mouth.

Rigo leaned forward slightly, wrists and elbows still locked. "Then what is it?"

"It's just what I do. I'm a midwife. I'm there for others when they need it."

He chewed his gum slowly, thinking about Gloria's words. She was loyal. Doggedly so. Sometimes she cared too much and she could come across as pushy. But you could always count on Gloria to be there.

Unfortunately, Gloria couldn't say the same for him.

It was past time to change that.

Lord, make me worthy of her forgiveness.

The prayer that had been on his heart the past few days now came into his mind without prompting. To be worthy of her forgiveness, he'd need to re-earn her trust.

He just needed to decide exactly how.

"In fact, Rigo, I'd probably better go. I haven't had a chance to stop by the clinic yet to see how it fared." She started gathering the trash from her meal. "I wish we had some kind of phone service. I want to know how Tanna's doing."

"I'm sure she's fine. She got to ride to the hospital in that helicopter in style. There are no better hands for her to be in—except yours."

She nodded. "I know. It's just so strange not to be able to check in with one of my moms after a birth. But I am going to check on the clinic. Thanks for lunch. It was good to see you between patrol shifts."

He'd take that as a good sign. "You, too, Glo. Leave a note in my room if you need anything. My schedule's going to be crazy for a while, and I'm not at Tía's house much right now. Speaking of Tía, I'm going to make sure she gets home safely, then I've got a few things to take care of myself."

He'd been desperate for a pillow before pulling up to the makeshift church service after a twelve-hour overnight shift. But lunch with Gloria had energized him.

So much needed to be done all over Port Provident. One thing at a time, he'd told Gloria.

Suddenly, he knew what his one thing was.

And he couldn't wait to get started.

All around, an island waited for hands to reach out and rebuild. Rigo had something even more pressing. He had trust to rebuild.

Chapter Eight

THE WALK BETWEEN THE church and the clinic could not be described as short. It took Gloria more than half an hour in the Texas September sun to make it all the way. But the steps and sidewalks gave her more than enough time to think about all the jumbled fragments in her mind.

Not only had Rigo stepped back into her life—run back in when she'd called him in a panic, truthfully—she was coming to rely on him. It was as though the hurricane had blown away the ugliest pieces of their past as it pushed inland.

"Gloria!" Dr. Pete Shipley stuck his hand out from behind a brown-stained refrigerator balanced near the curb in front of the birth center and waved. "I've been wondering about you. How's your parents' restaurant?"

"A mess. About like that break room refrigerator you've got there." She gestured toward the rings of duct tape circling the appliance, holding the doors shut.

Pete wiped his forehead with the back of a rough work glove. "That's for sure. I didn't have it in me to even open this thing up. I've spent my life in ERs and delivery rooms, and I just knew I couldn't take the mold and the smell of rotting food that would be in here. There's not a big enough emesis basin in the world for how I'd handle this."

Gloria nodded her head. "I was at Huarache's yesterday. About the same thing. Except I couldn't just move a commercial-sized fridge out to the street. I had to go in. I wished I'd had a Darth Vader mask."

"Luke. I am your freezer." Pete gave the James Earl Jones impression his best shot.

She let out a hoot of laughter at her boss's joke. "Something like that."

"It's good to see a smile on your face, Gloria. I was worried about you when I heard you'd stayed with Tanna." He continued picking up debris in the yard of the clinic and tossing it in a pile down by the curb. "Watch out. There are nails on the ground."

She tossed the shingles toward the pile and dusted off her hands. "Fair enough. My work gloves are at Huarache's. How's the clinic?"

Instead of answering, Pete turned around and faced the little green one-story cottage that housed the clinic. "Come on inside. We need to talk about what's next."

Gloria leaned against the doorway in what had been the waiting room of the Provident Women's Health and Birth Center. She'd known this was coming, but hearing the news for certain made her knees buckle a bit.

"I'm really sorry, Gloria. I know this is tough. I hate having to close the clinic, but the loss is just going to be insurmountable." Pete sat with a thud on the metal chair in the corner and focused blankly at his hands with a look of desperation. "Since the power failure was caused when the water swamped the substation, and business interruption insurance is tied to the windstorm policy, we're not going to get any kind of reimbursement for the days we'd be closed. It would take months to get the clinic reopened—months without any kind of income. And I just don't see us getting enough from the regular insurance once we finish repairs to cover the difference."

Although she knew Pete wasn't exaggerating the dire situation, and although she'd given serious consideration to her next steps, hearing once more about the changes in her life made her mind spin.

"I think my home is a total loss, and now to go along with that, my job is a total loss, too. And then there's all the mess from last night."

"What mess? Everything okay?" Pete stopped staring at his open palms and looked up. "Well, aside from the obvious."

Gloria could have kicked herself for letting that last part slip. She blamed it on the roller coaster of emotions. Pete had always been a great person to work with, a skilled doctor and a good boss. But she'd never discussed relationships or other deep personal matters with him, and it seemed strange to start now.

Then again, it wasn't like they'd be working together anymore.

"I've been staying with the aunt of my ex-boyfriend from high school, Rigo. He lives there, too. And he helped me safely deliver Tanna DeLong's baby."

A smile cracked Pete's face. "Gloria?"

"I know. I'm not sure what is more mind-boggling. Losing my house, losing my job...or wondering if I'm losing my mind."

"Well, what are you going to do about it?"

"Sell the house to someone who will tear it down and rebuild it so I don't have to. Take the MCAT. Apply to Lone Star University's medical school and eventually get a job with Provident Medical Center." She kicked at a red Lego piece from the children's area that had been swept to the waiting room.

Pete raised his eyebrows. "Really, Gloria?"

She nudged the Lego with her toe again. "Oh, you meant about Rigo."

"Yeah." He matched Gloria's slowly emerging smile with one of his own. "About Rigo. What are you going to do?"

"I don't know. Go with the flow, I guess."

Pete's smile jumped to a full-fledged boyish grin. "You? Go with the flow? You *have* lost your mind, Gloria Rodriguez."

They'd worked together for about two years. It hadn't taken the doctor long to diagnose her need for order and organization. "Probably so, Pete."

"There's a first time for everything."

"To everything there is a season." The quote from Ecclesiastes had never seemed more appropriate.

Her now-former boss nodded. "Indeed there is."

"So what are *you* going to do?"

He looked out the window framed by dingy brown curtains that had once been white with colorful polka dots, then back at Gloria. "I've already put in a call to the director of Global Medical Mission. I'll get the clinic cleaned up and closed up, put the property on the market and get the insurance paperwork in motion. And then I think it's time for me to leave Port Provident and move on. I don't know where they'd send me, but I'm open. You know it's been a dream I've had for a long time."

She knew about dreams, the ones that never strayed far from the corners of the mind. She'd tried for so long to put the memories of her relationship with Rigo to sleep. But time and circumstance had acted like an alarm clock in her life, wrenching her out of the motions she'd been subconsciously going through for so long.

"So I guess that's it." Gloria looked around the little clinic she'd grown to love. She'd started working here as a refuge from the worst moments in her life. Not having to work on the L & D floor at the hospital gave her a buffer from memories that, until this week, had brought her to tears every time she thought about them. The Provident Birth Center had restored her faith in birth and her ability as a midwife when she hadn't been able to save her own son.

She would miss this little clinic. But she'd never forget the lessons she'd taken to heart here.

Pete stood up and pulled a slip of paper out of the back pocket of his dirt-stained jeans. "I guess so. Here's your last check, Gloria. I'm sorry it had to come to this. I hope things work out for all of us in this new chapter we're being pushed into."

"I think they will, Pete." A smile pushed into the corners of Gloria's lips. "You know what they say—'That which doesn't kill you makes you stronger.'"

Losing liters of blood, her own child and her husband hadn't killed her. Starting over alone hadn't killed her. It took a hurricane to make her see the reality, but she would never deny the truth again.

"I know I'm stronger now," she said, and she meant every word.

In the time of her life that Gloria now thought of as "PH," or pre-hurricane, nothing settled her mind like an evening walk around the neighborhood. She would use the sidewalks of Port Provident to organize her thoughts about a birth she'd attended, something Gracie had said or even her sadness about being alone.

Today, though, walking back from the clinic, Gloria's mind raced at a pace far more quickly than her feet had ever taken her.

Pete had laughed at her declaration that she was just going to see where things led. But she'd witnessed a different side of Rigo lately and she didn't see how she could do otherwise. She'd seen a man who defied Mother Nature herself to bring people to safety. She'd seen a man who held her while she faced her deepest fears and opened up about his own.

And she'd seen a man who quite literally would have saved her and those who depended upon her from drowning if it had come to that, even though they hadn't talked for years or parted on good terms. Concentrating only on her thoughts and not stepping on scattered debris, Gloria realized her footsteps had brought her back to the place where they'd always brought her.

Home.

Right in front of her stood 909 Travis Place. But it looked very different than it had last time she saw it. Just as at the clinic, the refrigerator sat on the curb, sealed with bands of duct tape. All of her living room furniture had been pulled out to the covered front porch. Books lay open on a sheet of plywood, as though they were trying to dry out. Beige carpet, stained darker brown from sand and seawater, sat rolled intertwined with its blue-and–yellow-flecked under-padding. They looked like amorphous logs at the edge of the grass.

A flash of movement was visible in the open windows. Cautiously, she walked up the sidewalk to the front door, which stood wide-open.

Rigo came into view, dragging a jagged piece of drywall almost as tall as he was.

"Glo?" He rested the dusty rectangle of white against a corner of the living room wall. "I thought you were at the clinic."

"I was. I thought you were running an errand."

He wiped a hand carelessly across his sweaty brow. His dark hair clung to his forehead in damp tendrils.

"I am. More or less. I'm helping out a friend."

Gloria ran her fingers along the door frame, tracing the grain of the wood. A lump settled into her throat. She tried to swallow it away before speaking. "You've been here the whole time since we left the church?"

Rigo nodded.

"You did this for me?" She almost couldn't believe it. He'd made more progress in just a few hours than she had yesterday in almost an entire day at Huarache's, her parents' restaurant.

"You said it was going to be too hard for you to come over here for a few days. Mold is already setting in. I just didn't want things to get any worse than they already are."

Gloria looked up at his sweat-stained face. She'd seen him a million times in the heat of the day, usually killing time on the beach after surfing or getting in a workout by running up and down the sand. But she stared at him as if she'd never seen him before.

Truthfully, she never had seen him like this before.

Even when they'd been teenagers, head over heels for each other, he'd never done anything on this level for her. The old Rigo would have been more concerned about himself. He would have been helpful, but not all in.

"I don't know what to say," she finally got out.

He smiled. The confidence in that simple gesture spoke wordlessly, straight to her heart.

"You don't have to say anything. You don't even have to do anything. The electricity is scheduled to come back online in the morning and they plan to open the causeway in the afternoon. People can start coming back home. Take care of your parents. Take care of the restaurant, of Gracie's place. Do what you need to at the clinic. I've got this."

She shook her head. It didn't seem right. He'd done enough. She wanted to find a way back to friendship again. Not to be in his debt, or for him to be in hers. "I just need a little time, Rigo. You have a job to do. You don't need me in the way."

He pushed the sweaty hair back off his forehead. "You're right."

She was glad he saw it her way. Just friends. Clean slate. No one beholden to the other.

Rigo looked straight at her. He reached out a hand and lifted her chin so that their gazes met. A decade melted away in an instant as his eyes turned two shades darker, the iris almost matching the black of the pupil in the center.

She knew this look. She'd once lived for this look.

"I don't need you in the way, Gloria. I just need you."

Gloria's breath came short. That sounded like more than just friends, more than she was willing to give.

She opened her mouth to say something, to set him straight. He pulled the finger from under her chin and laid it lightly upon her lips, warning her to silence. She felt a tingle like a minty lip balm across the soft skin.

Rigo shook his head, telling her he wasn't finished. "And I'm going to do whatever it takes to prove I came back for the right reasons. I'm going to earn your trust back."

He trailed his finger off slowly. She stood perfectly still, unable to break that hard stare. Standing in the doorway of a house full of memories, she couldn't think of anything except that look.

"And once I do, I'm not stopping there."

Rigo couldn't believe he'd been so direct. The look on Gloria's face told him that he should have thought that one through before he spoke. But he couldn't help it.

"I came back to apologize to you, Gloria. To set things right between us." He needed her to know. "But I know now I'm not going to be right without you. Not ever."

She still didn't speak. The silence began to spread, threatening to shut down the hard-won emotional truce that had settled between them during the past week. His heart still pumped furiously, but the adrenaline began to turn to ice. In the past, Rigo dealt with overwhelming emotions and uncomfortable situations by just turning and walking away.

But he'd learned he was stronger than that. Rigo's counselors had shown him that he had never backed down from a wave, he'd never backed down from a bullet—and he used that knowledge to know he wasn't going to back down now.

"Glo. Please. Just say something. If I'm making you uncomfortable, tell me. But I'm not leaving. Not this time."

She spoke, so softly he almost missed it. "You can stay."

He watched the rise and fall of her chest. Measured, steady. Almost too measured, as though she were focused on the simple act of breathing.

"I don't want to upset you."

"You didn't upset me. You surprised me." She paused and ruffled her fingers through her hair, shifting her gaze downward. "You scared me."

Rigo nodded. That was understandable. He'd scared himself. "How so?"

"Because I don't think I want you to stop there, either." The words came out in a low-pitched rush, as though she were trying to get them out before she was tempted to take them back.

His heart sputtered a bit, it raced and then thudded with the realization of what he'd said. And with the responsibility. He knew the reason that their dreams had shattered rested on no one's shoulders but his own. He also knew that righting that wrong rested on his shoulders.

Lord, make me worthy of her.

"So where do we start?" Rigo wanted to be respectful of the hint of fear he still saw in Gloria's eyes. Clearly, she felt the same attraction he did. And clearly she still remembered the past. He was willing to let her take the lead. He owed her that much.

"Well, lunch today was nice. It was good to just share conversation and a meal."

He'd take her out to the best restaurant in town, three meals a day, to show her he meant what he said. But they were just days past a hurricane taking over their hometown, laying waste to electricity, buildings and fresh food.

Rigo let his gaze rest on Gloria softly. She'd always been pretty, but the years since they were teenagers had allowed her face to grow into true beauty. He loved that she was still petite enough to tuck perfectly under his shoulder and wrap his arms around. He wanted to earn the right to do that again. He knew that, in spite of the havoc the hurricane had brought, he needed to find a way to honor Gloria's request. He wanted them to rebuild in whatever manner brought her the most comfort. If that was over the quiet company of a meal, then he would make that happen.

"Meet me at the top of Inez's stairs at eight o'clock."

"Wait, what?" She gave a skeptical look from the side corner of her eye.

He broke into a grin as the plan came together in his mind. "I'd like to take you out on a date. Would you please do me the honor of dining with me tonight?"

Rigo's breath caught in his throat. It felt like asking her out for the first time all over again. Roll together all the times he'd asked her to homecoming and prom, and he'd still never been as nervous as right now. So much more was at stake than a dance after a football game and some high school popularity points.

"Rigo. There's a dusk-until-dawn curfew on. We can't go out to dinner. And don't you have to work?" The quizzical look in her eyes intensified and caught the light, giving them a glassy shine.

"Gloria. I help enforce the curfew. But I have a plan. And I don't have to be back on shift until eleven tonight." He couldn't keep the smile off his face. He felt like she was going to say yes, and it made him happier than he'd been in years.

Her lips pursed, bringing his thoughts back in time. He wanted to kiss her. For real. Not just the light touch to the head he'd given her in the nursery. But he knew he couldn't. Dinner was in the plan. Real kissing wasn't.

At least not yet.

"I have no idea what you've got up your sleeve. But that goofy grin tells me something's going on in your mind." She relaxed the curiosity in her stare.

"Do you trust me?"

The words were simple, but the answer was not. If she said no, he knew he'd have to live with that. His actions had brought them to this point, after all.

But his thoughts broke and the prayer of the past days flowed into his mind. *Lord, make me worthy of her forgiveness.* And then a postscript. *Give me the chance to show her the change You've brought about in me.*

"Not entirely." She pointed a slim finger at him, the bubblegum-pink polish roughened and chipped at the end of the nail. "Prove me wrong. You have one chance."

That was the Gloria he knew and had loved. Feisty. Issuing orders. Not the scared, shattered Gloria of late. He knew how to deal with sassy, secure Gloria.

He knew how to sweep this Gloria off her feet.

One chance was all he needed.

It felt silly, but Gloria rummaged through the upstairs closet at Inez's, looking for something nicer to wear than the sweaty and stained T-shirt and shorts that had become her defacto uniform. Of the few things she'd brought in her suitcase, she hadn't packed anything that fit the bill—because who expected to dress for a date during a hurricane? She felt exhausted, grubby and anything but date material.

A lightweight jersey dress that appeared to belong to one of Inez's granddaughters hung at the back of the closet. Judging by the style, it had probably been purchased about ten years ago. Gloria shrugged her shoulders—Rigo was a man, and a beach bum at that. He wouldn't notice if something was in style or not. And it was pink and summery and definitely not a dirty T-shirt. It made her feel special and dressed up after days of wearing muck.

She didn't know why thinking about this evening brought butterflies to her stomach, or why she'd want to spend any effort on salvaging a sundress that wasn't hers. Or trying to fix her hair into some semblance of order. Or to do anything to not look grubby and disheveled.

But it did seem to matter. More than she was comfortable admitting. And as the minutes ticked closer to eight o'clock, Gloria's butterflies began to dance and twirl even more noticeably.

At one minute until eight, a knock sounded at the door of the bedroom where Gloria had been staying.

Before words could even be exchanged, Gloria caught Rigo's gaze sizing her up from head to toe and in between.

"You look beautiful, Gloria. I don't know where you found a dress in the middle of a disaster recovery zone, but you did. You're amazing, as usual." Rigo beamed broadly. "I thought I would come and pick you up. I'm just glad I don't have to face your dad. He doesn't really like me."

"He doesn't like how you treated me. He used to like you just fine."

"Well, that's good. It means he'll like me again one of these days." Rigo put out his arm, like Fred Astaire leading Ginger Rogers to the dance floor. "Because I'm never going to treat you like that again."

Gloria hoped not. She'd accepted this invitation out of her new belief that she had to forgive Rigo in order to move on. If he inflicted one more bruise on her battered heart, she knew she'd never heal enough to trust or forgive again. The stakes were high and although she wanted to be positive, a part of her held back. It would be skeptical until proven otherwise, no matter what the rest of her wanted to believe.

"Come this way."

Rigo led her down the hallway to a small door at the end. Painted a polar shade of white, it was smaller than the other doors and didn't quite fit with the rest of the features of Inez's Victorian home. In her few days here, Gloria hadn't even noticed it.

"You're going to need to duck a bit," Rigo said, turning the heavy brass sphere of a doorknob.

The small door swung silently on matching brass hinges.

"It's like Alice's door to Wonderland," Gloria said.

Rigo nodded. "It's Inez's door to the attic. But it is definitely a door to all sorts of wonder. There are trunks and boxes up here filled with items that have been in my family for generations. Watch your step."

Gloria tiptoed around a narrow path between boxes and birdcages and rolls of old fabric, jewel tone colors subdued by years of dust.

"Why exactly are we up in your aunt's attic?"

He pointed at a staircase barely wide enough to hold two feet, side by side. "You'll see. Give me your hand."

This time it wasn't life and death. She didn't need to be saved from swirling waters. This time, the simple touch of Rigo's hand holding hers weighed upon her fully.

She could dress it up as forgiveness or second chances. But it was time to face the truth. She was here, with this man in this moment, because she had lived for far too long in a world like those bolts of fabric she'd just passed—neglected, muted and far from the original purpose.

Instead of being used, valued and admired, they were stuck in a corner of an attic. She'd been stuck in a corner, too.

She wanted to feel special again and connected to someone. To be a part of something greater than just herself.

Gloria wanted to be loved.

Holding Rigo's hand reminded her of a time when she had all of that. Could she find it again with him?

Could she trust him?

Could she trust herself?

She tightened her grip, feeling the curve of Rigo's fingers and the heel of his hand mold to her own. She followed his footsteps up the narrow stairs.

The door at the top of the stairs swung open as they approached it. A quick jolt ran through Gloria. Doors shouldn't just open.

"Good evening, sir, madam." A young man in board shorts, a T-shirt and a bow tie nodded at Rigo and then Gloria as he spoke. "My name's Kevin, and I'll be your host tonight."

Gloria stepped through the open door. "What's all this?"

"Welcome to Inez's Rooftop Grill," the young man said.

A small square table covered in an antique lace table cloth and framed by two nondescript metal chairs sat in the middle of the small patio area, which was ringed with a narrow white-painted rail topped with gingerbread-style trim. Candles were gathered in a small cluster at the center of the table, and they also graced the tops of other furniture and the porch railing. In spite of the pitch-black night, the stars twinkled and the white utility candles glowed warmly.

"I knew there weren't any restaurants back open anywhere on the island, but I knew of a really special place. Only a handful of homes on Port Provident have this rooftop deck—it's called a widow's walk. I've been coming up here to watch the stars since I was a kid."

"Widow's walk? What an odd name for a porch." Gloria had never heard the term, although she'd been on a few of these rooftop perches throughout the years. It made her think briefly of her own status as a widow. But she pushed the thought aside. As much as she would always carry her time with Felipe and Mateo with her, the past was not going to have a part of her mind tonight.

She would live in the moment and look to the future.

"The legend says that these little roof walks were where women would go and watch for their men to come home from sea, and they would often wait in vain. I doubt that's for real, but it's an interesting story. Can't you just see some turn-of-the-century woman out here in petticoats watching the horizon?"

Gloria nodded. "A very romantic legend, if a little tragic. I love the history that's all over Port Provident."

The makeshift maître d' gestured toward the folding table and chairs. "Will this table do, sir?"

There were no other tables on the porch. At only about twenty feet long, the little deck-like area made for a pretty solitary makeshift restaurant.

Rigo pulled out a chair for Gloria. "Yes, Kevin, this will be just fine."

As she sat down, he scooted her toward the table. The heavy antique lace tickled the tops of her knees exposed by the sundress's short hemline.

"Rigo?"

"Yes?"

"How do you know Kevin? Who is he?"

A smile broke the look of mild concentration on Rigo's face. Gloria could tell he was as nervous as she felt. Good. Strength in numbers.

"Kevin's one of my lifeguards. You've had his cooking before. He grilled the steak." Rigo beckoned the young man back to the table. "Sir? What do you have on special tonight?"

"I'm glad you asked. We have grilled flounder fillets, served over a steaming plate of ramen noodles, with a side of canned green beans from our legendary propane stove."

Kevin pointed to the edge of the narrow porch. Inez stood behind another small metal table. A tabletop grill blew a small line of smoke out the side. She stirred a pot on a two-burner propane stove and waved a black nylon cooking spoon in Gloria and Rigo's direction.

Rigo cupped his hand to the side of his mouth and loudly whispered to Gloria. "Chef Inez is well-known in these parts for her *caldo*, but we didn't have enough bottled water to make that tonight."

"How did she pull off flounder?" Gloria's mouth watered just thinking about a main course that didn't start off as powder in a box.

"Well, not only is he an amazing maître d' and rescued four swimmers over Labor Day weekend alone, Kevin here is an accomplished fisherman. He went down to the jetty earlier, and this is what he came back with. The catch of the day."

"This is a very special restaurant, it seems." She studied the glow of the candles. Gloria recognized them as the same white candles they'd used to light the room when Tanna was in labor. Only a handful of days had passed since that chaotic night, but it seemed like a lifetime.

She knew without a doubt that she was a different person than she was only days ago when she called Rigo in an act of panic. Hurricane Hope had come in and blown her winds and swirled her waves, leaving no doubt Provident Island was changed.

In those same hours, it seemed Hope had taken hold of Gloria's heart and changed it, as well.

"Whatever it takes, Gloria. If it's building you a restaurant under the stars because there aren't any others open in Port Provident, then so be it." Rigo's tone sounded measured—his patrol voice—and she knew he meant what he said.

Breaking her focus on the little flickers of light dancing on the candlewicks, Gloria looked up and smiled. "Thank you. You put a lot of thought into this."

"Sir? Ma'am?" Kevin came back over to the table with two bottles of water and two slim white packets. "May I offer you our house specialty? Fresh mixed powdered lemonade. It's an old recipe, purchased from the shelves of a big box store."

Gloria tried hard not to laugh. Kevin obviously had earlier directions from Rigo and took his job seriously.

"Yes, please. It sounds lovely."

Kevin cracked open each narrow plastic bottle of water, then poured a packet of bright yellow crystals in each, replaced the lid and shook each bottle dramatically off to the side.

For emphasis, he twirled one bottle around his head. Just as emphatically, water sloshed out of the bottle and cascaded over Gloria's head and down the front of the borrowed knit dress.

She closed her eyes. "Not quite the shower I've been dreaming of for a few days, but it'll do."

Rigo jumped up and brought a square of folded paper towel to her aid, pressing it to the top of her hair and down her face, soaking up the small rivulets still making their way downward. He knelt at her feet, his chin even with her shoulders. His presence felt so near she wanted to move away.

But she didn't.

She just sat there, quietly absorbing the moment while the flimsy towel absorbed the water.

"Well, there goes your tip, Kevin." Rigo cocked an eye at the erstwhile waiter.

"Sir, in my entire career of waiting tables, that has never happened." The teenager never broke character.

"How long's that been, Kev?"

Kevin brushed back floppy bangs from his brow line. "Well, sir, about five minutes."

"I knew I should have been stricter in the interview process." Rigo stood and handed Gloria the paper towel. "Can you get the lady a new house specialty—stirred, not shaken this time—and check on our flounder?"

Kevin nodded and took three steps over to the outdoor kitchen.

"You okay, Glo?"

She wished he hadn't moved back to his side of the table. "Sure. It's just fake lemon water. It's a little sticky, but I haven't had a real shower since I don't even know when, so this is probably the least of my problems."

"It doesn't matter." Rigo sat back down in his chair.

"What?" She was a little taken aback by his nonchalance. It wasn't a big deal that some lemonade mix had spilled on her, but she'd put forth a little effort to get ready for tonight. Maybe, in spite of what he said, her attempt at dressing up hadn't meant a whole lot. But still, that little part of her heart that was beginning to come out of hibernation wanted him to care.

He leaned back and looked at her with a measured gaze. "It doesn't matter. You're beautiful. Always have been. No sweat or lemonade will ever change that. It's not about what you wear. It's about who you are."

"Rigo, I've..."

He held up a hand, palm facing toward her, and spoke. "Stop. Don't say another word because you're going to deny it. I know the last few years have been rough for you. I know those days have put doubt in your heart. I know I helped put a lot of that doubt there. But you have to believe me when I tell you that you're the same person you've always been."

A few tears started to prick at her lower eyelid. She couldn't look at Rigo, so she looked at the candle glow and hoped the wetness would fade away. "I've changed. There's no two ways about it."

"Gloria, I've seen you call a person from your past that you didn't want to call in order to protect someone in your care—you put her safety ahead of your own comfort. I've seen you stay completely calm and deliver a baby in the middle of chaos. I know that you've put in countless hours at your parents' house and your sister's house to make sure they can salvage as much of their stuff as possible. And I know you walked an elderly woman to church so she could have the comfort of her faith and friends after a hurricane."

Inez waved her spoon defiantly. "I heard that. Who are you calling *vieja*?"

"Sorry, Tía. You're not old. Please don't burn the flounder in retaliation," Rigo called out over his shoulder without turning around.

Rigo lowered his gaze and met Gloria's eyes through the flames. "Even when you're bossy, it's just because you want what you see as the best for others. You're all heart, Gloria, and you give all you've got without realizing it—even to your own detriment. How many people have you helped in the last two years without stopping to ask for help for yourself?"

She couldn't cry in front of him. She just couldn't. But she couldn't speak, either.

"I know you haven't. The first person I asked about when I returned to *La Iglesia* was you. I wanted to know what time you came so I could stay out of your way for a while, until you'd had a chance to deal with the fact that I was back. Pastor Ruiz said you came to the late service every week, but he hadn't talked to you since planning Felipe's funeral."

She shook her head and hoped Rigo thought the solitary tear that snuck down her cheek was lemonade. "I just...I didn't have anything to say. Everything I'd lived for was gone. Praying about it wasn't going to bring them back."

"I understand. When my dad finally made me see I had a problem with alcohol, I didn't want to talk to anyone, either. I'd made mistakes, and they were my own, and talking to some counselor at a rehab center wasn't going to change the fact that I'd hurt you or that Felipe might still be here if I hadn't called him for backup. I have a lot of regrets, Glo. But through time and counseling and returning to the church, I've tried to make sure that my regrets don't become retreads."

"What do you mean?" He sounded so sure of himself, of where he'd been and what he'd learned. Their situations were obviously different, but she missed being that confident.

Oh, how she missed the old Gloria.

"I mean I don't want to keep making the same mistakes. I left Port Provident PD voluntarily, but I wasn't in a good place and it meant I didn't leave on the best terms. But I've come back and found a job that lets me still serve the community and keep the people who live and visit here safe. I didn't need a do-over. I needed the chance to do better."

Maybe they weren't so different after all. "Like how I moved from the hospital to the birth center after I lost Mateo.

I feel like I can do more for my patients there because of the way we're structured. I've even been able to really be there for clients who have lost a baby. It's almost become a passion of mine. I don't want anyone to ever feel as alone as I did that night, in a hospital bed, all by myself, knowing the whole world had changed for me."

"Gloria." Rigo reached out and took her hand. "That right there proves my point. You're all heart. And if nothing else comes out of tonight, but you leave here knowing that...well, that'll be enough for me."

She felt an active pushing on her heart, like the forward motion of a wave, nudging her back from the deep waters she'd called home for far too long. It was time to come back to shore. The years hadn't changed her irrevocably, as she'd feared. Instead, they gave her insight and compassion to do her job—her life's calling—even better. That was the gift of Mateo's short life. He made her a better person. Having loved a good man who first picked her up when she thought she couldn't give her heart to anyone again made her know that love wasn't just a one-time thing. She'd lost before and loved again. Maybe history could repeat itself.

And she had a most improbable lifeguard to thank for the realization.

Rigo couldn't believe the conversation they'd just had. So much had passed between them over the years that he wouldn't have been surprised if anger or frustration had come up when they talked about the past. He knew that was about God, not about anything he could have said on his own.

"Sir, madam. Your flounder."

Kevin presented two paper plates with a flourish. A filet of grilled flounder lay atop a pile of squiggly noodles flanked by a small group of green beans. Compared to the prepackaged food of the past few days, this looked like the best meal that had ever been laid on a table in front of him.

"Thank you, Kevin." Rigo opened the folded paper towel and laid it in his lap as if it had been a napkin made from the finest linen.

Kevin nodded, making his bangs flap. Rigo had no idea how he swam with all that hair in his face. But he was one of the stars of Beach Patrol. "And now, sir, if you don't need anything further, Chef Inez and I will leave you and the lady to your meal."

Rigo could see Gloria gently bite her lip, trying to stifle a laugh at the fake-haughty tone of Kevin's voice. If the beach patrol thing didn't work out, Rigo would need to remember to advise Kevin to look into acting.

"No, thank you, Kevin. I believe that will be all."

Kevin bowed solemnly, then opened the small door for Inez. She patted Rigo gently on the shoulder as she passed. Her eyes twinkled mischievously, reminding him of the stars above.

Heaven wasn't too far away in a place like this, and he could feel the answer to his repeated prayers being worked, even now, under these stars.

The door closed with a click, and they were completely alone on the small widow's walk. Alone with only the muted sound of rolling waves coming on shore a few blocks away and the glitter in the night sky.

Gloria must have harbored similar thoughts. "Look at them all." She waved her hand above, sweeping across the sky.

"Without the streetlights and such shining, they're so clear and bright. I can't remember ever seeing the stars shine like this."

Rigo leaned his head back. He could see several constellations he remembered learning about when he was a child. It was easy to pick out the Big Dipper and the Little Dipper. "There's the north star. Always pointing home."

Absorbed in the display above, Gloria's voice sounded almost dreamy when she spoke. "Always pointing home. I wonder where that is anymore."

"What do you mean, Glo? Your home is here, in Port Provident." Rigo twirled some noodles around the tines of his white plastic fork.

Gloria put a bite of flounder in her mouth and chewed thoughtfully before speaking. "I know. It's just that I've wondered today about my house. What do I do with it? The damage is extensive. And it's really more house than I need. We'd bought it to be a family place."

"Well, what were you thinking of doing?" He took another bite and washed it down with the lemonade.

"Maybe just putting it on the market. Tear out all the damage, of course, but sell it instead of fixing it up. I could use the equity and maybe even some of the insurance to start fresh. Get a condo on the beach."

He could tell by the look on her face that she was serious. "So you've thought about this?"

"I've thought a lot about fresh starts these days. I think it's time to do something different."

Rigo knew a lot had changed in the past few days. He hoped things weren't moving too fast. She'd already spoken of how her home and her job and her memories had changed. He wanted to support her but didn't want to see her newfound progress stalled out when she realized how much change she would be making. Sometimes those realizations led to progress-grounding fear.

"Are you sure?"

"I think so. There's not much left there to keep anyway. It's a good house with a nice floor plan. Plenty of people will be returning to the island and will need to make a housing change, too. I'd think someone could take advantage of fixing it up the way they want to." She chased the last green bean around the plate with the fork. "I have Felipe's life insurance in savings—I never touched it. And I still get his pension. I imagine the city will make sure salaries and things like that get paid. So even if the clinic doesn't open back up, I'll still be able to buy a small condo and be okay financially for a while. You've helped me see past my fears. The idea of moving on isn't so scary right now."

"I understand that feeling, Glo. I didn't really want to return to Port Provident at first. I'd made big changes in my life and I didn't want to come back here and have everyone think I was the same old Rigo. It kept me in Houston, working dead-end security-type jobs for a while instead of coming back here, to Beach Patrol. But then, once I realized I just needed to come and do what I needed to do—I gave myself permission to make necessary changes to my plan if things didn't work out—it made the decision a lot easier."

"And did things work out?" She laid her fork down and looked up.

He thought quietly for a moment. "Some things have. Others are still a work in progress. So far, I haven't needed to use Plan B."

"But you're happy with the changes you've made?"

Rigo stood and took a few steps to the railing. He leaned on it, looking toward the water. "I'm happy right now, here with you. And without those changes, I wouldn't have this."

Gloria left the table and joined Rigo at the white wooden gingerbread ringing the edge of the widow's walk. Rigo turned slightly and moved one step closer to Gloria. He felt it in the air, like the unavoidable siren call of the sea that had turned captains into dreamers and left their women behind on rooftop perches to watch the skyline and wonder.

"Sometimes change moves you forward," he said, putting his hand on the top of Gloria's shoulder and turning her. "Sometimes, it takes you back."

Like the roll of the waves, he leaned his head down and hovered briefly above her upturned face. When she didn't pull back, he found himself unable to stop the forward motion. Kissing her swept the years away, like the tide washing clean footprints in the sand.

Her hand reached up and slid around his neck, her short fingernails leaving behind a tickle where they danced across the skin.

The kiss felt at once both familiar and new, as if the years had changed them but left their spirit untouched. As he pulled away, he knew that no matter what change came out of this—good or bad—he wouldn't regret this moment and the chance to share a kiss with her just one more time.

As the kiss broke, Gloria's arm slid across the neckline of his shirt and over his shoulder. Rigo could feel her touch like an imprint left behind, a memory he'd carry forever. He stood still, trying to read her face. Although he didn't second-guess kissing her, he didn't want to make the wrong move now.

"Are we forward?" she said. "Or back?" Her words picked up where their conversation had left off.

"What do you think?" Rigo tried to match her measured tone of voice.

She brushed the hair back from where the light breeze had blown it in front of her eyes. "Not backward."

Rigo exhaled slightly. Good. He didn't want to have moved backward.

"And this is definitely change. But I don't know if we're forward, either." She turned away and focused on the faint lines of waves rolling in the distance. "I know that you've changed. I have accepted your apology, and I meant it. I've even told people that I can see the change in you—I've told it to myself. I want us to move on." She let out a jagged sigh, the uncertain edges of which nicked Rigo's heart. "But I don't know about us moving on *together*."

"I understand," he said simply.

His head understood. But his heart felt as though it had been put in one of the headlocks he'd been taught at the police academy, designed to subdue a suspect and restrict their motion.

Wait. That wasn't right. A *heart*lock. Designed to stifle newly growing feelings and restrict their expression.

Rigo'd been heartlocked.

And just like a suspect, he was going to have to accept it and deal with the implications of his conduct.

"Do you? Maybe you can explain it to me, then, because I don't." She spoke softly. He needed to concentrate to hear her over the night sounds from around the island. Without traffic below, the gentle *whuff* of the roaring surf could be clearly heard.

"You have a lot in front of you right now, Glo. I think you need to decide for yourself what changes you're willing to make and what changes you're not."

The *whuff* filled the silence again as he tried to decide whether to let his heart speak or not.

It wasn't much of a debate. If he didn't say it now, he might not ever have the chance again.

"I'm not running out on you again. I've made mistakes and I haven't been there for you in the past." He swallowed hard to clear the lump in his throat before it rendered him unable to get out the rest. "I may have been a fool, Gloria, but I've loved you all my life."

She reached up and wordlessly touched his sleeve, rubbing a small fold of the linen guayabera he'd pulled out of the back of the closet. Without a sound, she looked in Rigo's eyes, then nodded.

The brown of her irises looked glassy, like they were holding back a thousand secrets. The silence tightened its grip on Rigo's heartlock.

Gloria nodded again, opened her mouth to speak, then closed it without making a sound. She let go of his sleeve, then turned and squeezed awkwardly between the frame of the table and the railing. On footsteps that whispered, Gloria stepped through the tiny door and out of his life, taking Rigo's anxious, restrained heart with her.

Chapter Nine

AFTER STAYING AWAKE long enough to watch the moonlight creep through the blinds and across the ceiling, Gloria finally drifted off to sleep in the pitch-black that stole in just before dawn. Although she could not see the stars they'd watched together, their images filled her mind's eye and the soft touch of Rigo's kiss still lingered on her lips.

Gloria started awake at the sound of a large thump, followed by a low buzz. Turning her head, through groggy eyes she saw red blinking lights on the clock on the nightstand.

The electricity had come back on, just like that. Water would follow shortly, or so the word around the island said yesterday. Then the causeway would be opening around noon, bringing an army of curious residents and likely a few looky-loos out to see the aftereffects of a natural disaster for themselves.

Today would be the day when everything changed. People would return to Port Provident and begin to repair their homes and businesses. They'd see the curtain pulled back. Surely most residents who'd evacuated had seen the reports on TV, but even an HD picture couldn't replicate seeing face-to-face the two-by-fours turned to toothpicks across Gulfview Boulevard, the boats from the marinas across town now scattered on streets and in parking lots, the palm trees upended at the roots in the esplanades of the historic avenues, the black spots of insidious mold blooming on every wall that got touched by the brown sludge and water.

A lot of her friends and family would find their worlds rocked today.

Just like her own world shifted on its orbit last night.

Gloria sat up and ran her hands over her face, trying to head off her remaining urge to yawn uncontrollably. A slight, sleepy dizziness reminded her just how off-kilter things had become.

She stretched, feeling the pull of muscles that hadn't moved in a long time. Again, her thoughts turned back to last night. Gloria raised her arms over her head again and let her mind linger on the memory. And as her shoulders and her arms and her back all felt the warmth and tug of impending activity, so did her heart.

Her lips curved upward in a smile of acknowledgment. It was time to face the changes in the world around her without fear. Thinking about it too much would keep her from progress.

A knock sounded at the sturdy wooden door. "Gloria? Did you hear that?" Inez's voice echoed a bit in the hallway.

"I did. I think the power is back on." She scooted off the bed and wrapped the old bathrobe she'd borrowed around her. The early dawn light stained the floral pattern with a pink glow.

Gloria opened the door. "Did the city come by yesterday to check the breakers and such like they said?"

"Yes. After lunch. The tag they left is on the table Rigo put by the door."

"Is Rigo here?"

Inez shook her head, her hair still pinned tightly in curls. Even the hurricane's inconveniences couldn't shake decades-long bedtime rituals. "No. He left for his shift just before eleven last night. I believe this shift will end at eleven. He told me yesterday that they'd be going off those twelve-hour shifts as soon as the utilities came back on. So, I guess this is his last one."

"I wonder when the water will turn back on." Maybe sometime soon she'd be able to get clean and be as beautiful as Rigo told her last night she was.

"I hope soon. These curls are getting flat." She gently patted her hair twirled around the bobby pins. "What are you doing today, Gloria?"

Now that she knew the water could be back on any minute, the layers of salt caked on her body began to itch like the first peeling of a deep, red sunburn. "Well, if the causeway is opening back up, I assume my parents and Gracie and Jake will be first in line. So I'll probably go finish a few little things I was working on at my parents' house. And then once the water comes back on, I'm going to take a shower. I'm going to find a new bar of soap somewhere on this island, unwrap it and use the whole thing. Then I'm going to find a bottle of shampoo and squeeze so much of it in my hands that it runs between my fingers like liquid gold. I'm going to lather, rinse and repeat and repeat and repeat."

"*Ay, mija*. I completely understand. I dreamed about a bubble bath last night. I haven't had one of those in years, but I think I'm about to change that."

Gloria warmed a bit at the older woman using the word for "my daughter." She certainly had come to think fondly of Inez during the course of the past few days, and she liked knowing that Inez seemed to feel the same.

"*Mija*, that T-shirt you had on yesterday looked awful. Why don't you see if you can find another one? I'm sure Rigo has some in his closet and since they were all upstairs here, they didn't get destroyed like everything in your closet did. He won't mind if you take one of his to wear after your shower. No sense taking your first shower in days to have to put on that old dirty shirt." Inez pointed toward Rigo's closed door at the far end of the hall. "In fact, I can smell you from here. Just go in there now and get one for today and you can get another later if the water comes on. He's got plenty to spare."

Gloria didn't turn. Sure they'd shared a kiss, but she didn't know about sharing a T-shirt. It seemed against some kind of rule, somehow. She was sure there was something in the few items of clothing she'd brought with her that would do instead.

"What?" Inez picked up on Gloria's hesitation. "Just because you borrow a shirt from him doesn't mean you have to marry him, girl. It just means you won't smell."

Gloria could feel a red flush plucking at her cheeks from just under the skin. "Of course I'm not marrying him, Inez. That ship sailed, like, a decade ago. But I feel strange about walking in his room without his permission."

Had she really just said that? Clearly the caked on salt and sweat was getting in her head.

Not to mention that kiss. It definitely had already staked out territory in Gloria's mind and wouldn't leave. It just sat on Repeat, kicking up sparks like a July Fourth sparkler over and over and over.

"It's my house, my room. Not his. You're not there to snoop. Just walk in and find a T-shirt and walk out. *Ay yi yi, hija.*" Inez walked back to her room, leaving Gloria alone to contemplate that exasperative sound and Inez's true meaning behind it.

The older woman was likely right. Gloria had permission from Inez to go in there and it wasn't as if she was going to be poking around for dirt or anything. Just a shirt to go work in. No big deal. She'd worn plenty of Rigo's T-shirts in high school. Back then, she wore his letter jacket that he'd earned on the baseball diamond enough that it practically qualified as her own. This couldn't be much different.

With a tentative push of the door, Gloria walked into Rigo's room. In spite of days of total chaos, the room looked completely organized. A quilt in tones of navy blue, sky blue and white lay across the mattress. Two white pillows lay fluffed on top. The louvered closet door had been left open. Rigo had been right—the closet was tiny, but the clothes that did fit inside were hung in an orderly fashion. All the hangers were made of neat white wire, and they all faced the same way.

Averting her eyes from the linen guayabera and the memories it evoked in her mind and on her lips, Gloria pulled out two Beach Patrol shirts. She held Rigo's shirts in her hand and reflexively brought them to her face. She smelled the faint scent of pine and spice. It hadn't changed over the years.

But she had.

And she knew better now. She just couldn't let her wandering mind grab her heart and lead it astray.

She had a home and a career to rebuild, and all that came with it.

"I can't risk having to rebuild a heart, too," she said with a whisper, hoping her heart and her head would both hear and obey.

She walked out of Rigo's room and quietly clicked the heavy white-painted door closed behind her. The memories mingled with the idle dreams of what could be as she walked back across the hall.

Determined to get to her parents' house and get back to real rebuilding as quickly as possible, Gloria pulled off the stained, sweat-soaked shirt she'd been wearing and exchanged it for the one that smelled of pine and the past, powerless to keep her mind off of last night's kiss.

Rigo raised the hemline of his T-shirt and wiped it across his brow. Humidity was a part of life on the Texas Gulf Coast, but since Hurricane Hope blew through town, the water in the air felt more like a faucet. *Oppressive* seemed like the best word to describe how it felt to walk around in air that was thick enough to be served up in a bowl like soup or posole.

But as heavy as the air lay, the way Gloria left the widow's walk last night lay even heavier on Rigo's heart and mind.

He'd told himself not to expect anything from the evening. He'd promised himself he was doing it only to bring a smile to an old friend's face at a stressful time. He just wanted to prove she could trust him. He'd been ready to follow all his own advice and keep things simple.

Until Gloria walked out in that raspberry-pink dress.

Then everything changed. And even the heat and the humidity couldn't melt that memory of Gloria's petite curves hugged by that just-clingy-enough dress from his mind.

"Taking a break, Vasquez?" Rigo looked up from his thoughts to see Bradley Thorpe, the director of the Park Board. Bradley ran the island's beach parks and other tourist entities from a management standpoint, and Rigo was responsible for keeping them safe and secure. Brad had recently moved to the area from South Padre Island at the southernmost tip of Texas, but he and Rigo had immediately hit it off and become friends. Best of all, he hadn't been a witness to Rigo's downfall or heard any of the gossip of several years ago. It felt good to have a friend who knew him just as Rigo, with no attached baggage.

"Hey, Brad. Just evaluating these lifeguard towers. Believe it or not, there's not a lot of damage. I think lining them up here behind the building blocked some of the wind shear." Rigo gestured at the four-story brown brick tower behind them, the home of the Port Provident Park Board.

"That's great news. I've been digging through files, trying to see exactly how our insurance coverage stacks up. The downstairs of the building is flooded and a total wreck, just like everything else on the ground here. Both pavilions at the main beach parks look like they have structural damage."

Rigo nodded his head.

"You're a million miles away, Vasquez. Something's on your mind. Anything I can help with? Don't worry about the pavilions, man. You can use an office here for the time being. There are a few open spots on the third floor." Bradley leaned against one of the wooden lifeguard stands.

"It's not that, though I appreciate the offer."

"Then what's up?"

Rigo could see real concern in Bradley's eyes, overriding the tired glaze they all seemed to carry around these days.

Could he come clean with Brad? He liked that Brad didn't know everything about his past. While it would be nice to get a sanity check on these reemerging feelings for Gloria, Rigo just couldn't get comfortable with airing his dirty laundry right now with this colleague who'd become a steady friend.

"Do you read the Bible, Brad?"

"A little, why?" Bradley crossed his arms over his chest.

Rigo kicked at a small pile of muddy pebbles near his feet. "Ever heard of Jeremiah 29:11?"

"My sister has it up on a poster. Something about hope, right?"

The sun inched out from behind a cloud overhead, sweeping the lingering midmorning shadows off the lifeguard stands that stood all around them.

"Right. 'I know the plans I have for you...plans to give you a hope and a future.'" Rigo scuffed at the muddy mess he'd made under the soles of his feet. "I'm thinking about Hurricane Hope and wondering about the future."

"Okay, I'm not totally following you. From the look on your face, I thought you had trouble with some woman, though. Except that I've never heard you talk about a relationship or anything, so at least it's not that."

"Brad, I think it's exactly that." Rigo didn't want to change the dynamic of his friendship with Bradley, and he thought opening up would put them in a place he didn't want to be. But he didn't want to be evasive with his friend, either. Evasion was the first step on the road to dishonesty, and Rigo promised himself in rehab he wouldn't again keep secrets from those who cared about him.

"You remember the people I brought with me to the command center during the eye of the hurricane?"

Bradley nodded. "Your aunt and that mom and baby and the nurse?"

"Midwife." He may as well go all the way with this honesty thing. He knew Gloria's official title was Certified Nurse-Midwife, and it seemed worth making the distinction.

"Wait a minute." Brad's hazel eyes opened wide. "That baby was yours?"

A short laugh escaped Rigo, and he waved his hand shortly. "No, no."

"The baby belonged to the midwife?"

Rigo chuckled again. "No, the baby belonged to the young woman. The midwife, though, she used to belong to me."

"Wait. What?"

Rigo could tell he was throwing Bradley for a loop. Clearly, they all needed to get more sleep. Twelve-hour shifts in a disaster-damaged world took their toll on mind and body.

"Brad. Not literally. I dated her a long time ago." Seeing clarity in Brad's eyes, Rigo decided just to throw it out there. "And then I was a jerk and went to Mexico to surf and left her. She started dating a guy I'd been good friends with in high school. They got married. And when I came back to town and went to work on the police force, I got paired up with him. I tried to act like we were still friends, just like when we were younger, like nothing had changed. But it all had. The jealousy that he had her and they had a baby on the way—it ate me alive. I was there the night he died. It was all my fault. And then I messed everything up even worse than before."

Bradley uncrossed his arms, then crossed them behind his lower back and leaned against the lifeguard tower again. "So you killed this guy?"

Rigo waved his hands in front of him. "No, no. I was jealous. But not like that. I pulled over a car for a routine traffic stop, but as I questioned the driver, it didn't feel right. Felipe had gotten a call that Gloria had been taken to the hospital. But when I called him on the radio, he turned around and came back to help me. Gloria hadn't told him how serious her condition was, so she wouldn't scare him. He thought he had time to turn around."

He turned his head away. He'd kept this story inside for so long. Letting the words out took a flood of emotions with them. "My gut was right about the kids in the car. They were a group of small-time drug dealers and they thought they'd make a name for themselves. When Felipe got there, a guy popped out of the trunk that they'd rigged for defense. Neither of us saw it coming. Gloria was at the hospital upstairs, alone in L & D, when they rushed Felipe down to the ER. Their baby died that day from blood loss due to a ruptured placenta. I didn't have anything to do with what happened to the baby, but Felipe should have been with her. She lost everything because of me."

Bradley's brow furrowed with the weight of Rigo's words.

"So that's the past. You said you were thinking about the future. She's obviously talking to you. She was with you at the command center. I saw you two leave together. So something's changed."

Rigo nodded and recapped the past week for his friend.

"Look, Rigo, I haven't walked through the door of a church in a long time for a lot of reasons. But I grew up with a grandmother who went every Sunday, every Wednesday, and a few other times in between. And she used to always love to talk about how God would close doors and open windows."

"My *tía* Inez still says that all the time," Rigo said.

Bradley shrugged mildly. "Maybe this is your window. The past is past. The door is closed. You know your actions have hurt her, but you came back to make amends. Maybe when the hurricane blew out half the windows in town, it opened one for you, too."

Rigo let Bradley's words soak in like rain. "Maybe so. I just wish I knew what to do with my window."

"Do the right thing."

"Sure, Brad. That sounds way better than breaking her heart again." Rigo could hear the sarcasm on each syllable and he knew Bradley could, too.

"Hey, settle down, smart aleck. I just mean do all those things you meant to do. In a perfect world where you'd never broken her heart, what would you do?"

During all those nights in rehab when he'd laid in that stiff bed after curfew and thought about what he'd done to get to that point, Rigo rewrote history in his head over and over and over. He knew where he'd gone wrong. And it wasn't fair to blame the bottle or Mexico. They were symptoms of the problem.

He, Rodrigo Vasquez, was the problem.

He'd taken Gloria for granted. He'd accepted her and her teenage love for him as ordinary.

He'd been wrong. Her steadfast, loyal heart was extraordinary. And he should have treasured it.

"I'd make her feel special."

"So, what are you waiting for?"

Rigo pointed at the chaos around them. He knew what he was up against. "Gloria's lost her home and her job. I'm pretty sure she's been grateful for my help the last few days, but she's like everyone else—focused on one thing and one thing only right now. Not happily-ever-after. Rebuilding. I mean, Brad, are you crazy?"

"No. Are you?"

"What?"

"You're telling me you may have a second chance with the woman you've loved since you were a teenager. You're telling me that you believe a window may have cracked open for you. But you're also making excuses and telling me that some hurricane debris is in your way." Bradley locked his gaze on Rigo with a steel-like seriousness. "Let me tell you something, Rigo. My grandfather had known my grandmother for three weeks before he shipped out to France in 1943. But he never forgot her, just like you never forgot Gloria. He crawled on his belly on Omaha Beach, seeing her face in a haze of bullets and the ugliest side of humanity. He lost two toes to frostbite in the trenches in France. And he still made his way home to her. He's in his nineties now, and he'd do it again today if that's what it took to be with her. He said he didn't see the carnage of D-day as he came ashore. He saw her. What do *you* see? A hurricane? Or Gloria?"

His friend's words flew straight to his heart with the piercing accuracy of a sniper's bullet.

Since the moment he'd answered his phone Wednesday afternoon, everything tumbled in a constant cycle of change—it made him think of the careening roll and spin of socks in a dryer. In the time he'd been back in Port Provident, Rigo followed his plan to stay out of Gloria's way and make amends around town where he needed to. He'd been content.

Then his phone rang and a hurricane named Hope blew his past straight back into his present.

He used to feel so guilty about still having feelings for Gloria. He'd partner up with Felipe, day after day, feeling paralyzed by the ever-present fact that he'd never gotten over the woman who'd gone on to marry his friend. And then when his call for backup led to Felipe's death, the dark clouds crushed him stronger than any hurricane's destructive slap of wind.

Through rehab and a return to *La Iglesia,* he'd started to shed that guilt, but it sloughed off awkwardly, like a chameleon's shedding skin.

He didn't want to be a chameleon, ever changing. He wanted to be a rock.

And more than anything, he wanted to be that rock for Gloria.

"You're right, Brad."

"So, what are you gonna do about it?"

Rigo thought for a moment. "Man, I don't know. I made her a makeshift restaurant at Inez's house last night so she'd have a fresh hot meal. But there's just not much out there right now. My relationship with Gloria isn't the only thing that's a mess."

"Your options are limited. How about the First Responder Thank-You Dinner that Porter's Seafood is hosting tonight?"

Now that the basic services had returned, the oldest family-owned restaurant in town quickly put together plans to celebrate the efforts of Port Provident's first responders during the past week. They promised it would be simple, but they also promised it would be a time where the men and women who helped save the island could relax and enjoy a meal prepared with love and gratitude. Almost everyone Rigo knew in the police, fire and paramedic community would be there at least for a while.

And therein seemed to be the problem.

"No, man. I can't do that." His shoulders tensed up at the thought.

"I don't get it. You just told me you want to make her feel special. Take her out on a date that's not on your aunt's porch." Bradley's stare fell on Rigo so hard it landed like a punch.

He wanted to. He wanted to take the stress of the past few days—of the past few years—away from her. Wasn't that the whole point of the catch of the day on Inez's rooftop porch last night?

"There are limits to what I can do."

Brad's unwavering expression told Rigo he didn't believe a word of it.

"Really, Bradley. Half this town knows I broke her heart after high school and the other half knows I was there the night her husband died. I've got an unspoken peace with a lot of the guys on the force. I turned my life around. They can support that. But how much support do you think I'm going to get when I show up with my dead patrol partner's widow? And worse, what are they going to say to her? I'm not going to let them hurt her any more than she's been hurt, Brad."

Bradley took one measured step forward and pointed at Rigo. "I know you won't. But when you're on the beach, in the middle of battle, do you see those guys?"

"No. Of course not. Didn't I just say you were right?"

"Yeah."

His smugness lingered a bit in the air. It made Rigo want to fire back with his own short-clipped reply. "So?"

"Then you have to stand up to your past and knock it down. Treat her in such a way that they can't second-guess you now. Why are you letting excuses get in your way? Seems like you stood behind a big pile of excuses on a beach in Mexico and it didn't get you anywhere. Seems like maybe you think you see that window, but you've decided it's too small for you to climb through." Bradley took aim and fired with his words. "Seems like you're still not the man she needs you to be."

One. Two. Three seconds passed before Rigo caught his breath. Everything within him felt slow and deliberate.

Especially the realization that Bradley was right.

But it wasn't about one dinner with some of the guys at Port Provident PD who would immediately begin an investigation into what was going on. It was about showing Gloria he would be there for her, both in physical presence and emotional support.

"I'll ask her to come tonight. But what if she says no?"

"Then you've gotta keep crawling across the beach until you get past every single one of the bullets. She's worth the fight, right?"

Rigo wished he'd known then what he knew now. If he'd known what he'd lose, he'd have realized she was worth the fight—any fight it took—and he wouldn't have listened to all those lies he told himself in Mexico all those years ago.

Gloria was worth the fight. She was worth squeezing through whatever window God put in front of him.

If it took crawling across a battlefield or a field of hurricane debris, Rigo knew Bradley was right. He'd have to do it. Now that he'd had her back in his life, even for just a few days, he knew he couldn't let her go again.

"You mentioned your sister earlier. Does she still work at that print shop up in Houston?"

A wide stripe of sunlight cracked over the small cloud that had been playing peekaboo earlier. Bradley pulled his sunglasses from where they'd been folded over the neckline of his T-shirt.

"Yeah, she and my brother-in-law own it. From what I've heard from the control center, the hurricane really didn't do much damage over there in Sugar Land. Just a lot of rain and downed tree limbs."

Rigo smiled. "That's exactly what I was hoping to hear. Can you help me with something else? I have a window to crawl through."

Gloria felt something before she even heard the sound of tires in the parking lot at Huarache's. An awareness, a flicker of excitement, came over her and made her look up from the bag she was stuffing with wet table linens to take to the ever-growing pile of junk outside.

They'd come home.

Her whole family—the people she loved more than anyone on earth—were back on the island. Gloria couldn't have kept her feet from running toward them if she'd wanted to.

"Gracie!" Gloria wrapped her sister tightly in her arms as soon as she was close enough to touch her. They'd been apart only a matter of days, but something about being separated by a natural disaster—with no phones or open roads for a time—made the hours seem longer and more burdensome.

She could feel small streaks of wetness on her sister's cheeks. Gracie clearly felt the same weight of separation. "Glo. *Hermanita*, we've all been so worried about you. Are you okay?"

"I'm okay. Rigo made sure all of us in the house were all right."

"Vasquez?" Her father cleared his throat and Gloria thought for a split second he was going to spit on the ground in front of him. "Well, it's hard to run away when the roads are closed."

The words from her usually mild-mannered *papí* took her aback. She knew he didn't like what Rigo did after high school. What she didn't know was that he still carried it around with him.

Just like she'd carried it around with her for all these years. Funny how events could profoundly affect even someone who wasn't directly involved.

"I think he's changed." Gloria remembered the conversation they'd had in Mateo's room, where he'd opened up about his mistakes, his journey to rehab and his desire to prove to Gloria he wasn't the same person he had been.

"Gloriana. Don't be naive." Juanita Garcia stretched out her oldest daughter's name with about ten more syllables than it usually had, each very clearly enunciated. Gloria realized it made her uncomfortable because it sounded uncannily like how she herself addressed Gracie when she thought her little sister was making a big mistake.

Gloria couldn't think of how to reply. Before she put something past her tongue, *Papí* headed for the doors of Huarache's. *"Vamonos."*

Let's go. Indeed. Gloria would be glad to explain the mess from Hurricane Hope to her family instead of the time she'd been spending with Rigo Vasquez.

Mamí handed baby Gabi to Gracie, then caught *Papí's* hand as they walked through the door. Gloria lingered a few steps behind. She knew the heartbreak they were about to encounter and wasn't sure she could bear to see the emotions in their eyes.

"You know they just care about you, right? They only want what's best for you." Gracie's husband, Jake Peoples, stayed back with Gloria.

Gloria turned her head slightly and looked at Jake, while still monitoring her family's progress out of the corner of her eye. "What do you mean?"

"I mean the subject of you and Rigo Vasquez has come up about once an hour, every hour, since you briefly called to say you were staying at Inez's. I'm pretty sure they talked about it more than the actual hurricane." Jake nodded in the direction of his wife and in-laws.

Gloria gave a short, acknowledging nod of her own. "I just wish they'd understand it's between me and Rigo. Not them."

"Oh, you mean like when I took Gracie to the beach shortly after meeting her and you interrogated us both?" Jake's look told Gloria he remembered every single disapproving sister conversation she'd given Gracie at that time. And there had been more than a few. "I'm pretty sure that whatever he did to you in the past hurt them *for* you as much as it actually hurt you. Who picked up the pieces after he left?"

"Gracie. And Mamí. And Papí." Gloria lowered her voice. "They've always been there for me. Every single time. It's just what we do. We look out for each other. *Somos familia.*"

We are family.

And they always would be.

"I've never seen another family like y'all. My own family wasn't like that. My mother couldn't be bothered to care one bit about her children and my father—well, the man who raised me—couldn't see past his own anger and jealousy to do anything but scheme and hate. Your family is special, Gloria. Don't let yourself get mad because they care. Their biggest crime is maybe caring too much. But you wouldn't know a thing about that, would you?"

His slow smile showed the sarcasm in his words. No, she wouldn't know a thing about that. Except that it was her specialty. Especially when it came to her family.

Gloria shook her head. "I was wrong, you know."

"About what?"

"You. I misjudged you. I'm sorry. And I'm glad Gracie didn't listen to me...too much. I'm glad you're my brother-in-law." She tried to keep the emotion out of her voice but was pretty sure that he wouldn't have to listen too closely to hear it. She'd been so skeptical of the early days of Gracie and Jake's relationship, when Jake had been the interim CEO of his family's development company, and he'd been determined to evict Gracie's English-as-a-second-language school, La Escuela por las Lenguas, from the property she leased from the Peoples Property Group.

"I'm glad she didn't listen too closely, either." Jake leaned over and gave Gloria a quick but reassuring hug. "And I'm glad you're my sister-in-law. I remember Rigo. I didn't know him well, but we surfed together down by the Memorial Hotel quite a few times back in school. I don't know what happened between the two of you—and I don't speak Spanish well enough to keep up with all the names your mother called him in the car—but I do know that things are not always what they seem. A guy who finds out a family secret in a boardroom won't ever forget that lesson. I hope you'll remember that, too, Gloria. They love you, but if you think he's changed, sometimes you've got to just go with your gut."

"Or God."

"Exactly. I know now there was a reason why I decided to serve eviction papers myself to one Graciela Garcia de Piedra. I'd never served eviction papers before, and I've never served them since. Maybe it's the same reason you dialed Rigo's number for help."

Jake smiled at Gracie, a relaxed, knowing smile that stood out in the middle of the chaos of the hurricane-tossed debris that still covered Gulfview Boulevard—and the conflicting feelings that passed through her heart.

He could be right. There could be a reason she made that phone call a week ago. But her bruised heart just couldn't afford for her to be naive. She couldn't make a mistake with her trust again.

Gloria plucked at her brother-in-law's sleeve as they walked up the sidewalk to the front door of the restaurant.

"Jake?"

He stopped and turned toward her. "Yes?"

Gloria hesitated. But then realized her pause only underscored what she thought of herself and why she had to ask Jake the question on her mind.

"You've known me for a little while now. Do you think I'm a strong person? Or is it all an act?"

She swallowed strongly, trying to wash away the slightly metallic taste the words had left in her mouth. She really didn't know, and she feared the answer.

"Glo, no one could carry the burden of losing a husband and a child without having shoulders stronger than a linebacker. It's not a question of your strength. That one's not up for debate. It's a question of whether you can set the burdens of the past down."

Jake left her alone to ponder that question. Gloria looked blankly out at the waves rolling in on the other side of Gulfview Boulevard's narrow, raised black slice of pavement along the coastline.

A yellow-and-red truck pulled into the parking lot and parked slightly askew, next to the three-foot-tall pile of stuffed trash bags Gloria had thrown out over the past few days.

"I drove by your house, but you weren't there, so I figured I'd find you here."

Rigo jumped out of the truck. His black hair stuck together at the roots with a damp sheen of leftover sweat. She looked at his shirt, slightly damp with the same signs of physical exertion, then down to his shoes, scuffed with sand and mud. If she hadn't known better, she'd have thought he'd just stepped off the beach as a teenager. It surprised her to know that just looking at him caused the same feeling of excitement and awareness that it had so many years ago—just like a sparkler on the Fourth of July, glowing with a jumping golden electric spark.

"You've been working?" She tried to ignore the tickle of awareness that insisted on teasing her in spite of her conflicted stream of.

"Yeah. I've been at the beach patrol storage yard all morning, inspecting damage to our lifeguard towers. I've got a few hours off right now, then I'll be patrolling Gulfview until I get off tonight."

"Okay. So you'll be back to Inez's house late?"

"Well, actually, I wanted to talk to you about that. That's why I stopped by."

Gloria's heart did a small flip of anxiety. Was he moving out of his aunt's house? Going to stay with some friends from Beach Patrol? She'd miss the brief interactions with him, and the not-so-subtle matchmaking from their unofficial chaperone, Tía Inez.

"What do you want to talk about?"

"After I finish up my shift, there's a community dinner hosted by Porter's Seafood Restaurant as a thank-you to the first responders in town. They wanted to do something now that the utilities are back on and the roads are open. We can all bring one guest, and I'd like it if you came with me."

The sound of a throat clearing from the doorway a few steps away cut through the air before Gloria could answer Rigo's invitation. She'd heard that noise a thousand times during childhood. Usually when she'd been caught doing something she shouldn't have.

"*Papí?*"

"No, Gloriana. You're not going. Thank you for your concern for my daughter, Señor Vasquez, but we are home. We will take care of her. You are relieved of your duties, *Chief.*"

Carlos Garcia placed particular emphasis on Rigo's title. Gloria had never heard her father speak so harshly to anyone. A neutral tone of voice even when angry was almost second nature to Papí after years in the service industry. The customer was never wrong. But in this case, he made it clear that Rigo certainly was.

"Mr. Garcia, I don't think you understand." Rigo began to state his case.

"I understand perfectly, Rodrigo." Papí cut the younger man off before he could even get started. "Gloriana called you when she needed assistance. But if you think I've forgotten how you left after your so-called best friend got shot, I haven't. And I haven't forgotten that you never came back to Port Provident after you asked me to marry my daughter."

"Wait. What?" Shock like liquid fire pushed through her veins. "What are you talking about, Papí?"

Gloria took a step back from Rigo, toward the street side of the parking lot. She needed space.

And air.

And an explanation.

"I never told you, Gloria. I didn't want to make things even worse for you. But this coward..." Carlos pointed an accusing finger straight at Rigo's chest. "This coward, he came by this very restaurant two days before he left for that tournament in Mexico. He stood right there, in my office off the kitchen, and promised to love you forever, and asked my permission to marry you. And fool that I am, I believed him and said yes. I told him he could have my first born daughter's heart for the rest of his days. I told him we'd be proud to have him in the family."

"Rigo?" She followed the laser-precision point of her father and looked unwaveringly at the man who had held her heart in her youth, and who'd come close to capturing it again.

"He's right, Gloria."

In an instant, she tasted that bitter metallic taste again and tried to choke it down without letting her emotions out for everyone to see.

"And he's right about one more thing," Rigo continued. "I was a coward. I told you that the other day in Mateo's room."

Rigo walked with measured steps to where Gloria stood and took her hand in his. She could feel herself shaking with the trembles of memories and the secrets she never knew had been kept from her.

"But, Gloria, you've got to believe me. I'm not afraid anymore. I've been forced to see the ugly corners of myself and to learn lessons I'd never wish on anyone else. And I had to go through that battle so that I could stand here today and tell you this with certainty. I'm not afraid anymore, not of your dad or of the past. I know what I'm willing to fight for. It's you."

"How can I trust you? How can I trust any of you?" Gloria's harsh whisper sounded like the rasp of sandpaper. She looked up and pulled her gaze from Rigo, to Papí, then back to Rigo again. "Papí's right to not believe a word that comes out of your mouth. But, Papí, how could you not tell me the truth?"

"Gloriana. I did what any parent would do. I would never deliberately hurt you."

The unspoken—*unlike some people*—hung in the salty, humid air around them.

Rigo's brown eyes darkened as she watched. "Gloria. I don't deserve it, but I'd like the chance to prove I've learned those lessons. I'll do whatever it takes. But I can't show you if you won't take this first step. I said I'd never leave again, but if your dad is proven right, I will. I'll be out of your life forever. Will you just come with me tonight? Will you give me the chance?"

Gloria felt Rigo's grip tighten slightly on her hand.

She didn't *have* to give Rigo a second chance. Everyone would understand if she closed the door firmly, especially now that she knew he'd even asked for her hand in marriage, but still ran away.

But maybe, just maybe, she *needed* to.

Maybe that was the strength she'd been looking for. The strength to forgive. The strength to move on. Maybe it wasn't physical strength.

Maybe it was something even, well, *stronger* than that.

She nodded shortly and took a fortifying breath. In all her years, she'd never stood in front of her *papi* and openly defied his wishes. She needed a certain strength to do that, too.

But more than that, Gloria thought, she needed love. Or at least a chance at it. She'd been living scared and closed off from the world, from memories, from emotions, for too long.

"Pick me up at my house at seven."

The pungent smell of shrimp boil seasoning laced through the air. No nose in a multiblock vicinity could escape the smell of Gulf shrimp, mini cobs of corn and golf-ball-sized new potatoes. A dozen or more aluminum boiling pots stood on iron stands about waist high. A line of perpetually moving white coats piled the food on a series of tables a few steps away until the piles resembled a kind of food Everest.

And then, as soon as the peak would form, it would slide down like an avalanche as another hungry man in or woman would step forward, deposit a shovel of shrimp on a plastic plate, and head back to the table.

The dance would begin again, all executed under a gray banner attached to the front taupe-brick facade of Porter's Seafood Restaurant, which read in bright red letters We Will Never Forget that You Answered the Call.

Countless hours of frantic rescues, of pushing on in the face of imminent danger, of backbreaking work, of sweat and of tears were represented at the thirty or so tables that had been moved out to the parking lot.

Fire, Police, EMS, Beach Patrol, FEMA, National Guard, state, local, federal...they were all represented here. Although he'd lived every minute alongside these men and women—and there were moments he'd relive in his mind for the rest of his life—Rigo could barely comprehend just what was in front of him as the family behind one of Port Provident's most historic and well-known establishments used the language they spoke best—food and hospitality—to deliver a message on behalf of the whole town. The carpet they rolled out was stiff with salt and smelled of everything Hope spit ashore, but there was no denying it was red.

Rigo could see the appreciation on the faces of his colleagues. This mountain of shrimp meant more than just a full stomach and a hot meal.

He hoped it would mean something to Gloria, too.

"Do you want to grab those two seats over there?" Rigo pointed at two red padded seats on the corner of one of the far tables. "There aren't many places to sit left. This is a much bigger crowd than I thought. I'll go get a plate for each of us if you guard the table."

"Okay, that sounds good." Gloria plucked her way through the maze of tables.

Rigo couldn't help but notice all the little things about her. The slight sway of her hips as she walked, the smile she gave to a group of friends as she passed. She was everything he remembered and so much more. He'd been blind, so blind, before. But as he followed her every step, he knew he could see clearly now.

And he knew what he needed to do. And what he'd never do again.

Steven McLellan, one of Felipe's closest friends on the force, walked away from where he'd been talking to Gloria as Rigo brought back their plates. Since Rigo returned to Port Provident, Steven had maybe uttered ten words to him. And eight of them probably came while they were in the Grand Provident Hotel's command center during Hurricane Hope. There had been a time when they'd all been guys on the force, bonded together with life and death and everything that came in between.

Then the death of one of their own broke that circle and Rigo'd run off from the lives that remained. He didn't blame Steven for avoiding the interaction.

But once again, the weight of regret reached down and crushed straight on Rigo's shoulders. He'd made a mess of so many things, so many relationships. The fact that Gloria consented to come here tonight with him gave Rigo hope, though. If he could repair this relationship with Gloria, maybe he could make amends with others, as well.

"How's Steven?"

"He's good. Kathie and the kids should be returning to the island early next week. They went to stay with her mom up in Nacogdoches. Kathie said there'd been a lot of wind and rain, but otherwise Hope was pretty uneventful that far northeast."

"Good." Rigo meant it. He remembered Kathie as a woman who bestowed smiles with ease and acted as a doting mother on her twins. Knowing they'd been away from all the chaos of the past few days definitely was a good thing. "Did he say anything else?"

Gloria looked around, eyes shifting from one person she knew to another. Then she looked down at the table.

"What, Gloria? Did he say something about me?"

She shrugged a shoulder. "Yeah."

"Gloria? What did Steven say? I'm a big boy. I can handle it." He needed to know what he needed to answer for. It was almost like doing penance. He needed to answer the questions, he needed to atone for the impression he'd left behind when he left for rehab and gave the strict instructions that no one in town was to know where he went.

"He just wanted to know why I was here with you." Gloria raised a boiled shrimp and began to deftly separate the peel from the pink, cooked meat. "He said a bunch of the guys started talking after I showed up at the command center with you during the storm. They think I need to stay away from you."

Rigo knew this warning would reach Gloria sooner or later. The brotherhood in blue looked out for their own—especially the widows of their own—like that. And the fact that he was back leading the beach patrol division wouldn't give him a free pass from their well-earned skepticism. Rigo knew that and accepted it.

"He's just trying to protect you. Do you agree with him?" Rigo could feel the pressure at the back of his jaw as his teeth gritted together. He waited for her answer, dreading what it could be.

"No, I don't. Or I wouldn't be here with you right now." She flicked another translucent shrimp shell to a corner of the plate. "But I didn't have much of a defense to give Steven. For better or worse right now, Rigo, I'm just going with my gut. I use my instinct in birthing situations to help my mothers and their babies. I've already said a prayer or two that my instinct doesn't fail me this time. It's hard to tell friends and family they're wrong. Especially when they've been there for the last few years."

"And I haven't." He figured he might as well just say the unspoken.

"Right. Don't make me regret this, please, Rigo. That's all I ask."

"Gloria. I gave you my word today in front of your parents and Gracie. I'm all in or I'm out for good."

She picked up one more shrimp, then dropped it back on the small pile and looked up. "Then tell me you're all in. Let's stop talking about what was or what could be. I need to hear you say it."

"I'm all in."

"That's all I needed to know."

Rigo started to peel his shrimp. The steel of his jaw began to relax enough he thought he could eat. They both savored the fresh shrimp and popped the small, round red potatoes in their mouths—eating in a companionable silence for a few minutes.

"I had an interesting conversation today." Gloria broke the thin stillness between them. "I think I've got some big decisions ahead."

Rigo put down a potato he was about to eat. He could tell this had nothing to do with their earlier conversation. "What's going on?"

"It's my house," Gloria said. She fiddled with a miniature ear of corn, then set it down and salted it absently. "After I left Huarache's, I met Billy Patterson to talk about my insurance claim. And he said that based on his experience in Florida two years ago after Hurricane Carmencita, he thinks that they're going to call my house a total loss. He said FEMA will require it to be raised when it's rebuilt, and a bunch of other red tape. As my friend, he advised me just to sell it and walk away. He said he'd show me how to take care of everything."

He'd seen the pain written all over Gloria's face the day she had to confront that most everything in her house had been laid to total ruin. Now knowing even the structure itself couldn't be salvaged...it would be more than most people could bear.

"So what are you going to do?"

She twirled the corn on the cob a little absently as she collected her thoughts. "I'd told you earlier I thought I might just go get a condo. So I think I'm going to trust Billy's advice. Sell it. Move."

"And move on?"

"I think so."

The sun dipped into the Gulf of Mexico behind her. The red and orange sunset rays played with the natural highlights in her honey and cinnamon hair, making them shine. The fire and feistiness dancing around her face spoke to the strength Rigo knew she was gathering within so she could make this decision.

She started to speak again, then hesitated before finally getting the words out. "And I think you're a big part of that decision. I sat there for a long time after Billy left, weighing everything. And at the end of it, all I could think of was gratitude."

Rigo dipped a shrimp in the small red puddle of cocktail sauce on his plate. "Gratitude? For losing your house?"

Gloria shook her head. "No, for you."

"Me?" He couldn't quite make it all add up. "How?"

"I can make the changes I need to make because I have something to look forward to. I told you that all during the hurricane, the word *strength* kept coming to my mind. I know now I'm strong enough to come out of the shell I forced myself into."

She threw a translucent shrimp peel on the small pile between them, discarding it as surely as the chains of the past.

"Well, what are you going to do?"

"Maybe move out to the East End. Get something small near the beach. Watch waves roll in. If the clinic doesn't reopen, I think I want to go back to school."

Rigo could hear the old Gloria coming back with each syllable. The high school Gloria—fearless, always wanting to learn and do more. "Back to school?"

"Medical school. Pete has wanted to do a medical mission for years, and I think he'll take this opportunity to go do that. That leaves no doctors on the island who are supportive of a place like the birthing center, and we've had so many women over the years appreciate the opportunity for safe out-of-hospital birth. I want to go to the next level and be the one who fills in that gap."

Rigo couldn't keep the smile off his face. "I think that's great, Dr. Rodriguez."

"Really?" She ended the word questioningly, searching for true approval.

"Really." Rigo put his hand reassuringly over one of Gloria's. Her skin felt smooth and slightly cool from the night air. He was amazed that these two hands, these ten fingers, had been the first soft touch for countless little lives, cradling them as they made their journey into the big, wide world. He'd seen her gentle professional hands at work, delivering little Mateo as a hurricane swirled around them.

He squeezed lightly, then stroked the curve by her wrist once, then twice with his finger.

"Hmm." Rigo's inner thoughts came out as a mutter.

She didn't pull her hand away. "What?"

"I was just thinking. Your hands deliver babies. They bring new life into this world. But mine, they've been trained to hold guns." He pressed the finger gently along her wrist. "This finger is my trigger finger. I can end a life with mine."

"You've also been trained to rescue. Like you rescued me. If you hadn't been there when I called, things could have been so much worse for me and Tanna and baby Mateo."

Rigo laid his other hand, palm side up, like an offering on the table.

He met her eyes with his gaze, and she almost immediately looked down. Rigo felt his heart plummet with the speed of a passenger headed down a roller coaster's highest hill. He'd felt so much hope when she'd said he'd rescued her.

He closed his eyes. He just needed a moment to regain his control.

Like a feather, Gloria's fingertips grazed the heel of his thumb, where it connected into the palm of his hand.

Rigo's eyes opened to confirm what just happened. He saw her hand in his and swallowed hard.

Although her touch came lightly at first, once her hand landed fully on his, there was no denying its presence or significance. The contours of her palm still fit smoothly into his, and he noticed every curve and valley as they touched.

He opened his mouth to speak, but it had gone dry. Gloria smiled shyly.

"Remember that message you left me?"

"How could I forget? It was the single stupidest thing I've ever done in my life." If he'd just come home that summer, so many lives would be so different and so much time never would have been wasted.

"You told me to go catch my dreams."

He nodded. There didn't seem like anything to say. Nothing good, anyway.

"I loved Felipe. I loved Mateo before he was even born." She tightened her fingers around his, the fingertips pressing his skin. "But you were the first dream I ever had."

Rigo closed his fingers around Gloria's hand, connecting them as tightly as woven cloth.

"If you'll let me, I want to be the last." He looked in her eyes, gathering strength from the flecks of golden light in the brown irises. He needed it for what he was about to say. "Gloria, I want to kiss you. I want you to know how I feel right now about you, about us. But not here. Not now. Not with all these people around. But later...maybe...would that be okay?"

For the second time tonight, he held his breath. He didn't know what he'd do if she said no.

Gloria nodded. "*Sí, mi sueño.*"

She called him her dream. She said yes. That was all he needed to know.

The sound of a bottle clunking into a metal trash can interrupted Gloria's swirling thoughts.

"Hey, Rigo! Want a drink?" Officer Brock Carpenter held up a small personal cooler. Gloria felt certain it didn't carry cans of soda.

Knowing now that Rigo had been through rehab for alcohol issues, Gloria tensed as she waited for Rigo's reply.

"No thanks, guys. We were just about to head home." Rigo stood and started scooting the shrimp shells onto a plate to throw away.

"Hey, wait. That's Rodriguez's wife." Carpenter's voice boomed across the three tables between them and rang in Gloria's ear. "Glo! Haven't seen you in a while. What are you doing here?"

The force in the officer's tone nearly pushed her backward. What was the best way to answer that loaded question?

"Dinner. We came to have dinner, guys, same as you." Rigo jumped in. She knew the sound of a trained law enforcement official trying to diffuse a situation. She'd heard Felipe use this tone many times before.

Sometimes, she smiled slightly with the memories.

"That's interesting, Vasquez. Get her husband killed, then take off and when you get back to town, take her out on a date. Nice work." Carpenter saluted Rigo with a tip of the brown longneck bottle in his hand.

Gloria's blood began to heat up, bubbles crowding into her veins, feeling as though they would soon burst into a boil. She picked up her plate and plastic cup and turned to put them in the trash can. She didn't want to face Carpenter anymore. He'd always been a bully. She remembered Felipe didn't like to have anything to do with him. But if she recalled correctly, Rigo had gone out to the local bars with him a few times.

"Carpenter, shut it. You're letting that bottle do the talking and you're upsetting Gloria." Rigo closed two tables' worth of distance, putting himself squarely between Carpenter and Gloria.

"Upsetting? It's upsetting to see an officer's widow out with the man who was there the night her husband was killed, then didn't even show up for the man's funeral. It's like seeing something out of one of those bad chick TV movies." He leaned over to the officer sitting next to him, a man Gloria didn't recognize. His voice dipped low and smooth, like a mock television announcer. "He couldn't save her husband, but he was the only man who could save her...tonight on the Life and Love TV chick movie of the week."

A roar of laughter went up from the table.

"Good one, Carpenter," said the officer across the table from him. He took a slow swig from his own brown bottle.

"Yeah, Rigo was always there for the damsels in distress." Carpenter winked for emphasis. "What the ladies didn't know is he always worked it so he was the cause of the distress, then he could come in and save `em."

Ice began to form in the pit of her stomach. She couldn't believe it was staying there so solidly since her blood continued to boil at a fast roll. Surely Rigo wasn't manipulating the trust she had placed in him the past few days?

She wasn't being naive like everyone said. She couldn't be. She, the midwife, could sniff out problems like a bloodhound.

Rigo began to walk back toward Gloria.

"Come on, Glo, let's go. And you, Milton—" Rigo pointed at Ricky Milton, one of his friends on the force, seated at the end of the table. "You shouldn't even be here. I'm not your sponsor, but you can call me anytime. Don't do something you're going to regret."

"The only thing Milton regrets is not calling her first, since she's back to dating cops." Carpenter stood up and gave Rigo a forceful shove to the shoulder, knocking him off balance and into the table.

Like a well-timed SWAT attack, a swarm of officers leaped up from their own meals and pulled Rigo and the bully apart. Carpenter spewed a string of words that made Gloria, who'd spent the better part of her adult life around police officers, blanch with shock.

Especially since some of them were about her.

She felt as though the rogue punch had pushed *her* to the ground instead. The force of Carpenter's crude words hurt as surely as a fistfight.

"I'm done, I'm done..." Rigo said as he tried to shake an officer off of each arm. "Don't worry, McLellan. I'm not going to finish off Carpenter. Even though I should."

Gloria could see the heat in his eyes and the steel on his face. It was taking every ounce of self-control he had not to further defend her honor, but this time not just with words.

"You need to go, Chief Vasquez. Leave now and there won't be any further action." McLellan stared down Carpenter, daring him to object. "Gloria, you need to go, too. But remember what I said."

The implication with his simple sentence seemed clear to Gloria. He saw this as yet another bad situation Rigo found himself in. Another reason why Gloria couldn't trust Rigo's judgment. Another reason she shouldn't let him back into her life.

But that wasn't how she saw it at all.

"Come on, Rigo." She took him by the arm, then tucked her hand firmly into the crook of his elbow.

Carpenter's shove may have brought the assembled group of first responders to their feet, but Gloria's hand on Rigo's arm dropped their jaws.

And she knew without a doubt she was strong enough not to care what they thought.

"You okay?" Rigo reached out and patted Gloria gently on the leg as they drove down Gulfview Boulevard. There was no longer hesitation in his touch, nor in how she felt about it. He wanted to be with her. She wanted to be with him.

"That was some dinner, wasn't it?"

Rigo laughed, the sound tinged with gentle irony. "That it was. The shrimp sure tasted good. And I can't lie, seeing Carpenter get shut up felt even better. He's a jerk, Gloria. Always has been. Don't let him get to you."

"Oh, believe me, I'm not. This isn't the first time I've been around him. Felipe had words with him at a Christmas party several years ago."

"Really?" Rigo took his eyes off the road for a second to look at Gloria. "That was one of the greatest things about Felipe—nothing ever got to him. He was Unflappable Felipe."

"Maybe on the job, but he brought a lot of that frustration home with him." She stopped herself. She'd never spoken of Felipe's mood swings to anyone. She knew he'd kept them hidden well from his brothers on the force. He hadn't always been able to keep them hidden from her, though.

"Wait." Rigo hit the brake on his truck and pulled quickly into an open parking space along the sidewalk that twisted along the gulf's edge. "Are you saying he hurt you?"

"No, no. Not physically, nothing like that. But emotionally, not really. Some days were better than others. I knew he still loved me, but he didn't know how to deal with the stress of the job, then coming home to miscarriages and disappointment. He couldn't fix it and so he eventually tried to distance himself from it and threw himself into his work."

"But he didn't hurt you?" Rigo's eyes said more than his words. Wide, open, searching. He clearly focused on her face with a hyperintensity, trying to make sure she wasn't holding anything back.

The concern he showed pulled at Gloria's heart. She didn't want to speak badly of Felipe. He'd been a good man, a good husband—even if they'd had some problems in the last years.

But even more than that, she didn't want any more secrets between her and Rigo. No more misunderstandings.

They'd weathered enough mistakes that had changed the course of their lives. She didn't know where this newfound trust and redeveloping closeness was leading them. But she knew where she didn't want it to lead: right back to secrets and lies.

"No. But that night, when I learned he stopped to help you instead of coming straight to me..." She let her words trail off as she gathered a breath. She'd come too far to stop. "It hurt. I lost my husband and my child that night. And on top of that, I had to deal with knowing that backing up a suspicious traffic stop was more important than being at my side as Mateo and I fought for our lives."

"Gloria, I'm sorry. I didn't call him to cause a problem—I needed backup—but I'm the reason he wasn't there with you. My call is the reason he was killed. I've made so many mistakes, Gloria. I'd do anything I could to change them, but I don't know where to start." Rigo's voice was as flat as the glass-smooth water just beyond them. There was no wind tonight, no waves.

And no need to hold back anything in their hearts.

"Start here."

Gloria leaned her head past the center console of the truck. Rigo met her halfway, and the instant she felt the touch of his lips on hers, the past faded away where it belonged.

Rigo slipped a hand behind her neck and pulled Gloria a little closer, a little tighter. She let her head settle a bit on his hand, using his strength to fortify her own.

Her knees weakened a little, and she was happy to let the feeling take over. It meant she could still feel. It meant that spark could still light inside her heart and tickle as it rode through her veins.

She leaned in to Rigo, the solid wall of his chest giving her a strong place to land. She breathed in the faint scent of the cologne he'd put on this evening, the same notes of sandalwood and fir he'd worn since he'd started wearing cologne. It all felt and smelled and tasted so familiar.

She wasn't in this alone.

And she didn't want to be without him, without this strength, ever again.

Chapter Ten

"WHAT IS THAT SMELL?"

Rigo stepped through the half-open back door of the house on Travis Place the following afternoon and a toxic wave singed the inside of his sinus cavities.

Gloria was a sight for sore eyes. He'd been arguing with tourists who thought it would be fun to come see someone else's heartache. Disaster tourism just for kicks. The very thought disgusted him and he'd been pretty pointed in his dialogue with the tourists. But seeing Gloria set his emotions to right.

"Fertilizer."

"It smells like a bomb went off, Glo."

"Well, yeah, kinda." The angry tang of ammonia hung heavy in the house and Gloria pointed at the door that led to the garage. "Water got into the cabinet where I keep all my lawn and garden stuff. It melted the bag of fertilizer I had stored in there. When I opened it up, it all poured out. I thought it was going to burn my eyes out."

"Do you need some help getting it cleaned up?" Rigo looked toward the back of the house.

"No, I turned on the hose...after I found a mask to put over my nose. But even though the water's back on, there's not enough pressure to wash away this mess. I'll be glad when all this cleanup is over and I don't have to smell any other awful, nostril-searing scents." She waved her hand in a dismissive acknowledgment of the disheveled contents of the garage. "It's as much of a mess in here as it feels like my life is right now."

"There are some good things going on, though." He reached out a hand and when she laid her palm in his, Rigo tugged Gloria close.

He couldn't help himself. Now that the smoke of years of misunderstanding was clearing, all he wanted to do was keep her close and hold her.

Well, in the spirit of honesty, that wasn't all he wanted to do. Right now, he wanted to kiss her. For a long time. And then do it all over again. And again. And again. Until they had enough new memories to wash the old ones out with the tide that still churned and chopped higher than usual off the Texas shore.

Rigo ran his free hand up Gloria's spine and settled his palm at the base of her skull, cupping it gently. She didn't pull away as he pressed the curve of bone with his fingertips, coaxing her head closer to his own and finding just the right angle.

There were memories to be made.

He leaned down and lowered his mouth to Gloria's. Her lips slid softly against his. No liquid in any bottle had ever made him feel as wild as the sharp sword of adrenaline slashed through him, fueling his emotions. It drove him to pull Gloria more tightly to him, where he could feel the gentle sways and curves of her body pushing aside the hard weight of regret.

Rigo cursed the eighteen-year-old he'd once been for ever thinking he could have done better than this, for ever thinking he didn't need this above almost all else in his life, except his relationship with God. It was impossible to tell where his breath ended and hers began.

He let the tension flow out of his shoulders as he reminded himself she was here, now, in his arms where she belonged. And he would never let her get away again.

Gloria slid her hand up Rigo's chest and rested her forearm in the curve between his neck and shoulder, like two pieces of a puzzle coming together.

It just fit. Like Gloria's presence back in his life.

He pulled back slightly and Gloria took a half step back. The moment was over. But the lesson forged in the embrace would not be forgotten.

"Never again," Rigo said. His words came out crisply and sounded low—he'd used his police officer's voice by instinct.

Gloria began to move her arm from its spot on his shoulder. Rigo placed his hand on hers, gently but in a way that left no room for misunderstanding. Gloria stayed still.

"What do you mean?"

The humid September heat pressed heavy in the room and Rigo wiped a bead of sweat out of Gloria's hairline.

"I promise you, Gloria Garcia Rodriguez, that never again will I exchange the truth of what we have together for the lie of something that comes in a bottle. Never again will I give you a reason to shed another tear or find love in someone else's arms." He knew he should have hesitated. He knew he should have held back. He knew he shouldn't chance overwhelming Gloria with the force of what he was feeling. But he had to. He had to be honest with her. She had to know. "I love you, Gloria. I always have. I never stopped. Not for a minute—even when my actions said anything but that. I don't know what's ahead for this island or for us as we rebuild. But I want to be the one you come home to, wherever that is, whatever that is."

Gloria's first reply was a small sound, like a strangled sob. She leaned her head into his chest, and Rigo wasn't sure if the wetness that immediately pressed through his shirt was sweat or tears. It didn't matter—she was where she belonged, next to him, in his arms. With time, they could sort everything else out together.

He only hoped she saw things the same way, and he battled to keep his adrenaline in check as he waited for her answer.

Rigo felt her head shift up and down, nodding against his shirt.

"*Mi casa es su casa*, Rigo."

My house is your house. He let out his breath as he closed his eyes and thanked God for letting her see things the same way.

"Well, not this house." Gloria pulled away and looked slowly at the stained walls and the last roll of carpet and pad in the corner that was ready to be dragged to the curb for eventual pickup. "But wherever there's love, there's home, right?"

Rigo thanked God silently again. He couldn't believe his dream was coming true. After everything he'd messed up, he was getting a second chance. Maybe he was becoming worthy of her after all.

"So you feel the same way?" A mosquito buzzed somewhere in the room, the tiny hum breaking the silence as he waited for her answer.

"I do."

Someday, Rigo hoped to hear her say those words in the sanctuary at La Iglesia de la Luz del Mundo as they stood before their family and friends and finally took the vows he'd asked Carlos's permission to take a decade ago.

But for now, just knowing they were moving forward together instead of looking back would have to do.

Hopefully, though, not for long.

Another hour passed as they moved the soaked contents of Gloria's garage out to the curb.

The city had announced yesterday afternoon that they were working with a FEMA contractor to begin collecting the mountains of garbage residents were pulling out of their homes. As the day grew longer, Gloria's pile grew, too.

A drowned lawn mower that would never run again. Disintegrating cardboard boxes that once stored Christmas decorations, now devoid of their holiday cheer. A framed print of a sunset, the watercolor now waterlogged and warped, mold beginning to creep in a polka-dotted pattern across the faded brushstrokes. They were all there, standing in silent testament to the changes that had befallen Port Provident and all her residents.

Gloria made a few trips back and forth from the front door to the curb, throwing armloads of textbooks on the pile.

"Look at these. Can you believe it? All these huge, expensive nursing textbooks." She heaved four thick books toward the ground. "The covers look like they need to be ironed and the pages are all stuck together and smell like mold. Ugh. There's no saving them. I guess when I start medical school, I'll be starting from scratch in the reference book arena."

"So you're really going to do it?" Rigo couldn't keep the grin off his face. This sounded like the Gloria he'd fallen in love with so many years ago, a woman not afraid to take chances. A possessive pride took hold of his heart, seeing *this* Gloria, the *real* Gloria, eclipse the shadow of the angry Gloria who'd been shackled by the past.

"Yeah, I think so. I don't have any more obligations at the clinic. I have some friends in the admissions office at the med school. Once they get back up and running, I'm going to call Paula and see if she can guide me through the process."

"And you feel good about that?" She sounded confident, but Rigo wanted to confirm Gloria was truly onboard with this change of events in her life.

"I do."

She said it again, and Rigo's heart skipped a quick beat. He'd once hoped to hear those words from her in a church, a lifetime ago. It was driving him crazy not to just reach out and pull her close for another kiss. But he knew he couldn't. They were making progress—slow progress, but still progress—and he didn't want to risk that fragile bridge they'd built.

Still, it was hard to feel the way he felt about her and hold that back.

"We should do something to celebrate, Glo. This is big."

She smiled, a tinge of nervousness tucked into the corners of her lips. Rigo thought her shy smile was one of the most beautiful things he'd ever seen.

"I can't tonight. I promised Mamí and Papí I would meet them for dinner at Gracie's. They didn't have any flooding damage since they're still living in Jake's old apartment in the carriage house over the garage at the Peoples estate until the renovations on the main house are finished—I guess *that* will be taking a little longer now. I'd love to take you up on your offer, but I don't think the rest of the Garcias will feel very celebratory if you're around."

Rigo kicked at some of the trash in the pile with his shoe in order to stop it from moving down in a slow slide, then he laughed. "No, I'm pretty sure the next time Carlos sees me with you will be the last time. He'll lock you in a tower like Rapunzel."

"No, he won't." Gloria threw Rigo a sarcastic scowl. "Well, not that he wouldn't want to. I'm just not the kind to go into a tower willingly."

"No, you're not, and thank God for that."

For the first time since he'd showed up on Travis Place, Gloria looked uncomfortable. "Why did you say that?"

"Say what? That you're not the type to go without a fight?"

"No. The other part. The 'and thank God for that' part."

Rigo thought about it for a second before replying. He wanted to get this right. No more misunderstandings. It wasn't just a figure of speech. "I honestly meant it, Glo. I thank God for you and who you are and how He made you to be. You're one of a kind."

She subtly shifted from her right foot to her left, then back again, but Rigo didn't miss the motion.

"You don't believe me, do you?"

"It's not that I don't believe you. I mean, come on, I know I'm headstrong and all, but..."

"You don't know why I said I meant that I thanked God for you literally, instead of just meaning it as some common turn of phrase?"

She turned her head and looked down the street. "Pretty much."

"Because it's true. Because it's something I had to realize about myself." Rigo sat on the foot-long space of the curb that remained free of trash. "I told you I spent a long time running. From you. From myself. From God. While I was in rehab, my dad sent Pastor Ruiz to visit me. And the conversation we had that day helped me change how I viewed myself. Whatever my strengths or weaknesses were, they were there because God put them there. They're part of me—the good and the bad—because God has a purpose for me. And part of that is to use my strengths to fulfill what I'm supposed to do with my life, and to use my weaknesses to trust Him to help me grow. It's the same way for you. I thank God for everything about you because you are who He made you to be."

"I haven't trusted God for much in a long time, much less to grow or anything like that. I've just gone through the motions to try and get through the day-by-day and not let anyone—not my family, not my patients, not my friends—see how I really feel inside."

"I know." Rigo stood up and walked over to Gloria. He wrapped his arms around her, trying to be both strong and gentle at the same time. He wanted to support her, not push her. "But it doesn't have to be that way anymore. If I can do it, you can, too, you know."

"I wish I could. That would be nice." Her words floated out on a sigh.

He recognized that point of resignation, of reaching deep and knowing you'd been running from the truth, the inevitable.

Rigo shifted his arms a bit and turned Gloria so they were facing each other. He unwrapped the embrace and took her hands in his own. They were strong enough to bring new life into the world, but fragile enough that they trembled slightly as he brushed his thumb across the smooth skin that covered the back of Gloria's hands.

"Then let's make it happen." Rigo bowed his head about forty-five degrees and closed his eyes. He didn't pray much in public. It made him nervous enough sometimes to share these thoughts with God, let alone another person. But if he couldn't share with Gloria, pray with Gloria—pray *for* Gloria—then he realized he had no business praying to God to make Rigo himself worthy of Gloria.

A breeze stirred, blowing the heavy smell of mold from their immediate area. "Heavenly Father, give Gloria the grace to accept the changes in her life and to use them to fulfill the purpose You've given her. Help her to feel Your presence when those changes and the memories they bring back are hard to bear. And mostly, help Gloria to see her as I see her and as You see her. Help her to see the beauty inside and outside and to know Your promise, that beauty comes from ashes. Amen."

Gloria's eyes had opened before Rigo opened his, and they were filled to the brim with a mixture of caramel light and tears. "That's truly how you see me, Rigo? Beautiful?"

"Inside and out." He nodded with the full weight of his heart and soul. "And more importantly, it's how God sees you, too. You're a firecracker. You're one of a kind, Gloriana Maria Claudia Garcia de Piedra."

Her face softened as the guard she'd worn like a suit of armor for years fell to the ground. "You remembered my whole name."

"Of course I did. It's written on my heart."

Chapter Eleven

EVEN THOUGH THE AIR all around Port Provident was heavy with September humidity and the now-constant smells of mold and decay, Gloria pulled air into her lungs, filling them all the way until they pressed down her diaphragm. She felt like she could finally breathe again.

She'd been so wrapped up in holding her emotions tightly that she hadn't seen how they were locking her in like a girdle of strife and anxiety. She'd been so concerned with making her family and friends and patients think she was fine that instead, she'd created more problems.

And she'd been so focused on living day to day that she'd forgotten there was an eternal vision.

But as she looked up at the sky, streaked with pink twisted with ribbons of deep blue as the sun began to set over Provident Island, she knew God was up there, along with the people she'd loved so dearly and lost. She'd turned her back on God—and everyone else—but He'd never left her.

She knocked on the door to Gracie and Jake's carriage house apartment and heard the melodies of warm laughter coming from inside. It felt good to be back.

"*Mija*!" Gloria's mother opened the door, practically shouting the Spanish endearment for a daughter. She folded her into a loving hug.

Gloria had received more hugs since the storm than she had in years. She'd forgotten how it felt to give love as easily as one received it.

"*Holá*, Mamí. Whatever you're making sure smells good."

They walked hand in hand toward the kitchen.

"A relief agency opened a temporary food pantry in the parking lot at La Iglesia this morning. They'd brought fresh vegetables, rice, beans and believe it or not...tortillas. So, Papí is making a sauce and is pulling together some enchiladas. I don't know how he does it, but he always makes something work."

Gloria thought of Papí's last conversation she'd been a part of. Could her father make something work between himself and Rigo? She settled back into what had been habit for most of her life, the past few years excepted—she said a quiet prayer and tucked it in her heart.

"Go see Tía Gloria." As soon as she turned into the living room, Gracie placed Gabriela in Gloria's arms. "You've missed your *tía*."

The little baby stuck out her tongue and blinked as she focused on her aunt's face. Gloria leaned over and drank in the sweet scent of baby shampoo and milk. For the first time in years, the smell of gentle innocence didn't tug at her heart with memories of what could have been.

She closed her eyes and appreciated her sweet niece for exactly who she was, instead of mourning who she wasn't.

"Glo? What's on your mind?" Gracie asked as she pulled a diaper out of a square canvas tote.

Gloria shook her head just a bit. She wanted to keep this new feeling to herself. She felt that if she brought up the past, she'd be pulled into a whirlpool of talking about it all night and that would be a setback to her progress.

She pressed her nose to the top of Gabriela's downy head. "Just thankful that she smells like a baby."

Gracie wrinkled her nose. "I thought she smelled like tinkle when I handed her off to you. Diaper change time."

With confidence, Gracie picked up the little bundle, then laid her atop a blanket at the far end of the couch.

"Okay, well, there's obviously that. But at least it isn't raw sewage or mold. Natural baby smells—all of them—are far more my style than what my nose has been forced to handle this week."

"I'm sure it was awful, Glo." Gracie tucked the diaper together, then snapped the baby's onesie together. "I wish you could have come to San Antonio with us."

"I'm sure San Antonio was far more calm than it was here, but Tanna needed me. I couldn't have left her."

"I know you couldn't have. You've never been able to turn your back on anyone who needed you, no matter what." Gracie sat on the couch and arranged the baby for feeding time. "Which brings us to something else."

Her sister's voice trailed off slightly, but Gloria knew that wasn't the end of it. "What?"

Gracie looked down at the baby, quickly shifted her eyes to Gloria, then adjusted her gaze back to her daughter again. "You know what. Rigo. You haven't been able to leave him alone, either."

"Graciela. Just stop right there." Gloria pushed her shoulders down and back, straightening her spine.

"No, Gloria. Not this time. You've always looked out for me. You've always acted like big sister knows best. But this is one time your little *hermana* really needs to have her say."

Gloria turned her head slightly and looked at her sister's expression.

It seemed very familiar.

She'd seen it in the mirror on many occasions. The look Gracie was giving her was one hundred percent Gloria.

Gracie barreled ahead, seeming to sense correctly that if she didn't fill the pause in conversation, Gloria would.

"He's bad news, Gloria. He's in the past and you need to leave him there. It's fine that he was able to help you a few days ago—it was a hurricane, for goodness sakes, take whatever help you can get—but the storm's over, your patient's safe and your family is back here. You need to leave Inez's house and go home."

"Home? I don't have a home, Graciela." She couldn't keep the bile from rising in her throat and coming through in her voice. She hadn't realized just how bitter those words tasted. "I don't have a home or a job. Everything I had is gone."

"No it's not. *Somos familia.* We're family. Always. You can stay here with us. And you can always work back at Huarache's."

Gloria tried to push her hurt aside and be rational, but it was a struggle. "Stay here? With four adults and a baby in an over-the-garage apartment?"

"Hey, it's clean and dry and not destroyed." The baby squirmed in Gracie's lap as the sisters' voices raised slightly.

"Neither am I, Gracie. I don't need charity."

"Family is not charity, Gloria. I don't understand why you'd rather live at Inez's instead of here with us, unless you're really trying to start something up with Rigo again."

Gloria stood up abruptly. "Start something up? I'm not a high schooler sneaking around behind the bleachers."

Gracie tried to match her sister's motion but was moored by the feeding baby in her lap. "Well, the last time you were with this guy, you were a high schooler. He was bad news then and he's bad news now. Glo, I realize a lot has happened to you, but don't throw your common sense out the window."

"What window? Just about every window in this town is blown out."

"It's a figure of speech, Gloria."

Gloria jumped in before Gracie could finish. She barely recognized herself in her actions with her family since they'd come home. First she'd walked off from Papí. Now she was snapping at her sister. She felt a pounding in her veins, like a prizefighter in a ring, waiting for the chance to take a swing.

She knew she should be appalled by how she was acting. She knew she was getting caught up in her emotions.

She also knew that for the first time in a long time, she felt like fighting. She felt like fighting for something that mattered to her.

"I meant that everything's changed, Gracie. The whole island has changed. So has Rigo. And so have I."

There was no mistaking the tone in Gloria's voice. Gracie leaned back against the corner of the couch as the baby mewled and waved an arm in a wobbly circle.

"I just think you're smarter than this, Gloria," Gracie said, gruff exasperation riding on the syllables of her whisper.

Gloria looked toward the hallway. The rest of the family was cooking in the kitchen at one end. The front door was at the other. She considered both for a moment, then made her decision.

She knew she was about to hurt some people who loved her dearly. She'd always tried to do right by her family, to help Mamí and Papí at the restaurant, to support Gloria's school and to be everything she thought a big sister should be, and to never let the people she cared about most worry by knowing how much she'd been hurting the past few years.

Just as clearly as she knew she had never let them down, Gloria also knew she couldn't live the life she'd known before Hurricane Hope blew through town. She closed her eyes and silently asked God for that strength she'd been pursuing since the storm came and changed everything.

"I'm smart enough to fight for the people I love, Graciela." Gloria picked up her purse and walked in the direction of the door. "And Rigo is one of them."

Rigo knew that flash and howl coming from behind him all too well. He'd lost track of how many times he'd been part of a routine traffic stop as a patrol officer. His last traffic stop as a patrol officer was anything but routine, and it cost Felipe Rodriguez his life, Gloria her husband and Rigo his world.

When he first got out of rehab and began to get his life back together, he never even considered asking to become part of the rank-and-file of PPPD again, instead choosing to wait until there was a position open in the Beach Patrol. He wanted to be out with the sun and the waves and the lifeguards and put as much distance as possible between him and routine traffic stops.

As he looked in the rearview mirror and saw Carpenter getting out of the patrol car, the angle of his face washed in alternating streaks of blue and red, Rigo's stomach sunk. There was no reason to expect gunfire this time, but he was smart enough to know that what happened next could destroy everything he'd been working for just as quickly.

Carpenter would like nothing more than to see Rigo off the island again—that much was clear to everyone at the first responder dinner.

A tap sounded on the glass of the window, and Rigo rolled it down.

"License and registra—Vasquez. I should have known that you'd be behind the wheel of a suspected DUI stop."

Rigo handed the twin rectangles of driver's license and insurance card out the window. "I'm not drunk, Carpenter."

"Well, I've been following you since you left O'Boyle's, and you've made several questionable lane changes." Carpenter put his hands on his hips and spread his legs into a triangle stance.

"I was trying to get around the dump truck hauling all that debris to the temporary landfill so I could get on the causeway, and you know it."

A soft choking snort, then a lazy snore, came from the passenger seat.

"What was that?" Carpenter leaned inside the window. "Milton's with you?"

Rigo put his hands on the steering wheel and clenched them, since he wouldn't be able to answer Carpenter's questions with a tightly clenched jaw. He needed to direct his tension somewhere. "Pretty sure he's passed out."

"I'm going to need you to step out of the car, Vasquez."

Rigo turned his head so Carpenter wouldn't hear the words he mumbled under his breath. He faced Carpenter, who was still studying the flopping figure in the other seat of the truck.

"I told you, I'm not drunk. I haven't had a single drink. I went to O'Boyle's to pick Milton up. He called me and needed help. His AA sponsor is still evacuated. I'm taking him to a rehab clinic in Houston."

"You know all about rehab clinics, don't you Vasquez?"

"Cut it out, Carpenter. I don't have to answer that." Just like at the first responder dinner, it wasn't taking long in Carpenter's presence to make Rigo's blood pressure rise almost uncontrollably.

Carpenter tapped the door of the car. "You don't, but you do have to step out of the car."

Rigo tugged with deliberate, measured force on the door handle. He knew he didn't have any choice but to comply. What he didn't know was how far Carpenter wanted to take this. There was a probationary clause in Rigo's contract that didn't expire for another month. He served at the pleasure of the chief of police and the mayor of Port Provident. Any conduct issues would quickly lead to the displeasure of those two.

And then where would he be?

He'd lose his job and more important, his chance with Gloria. They'd made so much progress but it was still fragile. He knew they were on the path to being strong, but for right now, even the merest hint of him being back to his old ways would send Gloria back into her shell.

That much he knew for sure.

And it scared him to the core.

Rigo knew the different faces of fear. They'd been well-acquainted over the years. He'd been full of false bravado when he'd called and left Gloria that message from Mexico. He'd been numb with shock as he watched Felipe fall to the ground after the gunshot. But today, he knew acutely what was at stake, and his awareness wasn't dulled by drink or swept up in the middle of fight-or-flight instinct.

He stepped out of the vehicle, determined to get through this, get away from Carpenter, get Milton the help he needed. And then get to Gloria and kiss her and do whatever it took to move them from fragile to forever.

Carpenter motioned to the trunk of the car. "Empty your pockets, then put your hands there where I can see them."

Rigo did as he was told. He laid his cell phone and wallet on the trunk of the car, then laid his hands on the edge, clearly visible.

Carpenter opened the door to the squad car and fiddled with his equipment. "It's better for both of us if I have this on. You're a trained cop and I suspect you're under the influence. I don't know what you'll try, but you went to the same academy I did and you know the same holds and tactics I know. This dash cam is best for us both."

"I told you, I'm not drunk. You want me to say the alphabet backward or walk in a straight line, man?"

"No. I want you to do as you're told, Chief Vasquez, and quit being belligerent. It's really not going to look good on the front page of tomorrow's paper that the brand-new chief of Beach Patrol is driving under the influence and resisting law enforcement."

Carpenter was crazy, no doubt. But he was right. Any other cop in this town would bend over backward to not put a black eye on a chief of a department if he could avoid doing so. Rigo didn't necessarily expect special treatment—he just expected fair treatment—but he knew many an incident had been swept under a rug or two in order to keep someone with a chief's rank from being publicly embarrassed.

But that wasn't Carpenter's style. He'd always been a bully and he probably saw this as an opportunity to not only take down Rigo, but to bring himself some glory. He'd applied for the job at Beach Patrol, as well. But Rigo's strong lifeguarding experience made the difference. He understood all the aspects of the job—law enforcement and water safety. Carpenter didn't.

Carpenter wasn't the type of person to care about the details, though.

Rigo did. He cared deeply about the details. Because the details in this awkward situation could make or break everything he'd come back for.

One detail trumped it all. He *hadn't* been drinking. By any standard Carpenter chose to measure—field sobriety tests, breath tests or even a blood test—the results would all come back negative.

But if Carpenter dragged this out or word got out to the wrong people in the meantime, something else would come back negative—Rigo's reputation.

He'd done good work with Beach Patrol since coming back. But his reputation, especially among those cops who hadn't seen him since he returned and only remembered the night Felipe died and Rigo's no-show at the funeral, stood on no more firm a foundation than the one that bolstered his fledgling relationship with Gloria.

Rigo had so much to prove, to everyone. He couldn't let Carpenter take this too far.

As he thought through this very possible worst-case scenario, he could feel the sweat on his palms begin to form a slick barrier between his skin and the paint of the car.

A metallic buzz sounded, loud enough to jerk Rigo's head up and jolt his thoughts.

"Don't touch it, Vasquez. Keep your hands on the car." Carpenter strode purposefully to the trunk and looked down at Rigo's ringing phone. "Gloria Garcia." He read the name off the display on the phone with all the resemblance to the Grinch, as he bared his teeth and rolled out his green Grinchy antennae in anticipation of wrecking the celebrations in Whoville.

"You know her last name is Rodriguez, don't you?" He stared Rigo down and swiped his finger over the glass to connect the call. "Hello?"

"I did not tell you that you could answer that, Carpenter." Rigo gritted out the words angrily, then raised his voice, hoping he could be heard through the microphone. "Gloria, do not listen to him."

"Vasquez, you need to shut up unless you want to be in more trouble than you're already in." Carpenter fixed a stare on him, one that confirmed every fear that had run through Rigo's mind earlier. This was personal, and Carpenter was not going to back down until he found a way to ruin Rigo.

Rigo could hear Gloria speaking on the other end but couldn't make out the words, just the panic in her tone of voice.

"It's Carpenter, Gloria. I followed Rigo from O'Boyle's pub, where he and Officer Milton had too much to drink. Officer Milton is passed out in the car, and I'm about to take Vasquez in for further testing."

Rigo pushed on the side of the car so hard that the vehicle shifted its weight off the back left tire in front of him. "I'm not going to fail the field test, Carpenter. And you can't answer my phone."

"I'm sorry, Gloria. I wouldn't pull someone over without clear evidence. I saw how he was driving. And with Milton passed out, there's no question in my mind." He paused. "Yeah, sure. Here."

"She wants to talk to you." Carpenter punched the speaker button on the phone. Rigo made a move, but Carpenter's eyes narrowed to icy slits. "Keep your hands on the car, Chief Vasquez. I'll hold the phone."

"Rigo, what is going on?"

"Nothing. Nothing is going on." He tried to keep his voice calm, in the hopes of soothing some of the panic out of Gloria's voice.

"It doesn't sound like nothing." Her words were clipped, short and full of gunpowder just waiting to explode.

"Carpenter's a jerk, Gloria. You said it yourself."

Carpenter shook his head disapprovingly. Rigo doubted he could dig his hole any deeper with the patrol officer. At least maybe he could get Gloria to understand until he could explain things to her in person.

"Don't lie to me, Rigo, but if you answer yes to this, don't ever call me again. You were at a bar?"

Rigo had been wrong earlier when he figured there wouldn't be shots fired at this traffic stop. Gloria was taking aim.

He wasn't about to lie to her, that much he could promise. "Yeah, but..."

Carpenter tapped the screen with a fingertip. "Looks like you lost your connection."

"Why are you doing this, Carpenter? You turned on the dash cam. It's all there for evidence—the fact that I told you not to answer my phone and that whole conversation."

He looked down the shoulder of his starched black shirt. "I did turn on the dash cam. But it looks like I forgot to turn on the mic."

Carpenter gave a half shrug, then narrowed his eyes to steely slits. "Your word against mine, Vasquez."

Rigo couldn't fight the chill that came over him. It had nothing to do with the crisp September weather.

Carpenter placed the phone on the trunk, tantalizingly in front of Rigo's stationary hands. Rigo itched to pick up the phone and call Gloria, despite what she'd said. He needed to finish that sentence. She needed to know the rest of what he had to say.

As hard as it was to do so, Rigo pulled his concentration back to Carpenter. More than anything, he wanted to figure out a way to get to Gloria and make her understand. However, he knew that if he tried anything, Carpenter would make this mess even worse. Even if he got brought in front of the chief of police, he could explain away the suspicion of DUI easily by showing all the passed sobriety test results.

If he tried to make a run for it, to get to Gloria, then he knew Carpenter would find a way to charge him with resisting arrest. And he couldn't explain that away, certainly not with dash cam footage showing him fleeing down the street toward Inez's.

"I'm calling for backup to take Milton somewhere to sleep it off," Carpenter said with all the subtlety of a two-by-four upside the head. "Then I'm testing you."

"You can't do that. I can still refuse."

"Noted. Suspect refuses field testing. I guess you've forgotten that since the hurricane, a no-refusal order has been in place."

Rigo had forgotten. And he felt the press of the trap as it tightened.

"There's a mobile health clinic next door to headquarters right now. They're also set up to do blood draws. That's where we've been taking people like you in."

"People like me?"

Carpenter reached for the metal cuffs at his belt. "Yeah, guys who think the rules don't apply to them. You know, guys who would let their partner get shot and run off like a scared cat with its tail between its legs because he's a drunk and too weak to face reality."

Rigo *was* scared. Carpenter had that much right. He was scared of what everyone would think when he was paraded in for suspicion of DUI. He was scared of how that would affect his job. Only thirty days left of his probationary period, and this would surely leave a black mark. He'd given his word when he came back that he was sober. He'd signed paperwork to that effect. Sobriety was written in his probationary contract.

If he broke that pledge, his employment agreement was voided immediately.

Carpenter couldn't have known what was in that document. Only the chief of Port Provident PD, the mayor of Port Provident, and the attorneys for the department and the city knew what was in there.

In the end, it didn't matter if Carpenter knew or he was just poking at Rigo's weak point.

But as scared as he was for his job, he was a hundred times more scared of what was going through Gloria's head when the last word she heard out of his mouth was an admittance that he'd been in a bar.

Even though he stood braced against the car, he could feel himself falling. He could feel the insecurity of this moment.

The screen on Rigo's phone lit up in front of him. Carpenter jerked Rigo's arms behind him to fasten the handcuffs. Rigo's eyes, however, were still free to face forward and read the message on his phone.

I trusted when you said you'd changed. Meeting Milton in a bar to go drinking is backward. And I can't move forward with us in light of that. I meant what I said. Don't call. I'll be gone from Inez's by morning.

Carpenter gave Rigo a shove toward the curb. "Go sit there until my backup comes."

Rigo lowered himself awkwardly to a seated position, without the use of his hands for balance or bracing. He felt the position was fitting since he'd just been kicked to the proverbial curb by Gloria.

Immediately, his mind wondered why Gloria had so little faith in him, why she'd believe a jerk like Carpenter about anything.

But he knew the truth. He'd been that jerk to Gloria first, all those years ago.

He'd been so close to making amends for his callous ways and winning Gloria back. But all she'd heard from him was words so far. She hadn't yet had the opportunity to see him back it up with enough actions to drown out the voice of doubt when it came calling. She'd heard him admit with his own voice that he had been in a bar. He didn't blame her. He could only blame himself.

Not for going to the bar and trying to help Milton.

For going to Mexico and breaking Gloria's heart and her trust in the first place.

Rigo knew tonight would come to an end. He'd be released because there was no evidence to hold him on. Then, he'd make sure Milton got to the treatment center in Houston. And somehow, he'd find a way to navigate any questions that came his way about his ability to remain chief of Beach Patrol. He lowered his head and prayed silently for protection for his job.

And protection for his heart.

And then when this night was over, he'd have one last thing to do. Even though he knew it wouldn't make any difference now.

Gloria had stayed barricaded in the room designated as hers at Inez's all night for nothing. Rigo had never come back to his own guest room at the far end of the hall. If it had been a misunderstanding, he'd have been quickly released.

Since he was gone all night long, she knew the truth. He'd been booked for DUI and held overnight. He'd been out drinking again. And he'd gotten so drunk that he'd gotten caught. So much for that time in rehab and those lessons he'd said he learned.

As the sun took its position in the morning sky, Gloria took the stairs in Inez's house slowly, awkwardly carrying her few worldly possessions in the tiny suitcase she'd brought with her as Hurricane Hope bore down on the island. She felt a bit like a hobo, jumping from place to place without permanence. But it was time to start moving forward.

Without Rigo.

And that meant moving out from under his aunt's roof and away from the memories she'd formed in this place in just a few short days. Baby Mateo's birth, the howl of Hope and Rigo's rescue of them all. The makeshift restaurant on the widow's walk. That tender kiss that took away the years and the yearning.

Like everything else in Port Provident, they were all water under the bridge.

She would leave here and ask her sister's forgiveness for the way she'd acted last night. Hopefully Gracie and Jake would still have a couch for her to sleep on until the numerous government agencies and insurance companies flocking to the area could sort out temporary housing arrangements for Port Provident residents. Hopefully, soon she could get a hotel room or a trailer or something to call her own for a while.

But first, she had to find Inez and say goodbye.

Gloria placed her plain brown box at the bottom of the stairs and followed the scent of rice into the kitchen. Inez stood behind an ancient two-burner camp stove. Gloria recognized it as the one she'd used at Rigo's rooftop restaurant.

"He's not here, *querida*." Inez stirred something in a battered aluminum saucepan.

"I know he's not." A lump settled in her throat. She'd known Inez for years, had respected her as a matriarch of the neighborhood and a pillar of the church community. But now, after a bond forged by wind and waves, Gloria realized she loved the petite lady like her own *abuela*.

She'd said so many goodbyes in her life. Experience didn't make them easier.

"I'm going to stay at Gracie's. Will you be okay here by yourself, Tía?"

As she said that, a little fear gripped Gloria's heart. She couldn't leave this woman here by herself in a city turned upside down.

"Well, they're starting the work on the downstairs tomorrow. My grandson Raul knew some contractors in Houston and he was able to get them to come help quickly. I'll probably go stay with Raul's family while the work is being done. I'm glad your sister is back and that you have somewhere safe to go."

Gloria noted the older woman's omission. "What about Rigo?"

Inez turned off one of the burners, the blue flame shrinking lower and lower until it extinguished.

The slow diffusion reminded Gloria of her heart.

"When I told him about the crew coming, he said not to worry about him. He had some other plans."

Gloria nodded with irony. She couldn't believe Rigo had warned Inez he wasn't coming back. It felt worse knowing he'd planned to go out on some epic bender with Milton. Regardless of all his sweet-sounding promises, he'd gone back to his old ways, and once again, he hadn't cared about the effect on Gloria. And she was a fool for ever believing it could have been otherwise.

Gloria rolled her lower lip in slightly and bit down. Her top row of teeth felt sharp as they pressed against the flesh. At least she could still feel. Too bad all she was aware of was hurt.

"So he didn't call you last night?"

Inez shook her head, light wisps of gray hair swaying beside her temples. "Call me? No. He kind of rushed out of here yesterday afternoon and said he had some unfinished business to take care of. He gave me a quick kiss on the cheek, threw one of his *tío* Arturo's army-issued duffel bags over his shoulder and literally ran out the front door."

Gloria wanted to run, too. She wanted to run from all the "I told you so" admonishments she knew she deserved.

Her father's dismissal of Rigo boomed inside her head, rattling off the curves of her skull and echoing over and over again. *This coward...*

And then she heard Gracie's words from last night. *I just think you're smarter than this...*

Steven McLellan had warned her at the dinner. Even Carpenter had read the situation better than she had—and he'd been proven correct, right in front of his face.

So much for the intuition she'd always prided herself on. Everyone knew she'd been playing with fire. Except her.

Her emotions had been asbestos for so long that she didn't listen.

As usual, Gloria thought she knew best.

A Bible verse she hadn't thought of in years flooded into her mind. *Pride goes before the fall.*

She'd fallen for Rigo again. Then she'd fallen mightily.

And this time, she knew the scars would never heal.

The lack of sleep started to take a toll on Rigo. Last night had been one of the longest nights of his life, and on top of it all, he'd finally dropped off Milton at the treatment center early this morning and then gone to run his one precious errand while in Houston. He'd been let go as soon as the test results came back from the portable lab next to headquarters and the chief of police had personally assured him everything was just a misunderstanding and he'd see to it that it was kept from the media and city hall. Rigo had been running on stress and adrenaline and the crushing dread of a future without Gloria, the soul-searing dread that another hurricane had blown in his way and in one misunderstood instant, wrecked everything he'd built. All he wanted right now was a breakfast taco, a cup of coffee and a pair of toothpicks to prop his eyelids open. But he had a few more things to cross off his list before he could think about rest.

And he knew he'd never settle his nerves until he followed through on a plan he'd made a few days ago. Even though Gloria didn't want him in her life, and even though he'd decided sitting on that curb to respect the wishes she'd conveyed in that text, he still had one thing to do. He wasn't going to try and offer explanations, because although he knew he'd never drink again, he knew he'd disappoint her again—that was just part of life—and he couldn't bear to put her through that anymore, no matter how small it might be.

He'd just check this box—one that he'd been so excited about just a little over forty-eight hours ago—and move on. And then he'd let Gloria do the same.

The back door to Huarache's stood slightly ajar, propped open by a metal chair with red vinyl-covered padding.

Rigo had faced swirling surf to save drowning swimmers. He'd heard the loud volley of shots fired around him by a criminal determined to make a point. He was no stranger to stressful situations with questionable outcomes.

But nothing he'd ever walked into up to this point had made his throat go dry and his hands and feet tingle with a flood of adrenaline like preparing to face Carlos Garcia did.

Rigo poked his head around the edge of the door, feeling like an officer looking for a suspect. He saw his target right away, swinging at sodden drywall with a sledgehammer.

"Can I help you with that, sir?"

The heavy metal head of the sledgehammer dug into the wall and stuck as Carlos turned around.

Rigo felt like there was a similar lead mass in his throat as he waited for Gloria's father to acknowledge him.

"You want to help me destroy my life's work? That's fitting, since you've already destroyed my daughter." Carlos wiped sweat off his brow with a swipe of his forearm. "What are you doing here, Rodrigo? You're not supposed to be here."

"I know I'm not welcome, Carlos, but—"

The older man cut him off. "No, you're not. But—"

This time, it was Rigo's turn to jump in. They were both determined not to give much ground. "But what?"

"Gloria said you got arrested." He unscrewed the lid off a bottle of water and took a drink. "So what are you doing here? Did you forget something? Like telling my daughter you're drinking again?"

Rigo dropped the duffel bag on the ground. "I didn't get arrested, sir. I got pulled over and tested, but there was no alcohol in my blood. I assure you, sir, I haven't fallen off the wagon. I picked up my friend who needed help and was taking him to Houston for treatment. I told Gloria I wasn't the person I used to be, and I meant it."

"That's not what you said on the phone."

"I got cut off. She didn't get to hear the whole story. But I'm not here to make excuses."

"Then what are you doing here?" Carlos snapped at Rigo as light pushed across the kitchen and someone else walked through the back door.

"Rigo." Gloria's voice hit him with the force of a slap. "What are you doing here?"

A couple of other voices chattered, then fell silent, and Rigo knew Gracie and her mother followed right behind Gloria.

He stood between two groups of angry Garcias—a completely different type of sandwich than the Huarache's kitchen typically produced.

"Gloria." His voice caught in his throat at the sight of her, the woman he'd loved his whole life. He wanted to close the space between them, take her hand and reassure her that everything would be okay.

But he wouldn't do that. He wouldn't cause her any more emotional turmoil.

"If you're coming to tell me there's been a misunderstanding, you're right. It's been mine. I shouldn't have believed a word you said." Her jaw quivered slightly as she stopped speaking. She crossed her arms tightly over her chest.

"Gloria, I wasn't drinking. Carpenter cut off the phone call. He had the opportunity to mess with me and he took it. If you want to see the test results, I will get them for you. I have not lied to you since the moment you called me at Tanna's apartment."

Her brown eyes darkened, then broke the line of sight between them. The golden sparkle had fluttered out of her irises like glitter dropping to the floor. Years ago, he'd left her to deal with all these same emotions while he rode waves into oblivion off the coast of Mexico.

Rigo was not leaving her to deal with these emotions again. Mainly because he wasn't leaving. Ever.

And somehow, he would make her understand that one simple truth. He told himself he wasn't going to explain. But his heart wouldn't let him do otherwise. He knew that somehow, somewhere, he could find the strength to walk away. But he couldn't leave letting Gloria think he hadn't meant every word he'd said to her since she called him out on patrol before the landfall of Hope.

"Gloria, if I'd started back to drinking, I'd be at a bar again after all this mess. I wouldn't be here in the Huarache's kitchen." Rigo gestured behind him. "If I was going to lie to you, I wouldn't be within a mile of your father and a sledgehammer."

The left corner of Gloria's mouth twisted upward into the faintest beginning of a smile. She raised her head and looked at Rigo at an angle from beneath her lashes. He could see her hesitation as she struggled to trust him.

And then it hit him with the weight of the sledgehammer still propped in Carlos's hands. Rigo had resolved to walk away so he couldn't hurt her again. But that made him the liar he didn't want to be since those actions wouldn't line up with the promise that he'd never walk away again, no matter what.

Please, God, make me worthy of her. Make me a man who keeps his promises, a man she can trust. And open her eyes to see that.

With two steps, he covered the distance between them, hoping his touch could speak the truth more clearly than his words. He took her left hand in between both of his. He pressed the cool, slim fingers between his palms. He felt a faint pulse as he held on and wondered if it belonged to him or to her.

"The hardest thing I've ever done was come back. I came back after Mexico. I finally came back after rehab. And I've come back today, after you had every reason to believe the worst of me one more time. Every time I've come back, it's been tougher than the time before. This is the toughest of them all. But I came back for you, Gloria. I got Milton to rehab. He has to learn how to rebuild his life. I'm going to rebuild mine. But I can't without you."

She laid her right hand gently atop his. "So why did you come here to the restaurant?"

"To apologize." Rigo gave Gloria's hand a gentle squeeze, then let go. "And to bring this."

He turned to the duffel bag on the ground, knelt, then unzipped it. "I remember this from when we were kids, and I remember you'd said it meant a lot to your parents."

He pulled out a small black frame, then handed it to Carlos.

"It's the first dollar you ever made in America. I knew you kept it on the counter at the cash register. On my first patrol after the hurricane, I came in here to check the damage and I saw it. There was water inside the frame and the whole thing was soaked. The sister of a friend of mine owns a print shop up in Sugar Land. He took it to her and I picked it up last night after I got Milton settled. They were able to dry it out and fix it up and put it in an archival frame for you."

Carlos stared at the small rectangular frame and turned it over in his hands, then back again.

"I noticed it was missing. But so much was ruined, I thought we'd never see it again."

Rigo nodded. "I figured as much. I didn't really have a chance to tell you when we met in the parking lot the other day."

"No, I guess you didn't." Carlos's expression softened as he looked at the restored and protected symbol of his fresh start in America so many years ago.

"I know that's just a dollar bill, but I also know what it means to you. And I promise you, sir, that I know how much more your daughter means."

Carlos swallowed and nodded but remained uncharacteristically silent.

"All I'm asking for is the chance to prove that to you and to Juanita. And Gracie."

Rigo turned around and looked at the women in the doorway, then directly at Gloria. "And to you, too, *mí amor*."

He hoped calling her "my love" hadn't been too forward. Gloria opened her mouth to speak, but before she could collect her thoughts, Rigo decided he needed to finish what was on his heart, so he continued.

"You are, you know. The love of my life. Past, present and future." He bent back toward the duffel bag. "I have something for you, too."

He pulled out a small rectangular book. The front cover was a shiny silver, decorated with an engraved pattern of baby blocks and a teddy bear. The spine and back were wrapped in black velvet.

Rigo reached out and placed the book in Gloria's hands.

"Sophia couldn't save them all, but she scanned them into her computer and used Photoshop to bring them back as much as she could."

A tear rolled over the curve of Gloria's cheek, then another and another, clearing a track through the small amount of makeup she was wearing. She turned the pages wordlessly, studying the images as though for the first time.

"My pictures of Mateo. I thought they were ruined." Gloria's soft whisper was barely audible in the silent room.

Rigo saw matching tear tracks running down the faces of the aunt and the grandmother who had never gotten to know Mateo, either.

"I had to try. I didn't want the hurricane to take away everything you had left of your son."

Gloria held out one arm. Rigo walked into her embrace, like a surfer sliding into shore. He felt the brush of velvet against his neck as Gloria wrapped her other arm around him, still holding the book of her memories.

"I love it."

"I love you." Nothing but total honesty would do at a moment like this.

She stretched up on her toes and met Rigo's mouth with her own. He tried his best to focus on the kiss. He wanted to remember everything about this moment—the fresh relief of forgiveness, the sight of her, the smell of the air around them, the taste of the salt still wet on her lips.

Rigo pulled back just enough to ask her the question he needed to know. "Tell me we can rebuild together. Forever, this time."

He brushed a humidity-curled lock of caramel-colored hair from Gloria's forehead and gently tucked it behind the curve of her ear as he waited for her reply.

Gloria looked at the little book, at her family, and then at Rigo. Her eyes glowed and her smile was as fresh as it had been when they were eighteen and had the whole world at their feet.

"Yes. Together."

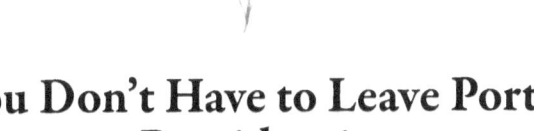

You Don't Have to Leave Port Provident!

Start Shelter from the Storm Now!

SOMETIMES THE PERSON standing in your way is your only hope...

As the director of the Port Provident Animal Shelter, Becca Collins had devoted her life to helping the furriest residents of Port Provident. When a special Labrador retriever, Polly, needs her help on the eve of Hurricane Hope, Becca can't say no—even if it means she'll have to ride out the hurricane on Provident Island. When she shows up on the doorstep of local veterinarian and Army veteran Dr. Ross Reeder, Becca throws a wrench into Ross' plans to evacuate himself and his combat-weary former service dog, Cookie.

Ross and Becca are used to disagreeing with one another, but they soon realize the only way they're going to survive the wrath of Hurricane Hope is to put their differences aside and work for the good of the animals who depend totally on them. As they discover they have more in common than they thought and work to rebuild the Texas beach town where they've both put down roots, Becca learns secrets about her past that threaten to change the whole direction of her life.

As Becca struggles with love, faith, and lies, will she still need the shelter she's found in Ross' arms or will the aftermath of the storm take away everything they've worked to build?

Start reading Shelter from the Storm to find hope, heart, and happily-ever-after today!

Best-Selling Christian Romance author Kristen Ethridge brings readers home to Port Provident, Texas for the Port Provident: Hurricane Hope series—sweet escape romances full of hope, heart and happily-ever-after. These clean romance novels with a light, uplifting thread of faith and love will sweep you up in the story and leave you with a smile.

Enjoy the complete Port Provident: Hurricane Hope series!

Shelter from the Storm

The Doctor's Unexpected Family

His Texas Princess

Holiday of Hope

https://books2read.com/ShelterFromTheStorm

Join Kristen's Reader Community Today and Receive a Free Port Provident Story

Join Kristen's reader community today for the latest and get A Place to Find Love, *a sweet escape romance that introduces you to Port Provident, Texas and the residents who find love on the island, for free!*

www.kristenethridge.com/newsletter[1]

Sneak Peek: Shelter from the Storm—Chapter One

TEN YEARS AGO, BECCA Collins caught a bus to Port Provident, Texas because it was as far south as she could get from Wisconsin without falling into the water. She never expected to take another bus to leave.

But today, she found herself standing in a line in front of Port Provident High School, waiting to board a school bus headed for San Antonio. Hurricane Hope was expected to make landfall overnight. This was the last evacuation bus scheduled to cross the Causeway which connected Provident Island with the Texas mainland.

The line had been moving consistently, but now there had been no progress in getting aboard the bus for a few minutes. The crowd, mostly made up of women and children, was beginning to get restless. Becca could hear it in the rustle of voices that were starting to rise above a whisper and in the stirring and stomping of feet as they adjusted the positions where they stood.

---

1. *http://www.kristenethridge.com/newsletter*

She could also feel it in the dense layer of humidity that had pushed ashore with the first bands of Hope's clouds and winds.

Damp circles were beginning to soak through the thin cotton of her T-shirt, and she felt a sticky clamminess working its way down her spine. She just wanted to get on the rattley yellow school bus and get moving. As the director of the Port Provident Animal Shelter, she'd seen the last dog in her care off the island this morning, headed to a shelter in a northern suburb of Houston. The final group of cats had departed around dinner time yesterday. The animals who had depended upon her would be safe.

The only thing left was to ensure her own safety before the storm arrived. If her compact Toyota hatchback wasn't on its last leg, she would have just taken matters into her own hands. But most days, she wasn't sure it would make it to the grocery store. A two-hundred-and-fifty-mile trip that was expected to take double the normal amount of time due to heavy traffic congestion? That was out of the question.

In fact, Becca realized, she might have had a breakdown before the little hatchback. The last few weeks had been so stressful. First the showdown at the board meeting with the president—and most unreasonable member—of the shelter's board of directors, Dr. Ross Reeder. Now Hurricane Hope.

She needed a break, and she needed it now.

She also needed to get on the bus. *What was taking so long?* Becca made a step to the right side of the line, trying to discern the cause of the hold-up.

"I'm sorry. The dog has to stay. We cannot take dogs on the bus or to the shelter." A blonde-haired lady holding a clipboard spoke with a stern voice that carried over the ever-strengthening gusts of wind.

"But she has to come. She's my grandma's dog. She requires a special diet. We can't leave her behind. She'll die." A teenager with a thick black braid down the back of her head spoke up, then gestured at a Labrador retriever near her feet.

"Then she'll have to stay behind with the dog. The Port Provident Animal Shelter is closed. Your only options are to get on board without the dog or to stay here with her. I'm sorry, but we can't make exceptions."

"But Grandma can't stay. She's not in good health. I take care of her." She gave another look down toward the dog's sturdy head. "And, so does Polly. We're all a team."

The woman with the clipboard shifted slightly, blocking a little more of the door to the bus. "I'm sorry. Those are the rules. You need to decide. We have to be loaded and en route in ten minutes and there's a whole line behind you."

A dog. A grandmother. Becca looked heavenward. She took a deep breath as the memories of Bess popped into her head like fragile soap bubbles.

"I'll take the dog." Becca picked up her backpack and slung it over one shoulder, then walked toward the Labrador and her visibly-shaking owner. "I'm Becca Collins, director of the Port Provident Animal Shelter. The shelter is closed. But I'll stay behind with your dog."

The girl turned her head slowly. The older woman's eyes released a stream of silent tears.

"You'll take Polly? But you don't even know us."

"I don't. But I know all about dogs and grandmothers. And hard choices."

Becca held out her hand for the leash. With deliberate, almost hesitant motions, the girl pressed the loop end of the leash into Becca's outstretched palm. Becca felt the worn weave of the purple fabric.

"Wait." The girl said, reaching into a reusable grocery store bag and pulling out a bag of specialized dog food. "There's a prescription label on the bag with directions for how to feed her. Oh, and we have to keep her well-hydrated."

"You said her name was Polly?" Becca said, giving the dog a scratch behind the flopped-over ears.

The grandmother spoke. The syllables cracked like popcorn. "Polly Wolly Doodle. I'll be back for her. Take care of her, please."

"All the day...all the day." Becca scratched the dog's ears again as her own throat tightened. Her own grandmother had loved Shirley Temple movies. As clearly as though it had happened yesterday, Becca remembered pushing a VHS tape in the recorder and snuggling on the couch with Bess, watching Shirley's little curls bounce as she sang Polly Wolly Doodle. "She'll be waiting for you when you come home. You'll find us both at the Port Provident Animal Shelter."

Before Becca knew it, everything was taken care of. Within two minutes of the last resident of Port Provident taking their seat, the bus was out of the parking lot, and the last group of evacuees was on their way off the island. The engine of the bus jumped to life with a diesel-fuel rattle...and then there was nothing but silence.

Becca stood in the parking lot, rooted. The last transport was gone, and she was not. She was still in the parking lot of

Port Provident High School. With a dog. And a less than half a bag of expensive prescription-only dog food.

She lifted the bag and looked at the label stuck in the center.

Dr. Ross Reeder.

Of course, Polly's vet was Ross Reeder. Because if there was one person she wanted to stay clear of today—well, every day, really—it was Port Provident's haughty, argumentative vet. The president of the board of directors of the Port Provident Animal Shelter, Ross had blocked Becca's plan to relocate the shelter from the old, outdated facility on Harborview Drive to a building in town that she believed in her heart would give them room to grow.

He'd made every step of the last two months feel like a twenty-mile hike in the mountains. Without shoes. Or a trail.

Dealing with him was painful.

But she'd committed to keeping Polly the Labrador safe and healthy—and she knew the half-empty bag of dog food was not going to last a dog of Polly's size very long. She also knew this specific, specialized brand was only sold in one place on the island.

Dr. Ross Reeder's office.

Ugh. The syllable pushed into every fiber of her body like some kind of green viscous slime. In fact, that feeling summed up her impression of Ross. Everywhere she turned with regard to the new shelter location, every idea she had...there he was, guaranteed to put a suffocating blanket of negativity over it all.

Polly thumped her tail on the ground twice, oblivious to Becca's internal dilemma. The simple canine gesture did remind her though that she'd promised to take care of this furry patient, and one of the basics of care was food.

Besides, most of Port Provident's citizens had already heeded the recommendations to evacuate. Ross Reeder was probably one of them. He was too uptight and by-the-book to go through a hurricane. He'd probably left before Mayor Blankenship's press conference yesterday that implored residents to leave Provident Island.

Becca didn't know Ross well—and she didn't want to know him well—but clearly, he didn't have an adaptable gene in his body. Becca assumed that staying on the island through a storm like this would take a lot of go-with-the-flow.

So, she'd knock on the door of Dr. Reeder's office, and when he wasn't there, she'd drive back over to the animal shelter and get some of the prescription food they had stocked in the back room. It was a slightly different formula, made by a different company—and a good rule of thumb was not to quickly change a dog's diet, especially a specialized one—but it was also highly recommended for canine kidney patients, and it should work for a few days until everything returned to normal.

She gave one more scratch behind Polly Wolly Doodle's furry ears. "Come on, girl, let's figure out our new game plan."

Polly let out a sound that was more bellow than woof. She hadn't really even expressed wariness at being left with a stranger. She seemed like a kind, trusting dog. You could see it in her tired, old eyes. Becca interpreted the dog's strong vocalization to mean that Polly was ready for what was to come. The idea made her chuckle. Polly the Labrador probably had more go-with-the-flow in her four chunky paws than Ross Reeder had in his whole body.

DR. ROSS REEDER PULLED the zipper around the perimeter of the suitcase where he'd put the last of the supplies he and his traveling companion would need in the days ahead. It was time to go. He didn't know when the Causeway would be closing, but judging by the strength of the wind, it would not be a viable evacuation route much longer. The Texas Department of Transportation had been very clear in a televised press conference a few hours ago that once winds reached a certain speed, it would be too hazardous for cars to drive across the tall bridge which spanned the more than seven hundred feet that separated Provident Island from the rest of the continental United States.

Ross locked the door on the room where he kept all his veterinary pharmaceuticals and supplies.

"Come on, Cookie. Let's get in the truck." Ross snapped his fingers and headed for the stairs with the attentive cream-colored Labrador retriever who was never far from his heels.

As he walked through the main floor of the house to ensure that everything in the clinic area was as secure as he could make it, Ross noticed he'd left the television on in the front room. Typically, this space served as a waiting room for his patients and their owners, but today—like much of the rest of the island—it was empty. He put his suitcase down and walked over to catch one last glance at Rick O'Connell's report on National Weather News, the country's leading twenty-four-hour weather network.

When Rick O'Connell showed up, that was shorthand for a storm that meant business.

Ross had seen enough excitement for a lifetime. After serving as an Army veterinarian in Iraq—where he'd saved a burned and bloodied Cookie after the furry hero's handler was killed by an IED—Ross was done with drama.

He'd moved to Port Provident a few years ago and wanted nothing other than to practice a more mundane form of veterinary medicine than what the Army offered, punctuated by watching sunrises and sunsets over the Gulf of Mexico from the widow's walk porch that crossed the roof on the back of the hundred-year-old house from which he operated his veterinary clinic.

Cookie was already waiting at the back door which led to the garage at the rear of the lot on which the distinguished Victorian house sat. Ross could hear the muffled thumps of Cookie's thick tail as it popped rhythmically on the hardwood floor.

Then Ross heard another thump from the front of the house—a pounding on the front door.

Who would be coming to a vet clinic in the middle of a hurricane evacuation?

Ross opened the door and couldn't believe what stood on the porch in front of him. One of his favorite patients...and one of his least favorite people.

But...Becca Collins did not own Polly McCaw.

"What are you doing here?" Ross knew his greeting sounded more like an outburst, but he was confused and running out of time. There wasn't really an opportunity for pleasantries. Not that anything was ever pleasant when stubborn, head-in-the-clouds Becca Collins was involved.

"Well hello to you too. I figured you'd be gone by now."

As usual, she made virtually no sense. "So why are you here? And what are you doing with Polly? Where's Eloise McCaw?"

A wind gust freed several strands of hair from the front of Becca's dark ponytail and blew them across her face. She tucked them behind her ear, where they promptly blew askew again. "She's on a bus to San Antonio with her granddaughter. They wouldn't let her take the dog."

"So, someone from the city called the shelter?" Ross kept watching the flutter of the wayward locks of hair.

"I volunteered. I was behind them in line. Polly's owner wouldn't go unless she knew Polly was safe. But she's in bad health and couldn't stay behind with Polly. The shelter is closed. The last dog left the island earlier today, headed up to a shelter in Montgomery County. I was following behind."

"On the public evacuation bus?"

She pursed her lips and nodded briefly. "Yes. We don't all make a doctor's salary. Some of us have to take advantage of other available resources sometimes."

Ross could hear the bitterness in her words. It was like listening to a lemon.

"What do you need from me?" Now he knew how Becca and Polly came to be together. He still wasn't sure, though, why they were on his clinic's porch.

She reached into a bag at her feet and pulled out a folded-up white bag. "Dog food. They didn't leave me with enough kibble, and I'd rather not change Polly's food if I can avoid it since she's on a special diet."

"Dog food? That's it?" This was far less complicated than most of the plans Becca dreamed up. "I've got some in the back. You two can come inside if you'd like."

Becca shrugged, then leaned over and picked up the bag at her feet. "Okay."

Ross held the door open as the pair walked in, then went back to re-open the storage room he'd just locked. When he came back, carrying two bags of Polly's prescription food, he saw Becca standing in front of the television in the waiting room. Her shoulders slumped under the straps of the backpack. Her whole demeanor changed from what it had seemed to be only moments before.

Ross placed the bags at Becca's feet, and Polly gave each a hearty sniff.

"What's wrong?" He asked.

Becca waved a hand at the TV screen. "They just closed the Causeway. We're stuck."

"No, they aren't closing the Causeway until four. TxDoT had a press conference a couple of hours ago. They won't close it until the wind hits a certain speed."

She shook her head and pointed at Rick O'Connell. "It wasn't the wind. It was the storm surge. Provident Bay is rising faster than they expected. The waves and current are proving to be too much for the Causeway. They are saying there may be structural damage below the surface of the water now. It's definitely closed. We're trapped."

Trapped. He thought back to Iraq and one particular ride in a convoy where he felt the eyes of insurgents on the back of his neck at every turn. He'd never felt more trapped in his life—a sitting duck, just waiting for whatever was going to happen. The memory poked at the deepest corners of his stomach, filling his whole body with a sense of unease.

Instantly, his thoughts turned to Cookie. Cookie had seen more and lived through more in Iraq than Ross had—and suffered the effects of it. Staying through a hurricane wasn't an option for Cookie. It would be more stress than Cookie could handle.

"There has to be an option."

"There isn't. Listen to the report. There's the head of the Texas Department of Transportation being interviewed. And that's the mayor standing next to him." She turned and looked Ross straight in the eye. "Do you have to disagree with everything I say?"

"You're picking the wrong fight on the wrong day."

"I'm not picking a fight. I'm reading the crawl at the bottom of the screen—also known as the very clear writing on the wall. It is what it is, whether you like the fact that I'm the one who told you or not." Becca leaned over and shoved one of the food bags in with the half-empty bag she'd been given by the McCaws. She slung the blue carrying bag over her shoulder and picked up the second bag Ross had handed her and tucked it in the crook of her arm. Becca gave the purple leash a tug. "Come on, Polly, let's go. We've got to figure out a plan."

Even loaded down with dog food and Labrador, she still looked like the same stubborn Becca that she was at every single board meeting for the Port Provident Animal Shelter. She carefully reached one hand out as far as she could without toppling her carefully balanced load and turned the doorknob. The heavy, solid wood door blew back in her face.

Polly jerked off to the side, and Becca lost her footing, tumbling to the floor amid a pile of bags.

"Are you okay?" Ross didn't like her, but he certainly didn't want her hurt. Especially not with a hurricane coming.

"I'm fine." The syllables were short and static. She adjusted the mess around her, propped herself up carefully, then stood.

Ross watched her struggle with rearranging her load and grabbed a bag of dog food and returned it back to its place.

"What's your plan?" he asked.

"My plan?" She cast a glance over her shoulder as she stood in the doorway.

"Yeah, where are you going?" Watching her fall to the floor made Ross realize he needed to set aside his usual opinion of Becca for a few moments. As much as he wished the breaking report on TV wasn't true, the simple fact was that they were both in the same boat now. Stuck on Provident Island. Stuck in the crosshairs of Hurricane Hope.

They weren't stuck together—thankfully, because he knew he couldn't handle that—but he did need to make sure she was going to be okay for at least the hours to come. That was the right thing to do.

It was the honorable thing to do.

He'd been out of the Army for a while, but honor and duty still remained the backbone of who he was. That was true in the dustbox of Iraq, and it was no different here in Port Provident.

The leash pulled tight as Polly kept trotting along while Becca didn't.

"I don't really know," she said, shoulders rounding again. "Plan A was to take the city-organized evacuation bus. So was Plan B. And Plan C. I don't think I can go home."

Her voice had softened, and it made Ross take note. This wasn't the combative Becca he so often encountered.

"Where's home?"

She turned to face him. "A studio apartment at the back of the shelter."

The Port Provident Animal Shelter backed up to one of the marshiest spots on Provident Island. Stuck between Harborview Drive and the harbor itself, there was virtually no doubt that the building would take on water, and probably a lot of it.

"You're right. That's probably not an option."

"I guess they'll open up the high school as a shelter. I'd heard some city officials talking about that as I waited in line. Councilwoman Angela Ruiz was there with her daughter, and she said there would be someplace safe for families to go."

Ross looked past Becca and Polly, to the almost totally deserted curb and street. "Where's your car?"

The rain had picked up significantly just in the few minutes they'd been inside. The curbs in this area of town had been laid during an era where the residents of Port Provident traveled in horses and buggies and carriages and needed a higher edge to step onto.

Ross could clearly see the water puddling over the top of the tall curb—which meant anything on the street was about to flood and be useless.

"I had a spot at the highest point in the parking lot over at the high school, so I left the car there. You weren't too far away, and the rain wasn't too bad, so Polly and I walked. But look at the storm now." She bit her lower lip and twisted it slightly between her teeth. "There goes Plan D. And probably my car. This is getting a little too real, too fast."

"Tell me about it." Ross watched the motion of the gray clouds overhead and the sustained shaking of the branches in the trees. "How about I drive you over there? I've got a truck with four-wheel drive. That should be able to get us through this. The high school isn't too far away."

A small light caught in her eyes. They were a rich velvet brown. Ross had never noticed that before.

"You'd do that for me?"

"For Polly," Ross said, then grinned broadly. "She's one of my favorite patients."

IN THE TIME THAT BECCA had been gone to Ross' office, another line had formed at Port Provident High School, this time leading up the front steps to the entrance of the school.

The rain slapped against the windshield of Ross' truck, and the wipers beat out a fast tempo, but couldn't wipe away the water fast enough. In the last hour, things had really taken a turn for the worst—a harbinger of things to come. There wasn't just wind and rain in the air, there was a thick shroud of tension. Becca could feel it in every cell of her body.

She hadn't been this nervous about anything in a long time. Certainly not since she left Milwaukee.

Cookie and Polly huddled together on the bench-style seat behind Becca. Canine intuition. The dogs knew something was coming, too.

"You can wait here for a second until the line goes down if you want," Ross offered. "It looks like the line is starting to move faster, but there's no reason to stand outside in this mess."

"I think we'll be okay." Becca reached down toward the floorboard, where she'd placed her backpack and all the dog food. "Thanks again for bringing us over here. Good luck to you, Dr. Reeder."

Becca stuck out her hand, feeling somewhat ridiculous—but not knowing exactly what to do here. She and Dr. Ross Reeder were never on the same side of anything. It felt a little awkward to know they were basically in the same boat right now—figuratively speaking—right down to a companion Labrador retriever for each of them.

Ross took her offered hand. Becca never thought she'd have expectations of a handshake with Ross Reeder, but it definitely took her by surprise that she noticed how smooth his hands were.

"You sure you'll be okay here?" He looked at the door to the high school, then back to Becca.

"Here? Of course. You wouldn't believe what I've seen in my life. A hurricane doesn't scare me." She put one two fingers behind the door latch and tugged, popping the door open. "Well, not that much."

Polly hesitated after Becca got out then opened the back door. She wiggled her big brown nose and sniffed at the rain-soaked air, giving Becca a look of chocolatey wariness.

"Come on, Polly. I'm getting soaked." Becca gave the leash a tug, and Polly pushed up from her seated position and placed one paw slowly in front of the other, then hopped.

Becca closed both doors quickly and gave a quick half-wave back at Ross and Cookie as she headed straight for the open glass door, Polly in tow.

"Stop, ma'am. The dog can't come in here." A police officer stood at the top of the steps and held up his hand.

"Can't come in? This is the shelter of last resort. Where else am I supposed to go?" A feeling like claustrophobia began to crowd in on Becca. She couldn't breathe properly.

"You can go right on in. The dog can't." The police officer didn't even crack a sympathetic smile.

"But she's old, and she has health problems. I can't leave her alone in a hurricane. She could die."

The man shifted slightly, positioning himself more directly between Becca and the door. "I'm very sorry about your dog, ma'am, but those are the rules. For a number of health and safety reasons, animals of any kind are not allowed in the shelter."

Rain started to blow almost sideways, throwing a wall of water directly under the overhang where Becca and Polly were attempting to stay as dry and calm as they possibly could.

It wasn't working.

Nothing was working.

Suddenly, Polly sneezed, coating the back of Becca's leg with a fine sheen of dog-mist. Becca barely noticed.

Becca's heart squeezed. She couldn't let Polly's family down.

She couldn't let Polly down.

Since the minute the worn purple leash had been placed in Becca's hand, Polly had been a trooper. She'd remained calm and had looked up at Becca with deep brownie-colored eyes filled with warm trust. She'd instantly sensed that Becca would help her, would take care of her.

Becca took the trust of dogs seriously.

A loyal basset hound named Rupert had taught her that valuable life lesson almost two decades ago.

She knelt down in front of the creamy-colored dog and put a hand on either side of Polly's face, then leaned down so her forehead touched the wide, flat top of Polly's head. Becca's grandmother, Bess, prayed about everything. But Becca hadn't seen much use in it. Her childhood had shown her that prayers went unanswered.

But maybe just this once...

Her tears mingled with the drops of rain soaking Polly's fur. "Please God, I don't even know what letter we're on anymore, but we need a plan. A real one. One that works for both of us."

A horn honked in the distance. *Beep. Beep. Beep-beep-beeeeeep.*

Becca broke her prayer off and hoped that God wouldn't hold the impatience of some jerk in the parking lot against her. She'd tried to pray a real prayer. It clearly just wasn't meant to be. She hadn't even gotten to say "amen" or any of that stuff you had to do for the prayer to count.

She heard another *beep* and looked up, turning her head toward the sound.

The headlights on Ross Reeder's truck were flashing on and off, then on and off again. As she stared, the truck drove toward the door. Ross rolled down the window.

"What's going on? You need a Plan E? Or is this Plan F? I can't keep track anymore."

Becca looked at Polly, then up at Ross, then back at Polly again. The dog stared soulfully, then pointed her muzzle toward the door of the car and stood.

Becca stood too, wiping her forearm across her cheeks, trying to get rid of the tears that had snuck out.

"I think this might be G," she said.

Ross nodded. "You may be right. At any rate, grab that dog food and let's G-O." He pointed at the clouds in the sky, lined up in gray rows for as far as the eye could see. "I don't think we've got much time to lose."

Keep reading Shelter from the Storm
Click here:https://books2read.com/ShelterFromTheStorm

Want to extend your stay in Port Provident?
Start a new book now!
The Home to Love Series
Language of Love[2]
Legacy of Love[3]

---

2. https://books2read.com/LanguageOfLoveBook

3. https://books2read.com/LegacyOfLoveBook

Labor of Love[4]
The Holiday Hearts Series
The Right Resolution[5]
The Cupid Caper[6]
Lucky in Love[7]
May I Have This Dance[8]
First Kiss Fireworks[9]
Falling Forever This Time[10]
Thankful for Love[11]
Mission: Mistletoe[12]
The Hope and Hearts Series
Shelter from the Storm[13]
The Doctor's Unexpected Family[14]
His Texas Princess[15]
Holiday of Hope[16]
Other Books by Kristen

---

4. https://books2read.com/LaborOfLove

5. http://www.books2read.com/TheRightResolutionBook

6. http://www.books2read.com/TheCupidCaperBook

7. http://www.books2read.com/LuckyInLoveBook

8. http://www.books2read.com/MayIHaveThisDanceBook

9. http://www.books2read.com/FirstKissFireworksBook

10. http://www.books2read.com/FallingForeverThisTimeBook

11. http://www.books2read.com/ThankfulForLoveBook

12. http://www.books2read.com/MissionMistletoeBook

13. http://www.books2read.com/ShelterFromTheStorm

14. http://www.books2read.com/TheDoctorsUnexpectedFamily

15. http://www.books2read.com/HisTexasPrincess

16. http://www.books2read.com/HolidayOfHope

Love Hallmark movies? Pick up Kristen's book October Kiss, based on the Hallmark movie viewers love! Available anywhere books are sold—in paperback, digital, and audio! October Kiss from Hallmark Publishing[17]

---

17. https://www.books2read.com/OctoberKiss

About Kristen

USA TODAY BESTSELLING Author Kristen Ethridge loves watching waves at the beach, eating the perfect taco, and reading books that leave her with a smile. Some would say her superpower is keeping alive one husband, three children, and six guinea pigs during their adventures across Texas—but that's not entirely true. She actually earned her sparkly cape for writing her signature style of Sweet Escape Romances—stories with hope, heart and happily-ever-after—for Harlequin's Love Inspired line, Hallmark Publishing, and Laurel Lock Publishing. One reader (who wasn't her mother) called Kristen's books "very good escape fiction" and that's pretty much the nicest thing anyone's ever said to her.

Kristen always wants to make new book best friends. Receive an exclusive free story by joining her mailing list at www.kristenethridge.com/newsletter. You can also follow her adventures in writing at www.facebook.com/kristenethridgebooks[1].

Keep up with Kristen through her author pages on Bookbub[2] and Facebook[3]. If you can't get enough of Port Provident, come join the Port Provident Community Center[4] on Facebook, the official gathering place for Kristen and her fans.

www.kristenethridge.com[5]
Facebook[6] Instagram[7]
The Port Provident Community[8] Center
Don't forget...if you love sweet escape romances, join Kristen's newsletter[9]!

---

1.   http://www.facebook.com/kristenethridgebooks

2.   https://www.bookbub.com/authors/kristen-ethridge

3.   http://www.facebook.com/kristenethridgebooks

4.   https://www.facebook.com/groups/2422381554654795

5. http://www.kristenethridge.com

6. https://www.facebook.com/KristenEthridgeBooks

7. https://instagram.com/kristenethridge

8. https://www.facebook.com/groups/2422381554654795

9. http://www.kristenethridge.com

LAUREL LOCK PUBLISHING

Publisher's Note: This is a work of fiction. Names, characters, places, and incidents are a product of the author's imagination. Locales and public names are sometimes used for atmospheric purposes. Any resemblance to actual people, living or dead, or to businesses, companies, events, institutions, or locales is completely coincidental.

Scriptures taken from the Holy Bible, New International Version®, NIV®. Copyright © 1973, 1978, 1984, 2011 by Biblica, Inc.™ Used by permission of Zondervan. All rights reserved worldwide. www.zondervan.com[10] The "NIV" and "New International Version" are trademarks registered in the United States Patent and Trademark Office by Biblica, Inc.™

Book Layout ©2013 BookDesignTemplates.com

---

10.   http://www.zondervan.com/